ROMANTIC TIMES PRAISES
JANEEN O'KERRY!

SPIRIT OF THE MIST

"Janeen O'Kerry breathes the misty atmosphere of ancient Celtic Ireland into a tale that mixes warriors, magic, legend, and a love that will not be denied into a romance that satisfies."

SISTER OF THE MOON

"Janeen O'Kerry casts a delicate spell of wonder and wishing in this tale of ancient Ireland."

MISTRESS OF THE WATERS

"*Mistress of the Waters* is a moving tale of ancient rites and beliefs. . . . Readers who like Gothic and magic will love this story."

QUEEN OF THE SUN

"Ms. O'Kerry draws the reader into the midst of her tale with accurate historical detail and well-crafted characters."

LADY OF FIRE

"Readers are whisked into the land of mists and warriors, druids and legends, as Ms. O'Kerry spins a delightful yarn of undeniable love."

THE KING'S CHAMPION

"He betrayed you."

Rioghan glanced down at the road. "It is the most common of stories. He was simply another man who thought to keep a wife at home and as many women as he wished elsewhere." She paused, glancing toward the forest as a night-black raven flew off over the pines. "I thought him special. I thought him different. I thought him a hero. But he was just like any other man, and the fact that I loved him could not change what he was."

The stallion's hooves thudded softly on the road as they traveled.

Donaill cleared his throat. "The day will come when you will find the man who is worthy of you. But I am not surprised to hear that you have not yet found that man."

Rioghan rode in silence. "Why do you say this?" she asked at last, keeping her voice as even as she could.

Again, he glanced over his shoulder. She could see him smiling. "Only because you are, as you say, so different from all other women. You are secretive and mysterious, and that is always an attraction to men. You are independent, far more than any woman I have ever known. . . ." He halted the horse and twisted around to look at her. "And you are very beautiful. I only wish I had known who you really were before now, for you have certainly caught the eye of the king's champion."

Donaill's face moved very close to her own. His breath was warm on her face in the cold damp air. His eyes began to close, and his lips approached hers. . . .

Other *Love Spell* books by Janeen O'Kerry:

SPIRIT OF THE MIST
SISTER OF THE MOON
MISTRESS OF THE WATERS
QUEEN OF THE SUN
LADY OF FIRE

JANEEN O'KERRY

LOVE SPELL

NEW YORK CITY

. . . for all those facing the timeless struggle between the darkness and the light.

LOVE SPELL®

January 2003

Published by

Dorchester Publishing Co., Inc.
276 Fifth Avenue
New York, NY 10001

ISBN 0-505-52528-3

Printed in the United States of America.

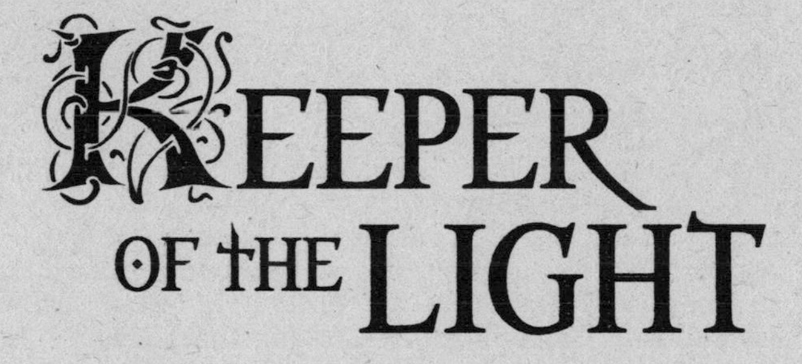
KEEPER
OF THE LIGHT

PRONUNCIATION GUIDE

Airt—art
Beolagh—BAY-oh-lah
Bran—brahn
Cahir Cullen—KYE-er KULL-en
Ceo—kyoe
cetmuinter—KET-min-ter
Cogar—KO-ger
Coiteann—kah-TENN
Donaill—DON-all
dormuine—DOR-min-eh
Eire—AIR-eh
fidchell—fihk-YEL
Irial—EER-eer-ell
Ita—IH-tah
Kieran—KEER-an
luaidhe—LOO-ih-yeh
Luath—LOO-eh
madra—MEH-drah
Rioghan—REE-gan
Sabha—SAH-vah
Scath—skawth
Sidhe—shee
Sion—shee-AWN

Chapter One

On a winter's night at the dark of the moon, three men guided their horses through the frosty pine forest and kept their swords at the ready.

"Marauding wolves and thieving Little People," muttered Beolagh, "and we ride out in pitch blackness—for what?"

Donaill kept his eyes on the faint track in front of him. He could see only a few steps beyond his horse's black ears, and he did not want to lose the way in the darkness. "To save a woman's life," he said over his shoulder.

"Save her life?" Beolagh snorted. "There's nothing wrong with her, save what's in her mind! Why send the king's champion and two warriors just to fetch the Little People's midwife? We have druids and physicians of our own at Cahir Cullen, and no need to ride anywhere to find them!"

"This woman cannot be helped by the druids," said Irial. "Even they said that the Sidhe's healer should be sent for."

"My brother is right," said Donaill. "Some things cannot be cured through normal methods. The druids—"

"Are surely much more learned than an old hag of a midwife living alone in a cave! Aren't the servants sent out to bring her when she is needed? Why send us? And why can't we take the road instead of this dark and miserable trace a badger couldn't follow? And why—"

Donaill stopped his horse and turned it around. His brother Irial did the same. "Your mouth is attracting the wolves, Beolagh," he snapped. "I suggest you shut it and follow this path along with us."

He turned his horse once more, and continued riding. "Besides, the servants walk along the road to Sion whenever they are sent to bring the midwife. But this is an urgent time on a dark winter night. So the king has sent his champion and two of his *very bravest warriors* to take the faster but more dangerous way."

Beolagh snorted at the thinly veiled sarcasm.

"If you would rather be a servant," said Irial, "and take the long safe road, I am sure King Bran will be pleased to let you do just that."

"Of course I am not a servant! I just think—"

"Quiet!" Donaill held up his hand. "Listen now."

They halted again and silence descended over

them. It was broken only by the breathing of the horses and the rattle of bridles as the beasts shook their heads—and then, floating through the black branches of the tall pine trees, came the faint sound of music and singing.

"This way," said Donaill, and guided his horse forward.

The delicate song, and the sweet sounds of harp and drum, were both beautiful and unnerving all at once. It seemed to Donaill that the music itself had eyes, that it watched him and his two men as it floated through the dark woods.

Donaill would not give Beolagh the satisfaction of hearing him say it, but he too would have preferred the good wide road to this narrow, twisting, barely discernable path through the heavy forest. It allowed a short route from Cahir Cullen to the home of the midwife, or so the servants and farmers said; but it also provided close cover for any wolf or outlaw or Sidhe who might be watching three of the king's men out on their late-night errand.

Of course, wolves almost never attacked men. And there was no rogue or thief that Donaill and his two companions could not handle. Yet thoughts of the Sidhe—the ancient, secretive, small dark folk of Eire who lived in seclusion in the deepest forests—filled him with unease. The people of Cahir Cullen had had little trouble with the Sidhe in recent years. Indeed, this midwife they were on their way to fetch was rumored to be one of them. And there were still the old and disquieting tales of men who disappeared while trespassing on Sidhe territory . . .

men who became hopelessly lost and were never seen again. . . .

At last they came to the edge of the trees and emerged in a small open meadow. Donaill was sure that the music came from here—but just as the three riders trotted their horses into the dry grass, it stopped.

The riders halted. All three men glanced around at the surrounding forest and at each other. Their horses shifted, their breath forming plumes of white mist in the darkness, as the faint starlight revealed a circle of nine standing stones out in the dark floor of the meadow.

"What's this?" demanded Beolagh.

"The stone circle of the Sidhe," said Donaill. "I have heard of it in tales, but never seen it. I was not even sure it was real."

All of them sat very still and looked at the brooding stones. The druids of Cahir Cullen had their own great stone circle far on the other side of that fortress, but it was made of large, smooth rocks standing out in the open on the top of a hill. This place was lonely, eerie, hidden away from the eyes of men, with stones that looked worn and crooked and bent, and must have been far more ancient than their own.

"It's so far inside the forest that it would be almost impossible to use," Irial said. "It hardly seems the sun's rays could reach it, or that the moon's rising could be marked."

"Yet the ground is clean and the stones are free

of weeds," Donaill noted. "*Some*one is using this circle."

They heard the faint, sweet music again, this time coming from across the clearing where the forest once more began.

Donaill's mouth tightened. "We're almost there. Keep ready." He cantered his horse across the rest of the meadow, picking up the path through the trees. Irial and Beolagh followed close after.

Donaill focused his mind on keeping to the faint trail and getting to the old midwife's cave, cantering his horse as quickly as he could and ducking beneath the dark needles and branches of the trees that reached out to grab at him. The other two men stayed close behind, and for once even Beolagh kept quiet.

The music faded away as another sound reached them: growling, howling, baying—almost like a roar. "Wolves!" cried Beolagh, trying to drag his horse to a stop. "Don't you hear them?"

"Not wolves," said Donaill, keeping his horse moving through the trees. "They're barking. Wolves do not bark. Those are dogs. And there are a lot of them."

"Oh, *much* better," Beolagh said with a sneer, but he allowed his horse to plunge forward after his companions. "I'd sooner face a little pack of wolves than a hundred snarling dogs!"

He may be right, Donaill thought as they drew closer to the growling and barking. The midwife was apparently well guarded, for the source of the sound did not appear to be moving. It was coming from just one spot directly ahead of them: their destination.

Donaill allowed his horse to slow down. In a moment he and his men reached another break on the trees, and he was forced to shield his eyes from a sudden bright light.

Far across the clearing a huge fire burned in a rock-lined pit. In its glare, a mob of long-legged dogs ran back and forth. The enormous animals, all of them black or gray with thick wiry coats, barked and snarled and showed their teeth, but did not turn on the warriors, who kept their distance and remained beneath the trees. The dog's collars, all of thick black leather, were plated with gold and bronze that gleamed in the firelight.

As his eyes adjusted to the spot of brightness that was the fire's light, Donaill became aware of a great darkness rising up behind it. With a start he realized he was looking at one of those enormous, grass-covered mounds of earth which could be found in many of the old and secret places of Eire, places where the Sidhe had once lived in great numbers.

Some insisted that these mounds were natural formations, but others, like Donaill, could only look at the perfectly curving structures rising in isolation out of flat and empty ground and feel that they must have been built by human hands . . . built by the Sidhe, long ago, or by their even more ancient and mysterious ancestors.

And here was the old midwife making her home in one of those mounds.

The entrance to the midwife's cave lay just beyond the flames. Pieces of shiny black cowhide hung down over the opening, backlit by what must have been lamps inside.

The dogs continued to hold Donaill and his men at bay. Their howls were enough to wake every living thing in the forest, yet there was no sign of movement inside the cave.

The trio's horses began to snort and dance, having had more than enough of the menacing dogs. "Well, where is she?" asked Beolagh. "This is the place, isn't it?"

Donaill moved his horse forward as close as he could get without antagonizing the dogs, and he cupped one hand alongside his mouth. "Midwife!" he shouted as loudly as he could over the frenzied canine barking. "Midwife! Come out to us!"

As one, the dogs raised their heads to the sky and howled: a long, drawn-out sound that raised the hair on the back of Donaill's neck. The pack fell silent, then, and the cowhide hangings in front of the cave were slowly drawn back. A small figure in black emerged.

For a moment, the three warriors could all clearly see inside the cave. Donaill caught a glimpse of scattered bronze and stone lamps casting their light over heaps of clean straw. Across the back of the cave was a sleeping ledge covered with slick black cowhides and soft, thick furs, and beside it a stood a beautifully carved wooden chest.

There was also, scattered throughout the dwelling on ledges and niches and low fur-draped benches, a collection of shiny objects—cups and plates and figures of animals—in gleaming gold and reflective bronze and bright, sparkling crystal.

Beolagh's eyes widened. He leaned forward over his horse's neck. "Where did she get all that? Maybe it's true what they say about the Sidhe—that they've got treasure beyond anything we've ever seen!"

Donaill glared at him. "It's nothing but an old woman's trinkets. Hardly what I'd call treasure."

"Ah, but think of how many *young* women's favors we could trade for, if we had those trinkets for gifts!"

"Do you think of nothing else? And do you truly have such a low opinion of the women of Cahir Cullen?"

"Pity you must win their favor with trinkets," added Irial. "Most of us don't find that to be necessary."

Beolagh just laughed. "That's what you *say*—but everyone knows women are all the same. They love beautiful things, and they love any man who gives them such. And besides, what else is there to think about?"

"Quiet," said Donaill. "There she is."

The woman from the cave walked slowly toward them, her dogs frisking about her feet. She put out her hands to quiet the animals as she approached.

"I presume you are the midwife," Donaill called. "You are needed at Cahir Cullen."

The woman paused, and though her black cloak hung down over her face she seemed to be studying them. "Tell me your name," she said.

Donaill blinked. Her voice was youthful and soft, nothing like that of the old crone he had expected. He glanced at his two companions before looking back to the woman.

"I am Donaill, champion to King Bran of Cahir Cullen. This is my brother Irial, and another warrior, Beolagh. Now . . . might we know your name?"

She nodded at his answer, still surrounded by her milling pack of enormous black and gray dogs. She dropped the black cloak's hood back from her head. "My name is Rioghan."

By the stars and by the distant light of the fire, Donaill saw a young woman with smooth, fair skin, strong, determined features, and large green eyes. Black hair cascaded over her shoulders and most of the way down her back. As she clutched her heavy black wool cloak close around her, Donaill saw that her hands and wrists and throat were bare of any jewelry; she had only a circular bronze pin inlaid with shining black jet to fasten the garment. Yet her eyes were so bright, so jewel-like, that they seemed to be more luminous than any adornment she might have worn.

"Rioghan," he said. He could not take his eyes from hers, and found himself wondering why.

Perhaps it was just the surprise of seeing such a fair face and youthful figure when he had been expecting someone old and withered. Perhaps it was just the strangeness of this wild and lonely place, with its menacing dogs and brooding stone circle and ancient, Sidhe-built, mysterious mound.

Or perhaps it was her eyes meeting his with equal fearlessness and equal curiosity. Donaill had never seen any woman with eyes so large and bright, whose gaze held such an intensity.

She did not respond, but went on looking steadily up at him. Her pack of monstrous dogs stayed close around.

"I must confess, I thought you to be an old crone. I did not expect to see a beautiful young woman."

She kept right on staring at him. "Do you not know me, Donaill?" She took a step forward through the sea of her protectors. "You have seen me often at Cahir Cullen."

He gazed down at her and shook his head. "I recall only a silent figure in black, coming to care for the women from time to time. But that is all."

Rioghan took another step forward. "It is true that I come most often in the night, but you have seen me many times. I know you, Donaill, though I am not surprised that you do not know me. You were always busy in that high place that all important men occupy, and so you took me for just another servant. You have *seen* me many times, but you have never *looked* at me."

Donaill started to speak . . . but found that no words were at hand. His horse shifted beneath him.

Rioghan reached down to stroke her dogs. "You say I am needed at Cahir Cullen. Yet there is no woman there whose time is near, so far as I know."

"You are right. This is not about a birth. But it is about a woman."

The midwife frowned, drawing her soft, dark

brows together. "Is this woman ill? Is she hurt? Can your druids and physicians not help her?"

"They have tried. But she has lost her reason and will not speak to anyone. The other women asked that you be sent for. Will you come and help?"

"What woman is this?"

"It is Sabha."

"Sabha . . ." Rioghan stood straight and folded her hands once more. "I will come. Please wait here for me."

As the three men watched, Rioghan returned to her cave, briefly pushing the hangings aside so she could enter. Beolagh leaned forward as far as he could, straining to catch another glimpse of her crystal and gold in the firelight. Donaill turned to glare at him until, reluctantly, the man sat back.

Rioghan soon emerged from the cave. She carried a small black leather sack in one hand, and with the other signaled to her dogs. They parted to let her pass, though two remained close at her side—one huge black beast whose collar was plated with gold, and another with a dark gray coat and a collar of bronze.

Donaill moved his horse so that it stood alongside a fallen tree, thinking to let Rioghan stand upon its trunk and then slide behind him on his horse. But she walked up alongside him, reached for his hand, and swung up without any further ado.

The group turned their mounts back into the starlit woods. Rioghan's two dogs followed closely.

* * *

The horses trotted as quickly as they were allowed through the silent darkness of the forest, eager to get back home. Rioghan tried to think only of the task ahead of her, but such was difficult to do when she was forced to sit so close behind Donaill and hold him tight around the waist.

She did know who he was, as she knew of most of the men at Cahir Cullen. If nothing else, she knew them as the husbands of the women whose newborns she helped bring into the world. But she felt quite certain that this man, Donaill, had no wife.

It seemed strange to her that he remained unmarried. Donaill was the king's champion, the best warrior at Cahir Cullen, and would surely be the object of many a young woman's affections. He was tall and handsome, with light brown hair and clear blue eyes, and his easygoing manner almost made one forget the power in his broad shoulders and well-muscled arms.

Even now he felt as strong and unmoving as one of the standing stones in the circle outside Sion. He seemed not to notice Rioghan's sudden tight hold on his waist when, at last, the horses burst out of the forest and took up a gallop toward home.

Rising before them, in the center of a wide meadow, surrounded by the tall black silhouettes of widely spaced holly trees, was the circular earth-and-stone fortress of Cahir Cullen. Its tall wooden gates opened as they approached, and the three warriors cantered their horses inside. Rioghan's two dogs stayed right along with them.

There were some twenty round houses, made with heavy wicker framework thickly covered with clay, scattered across the torchlit fortress grounds. As always, Rioghan could not help but think of how insubstantial they seemed compared to the cave that was her own home. Donaill jogged his black stallion in and out among the houses until he reached one near the rear of Cahir Cullen's curving inner wall. Quickly Rioghan slid down to the ground.

"Thank you," she said, looking up at him. She could see him better now in the soft light of the torches. His fine features and strong jaw were quite familiar, for she had indeed seen him before at this place; but it was strange to see those same blue eyes and warm smile directed at her.

"You are most welcome," he said. "Thank you for coming here to help us." And with that, he reined his horse in a half circle and rode away.

Rioghan took a deep breath, lifted her black leather sack to one shoulder, then turned toward the house, signaling her dogs Scath and Cogar to stay outside.

Two women opened the door as she approached it. "Rioghan, we are so glad that you are here," the first one said, reaching out to take her by the shoulder.

"Please, come in, come in," said the other. "She is here, but we do not know what to do for her."

Rioghan followed them into the small round dwelling. A low fire burned in the central hearth, and a scattering of flat stone lamps held flickering flames of light. Three other women waited inside, two of them sitting on one of the fur-covered sleeping ledges and another standing near the main fire. All of them were clearly anxious. "Here," said the one at the hearth, and gestured toward the floor.

Rioghan stopped. She kept her face very still and calm, but could not stop the cold feeling in the pit of her stomach.

The young woman, Sabha, lay curled up like an infant on a bed of thick, clean straw. Someone had placed a blue-and-green plaid cloak over her, but she seemed not to notice. "Airt," the woman whispered in a shaking voice. "Airt . . ."

"Airt is her husband," one of the others informed Rioghan. "But he is here at Cahir Cullen. He is well; nothing has happened. The men took him away from the house when she would not respond to him. He is nearly as distraught as she."

Rioghan nodded. "They have been married barely two years. Sabha has been a great help to me whenever I have come here." She glanced around at the others, then nodded toward the door. "Please go now. Leave me with her. I will do what I can."

The women all looked at each other, and then, each with a final kiss for Sabha, they left the round house and quietly closed the door.

Rioghan moved to sit down in the straw beside her patient. Throwing back the blue-and-green wool cloak covering the younger woman, she leaned down to speak to her. "Sabha, come now and help me. Help me to understand what has happened to you. Come now; sit up—sit up; there, that's it. Sit beside me and tell me what has happened."

The two of them sat together against the sleeping ledge, though Sabha slumped over so that her head rested on Rioghan's shoulder. "Let me help you," Rioghan said again. "Tell me what has happened."

But Sabha would say nothing except her husband's name, over and over again. She seemed not to know that anyone else was there.

Rioghan reached beneath the neckline of her own black wool gown and lifted out a slender chain of gold. The chain was Sidhe made, delicate and beautiful, and hanging from it was a long, slim pendant of polished crystal.

Holding the pendant with one hand, Rioghan sat up and placed her other hand on Sabha's head, smoothing the woman's long dark hair back as she did. "Now, Sabha," she said softly, "show me what you wish me to know. The crystal of seeing will allow me to see it, too. It will show me what you wish me to know. It will show me all that I *need* to know."

"Airt," whispered Sabha, and Rioghan closed her eyes.

Into her mind came the image of a house—this very house, Rioghan realized, for the arrangement of doors and windows and ledges was identical. The same bunches of dried primrose and red clover hung on the wall near the window, the same dented bronze pan rested beside the hearth, and the same gray-black tunic lay in the straw near the head of the sleeping ledge.

On that ledge, lit now by the pale, filtered light of the late-afternoon sun, were the same fur cloaks stitched together from the skins of badger and hare, and the same soft leather cushions stuffed with straw . . . but on those furs lay a slender blond woman, naked in the cold winter air, moaning in pleasure and grasping her lover's back as the young, dark-haired man kissed her hard on the neck, pinned her down, and mounted her.

There were no gentle caresses, no words of love between the pair. They grunted and groaned and coupled like animals.

Rioghan realized that there was something strange about this man: there was a faint discoloration to his bare skin, a grayness, as though something unclean, something poisonous, had come over him. She frowned, even as she kept her eyes closed—and then, in her vision, the door of the house opened and Sabha walked inside.

Rioghan could feel rather than hear Sabha's wail of despair. The man in these images was her husband, Airt, and on this day he had brought another woman into their house and the furs where they slept.

Rioghan released the crystal. "Oh, Sabha," she whispered, and held the other woman like a child. Sabha collapsed with her head on Rioghan's lap, clutched her around the waist, and wept at last.

Chapter Two

Rioghan lifted a small bronze cauldron from the fire and placed it on the hearth. The water inside was boiling. Opening her black leather bag, she took out a handful of dried white-and-yellow flower heads and added them to the pot. A brief search of the house yielded a clean wooden cup and a little honey.

After the flowers had steeped for a time, she poured some of the cauldron's mixture into the cup, added some honey, and stirred it with a slender wooden paddle.

Sabha still lay in the straw, though now she wept instead of chillingly calling her husband's name. Rioghan carried the steaming cup over to her and sat down on the carpet of straw. "Sabha," she said, giving the woman a little shake. "Sabha, sit up now.

I have brought you something to drink—and I must ask you a question."

Slowly Sabha opened her red and swollen eyes, and then she sat up to look at her visitor. "Rioghan," she said. "Oh, Rioghan—what has he done?"

"I know, I know. I have seen it all. You need not tell it again. Here . . . drink this."

Sabha took the cup and sipped at the strong, sweet tea. In moments the cup was empty, and she allowed it to fall to the straw and roll away. She turned back to Rioghan. "You said you wanted to ask me a question."

Rioghan reached out and took Sabha's hands. "This thing your husband has done . . . I can tell you it was not his choice alone. I could see the touch of dark magic on him. This woman, whoever she is—"

"Coiteann." Sabha's voice held the utmost contempt. "She is the servant who makes dyes, and spends all her working time over the reeking dye pots. She is—"

"I know what she is." Rioghan glanced again at the dingy, gray-black linen tunic beside her on the straw. It looked like as if it had been dyed with some noxious substance: soot, perhaps, or even a little blood. "Not one who is so powerful that she could take him against his will. She used just enough of the dark side of power to persuade him to bring her here, instead of to some hidden place in the forest as he would have preferred. That is why he brought her into your house and into your bed."

Sabha closed her eyes. "But why here, why in the late afternoon? They both knew that I would be returning from the hall at just that time!"

Rioghan shook her head. Fury burned inside her. "Dear Sabha. This woman did know, though she made your husband forget. She *planned* for you to find them together. She hoped you would divorce your husband and leave him free to marry her."

"I think she may well have succeeded . . . though I hate the thought of giving her such satisfaction."

"Then consider the question that I ask you now: Do you wish to exact justice? Do you wish to teach them both a lesson they will never forget?"

Sabha looked straight at Rioghan. Her voice was steadier than it had been. "Tell me what I must do."

A short time later Rioghan pushed open the door of Sabha's house with her shoulder, holding an armload of hare and badger furs, and the black linen tunic against her chest. The other women hurried over to her, but she held up her fingers to request quiet. "She sleeps now, in the warm straw. I have given her a drink to help her rest."

"Will she be all right? Is she rational now?"

"She will recover. Please let her sleep. It is the best thing for her. I will stay until dawn, and we can give her more of the tea that makes her sleep should she need it again."

With that, Rioghan let go of the bundled furs and the tunic she carried, and let them fall to the muddy ground. "Give these to the servants," she said, "and tell them to throw them to your dogs—if the dogs will have them."

The eastern sky had turned the faintest gray when Rioghan and her two hounds walked across the yard of Cahir Cullen and approached the tall wooden gates. The gates opened for her just as she reached them, for the night watch was accustomed to her quiet presence and knew that she preferred to leave at dawn whenever possible. A moment later she, Scath, and Cogar were walking down the wide road toward home.

Long ago—so long that none of them nor their children nor their grandchildren were still alive—the Sidhe had built this road between Sion and the holly grove where Cahir Cullen now stood. The road had been made from beams of timber laid both straight and crosswise to form a true, solid framework. Then the beams had been pegged together, filled in with twigs and rock, and covered over with earth to make a good surface for animals and chariots alike.

It served humans on foot just as well, Rioghan had found, and it allowed her to make the journey to this fortress with relative ease whenever she was needed. Only in an emergency was the shorter, but more difficult way through the deep forest taken—for while the dense, dark needles of the pines offered shelter and screening even in winter, they could also house terrible danger.

Donaill had been bold to bring his men down

that nearly invisible path in the deep darkness last night. Even Rioghan, accustomed as she was to the forest, always found herself picking her way very carefully through that wild, thick, confusing stand of tall trees and heavy brush, with its uneven ground and haphazard rocks. Yet Donaill had done it without hesitation when someone at his fortress needed help, though Rioghan knew well that even the boldest of men were apprehensive at the thought of meeting any of the Sidhe . . . especially at night in the dark and misty forest.

The Sidhe were the small, dark-haired folk who had always lived in Eire. They had built many wonderful things and had their own powers, but their gentle magics and fragile bronze weapons had proved to be no match for the tall, fair, iron-wielding invaders who had overrun their land and killed any who dared to interfere.

Most of the Sidhe were gone now, either long dead or through having their lines absorbed by the families of Men—but there were still some who existed in secret in the deepest part of the woods, living as best they could and keeping their magic alive wherever they could find a way to do so.

Rioghan followed the road, this time, and she was soon out of sight of Cahir Cullen. She felt a sense of relief, as she always did, when on her way home . . . though she made herself ignore the small tug of loneliness, the little sense of loss, that always accompanied her when she bade farewell to the people of the fortress. No matter how much she looked forward to being at Sion once again, there was part of her that missed companionship.

Yet her true home waited for her at the end of this road, she reminded herself, a safe and comfortable home guarded by some thirty fiercely loyal dogs and surrounded by the gentle and beautiful people called the Sidhe. Rioghan smiled down at her pets and walked faster, anxious to see Sion once more.

Just as she rounded the first curve in the road, there was the sound of galloping hooves behind her.

In a heartbeat, Rioghan and her dogs were in the cover of the forest. Her black gown and cloak blended with the bare black trunks and deep shadows of the pines, as did the black and gray coats of the dogs. All three of them stayed very still as a stallion and his rider came around the curve.

"Rioghan!" cried Donaill, slowing his horse to a trot and then to a walk. "Rioghan! I know you must be near. You could not have gone much farther than this. Please come out. I will take you back to Sion, if you will allow me."

He halted briefly, but when he got no answer he urged the black horse on again. "Rioghan!"

"Donaill." He turned the horse around to see her standing in the center of the road, Scath and Cogar close at her side. With a wide smile, his blue eyes shining, his heavy red cloak flowing out behind him, he reined his stallion back down the road to halt in front of her.

Rioghan looked up at him as he smiled down at her, and it seemed that she was seeing him now for the first time. He was a man in the full strength of maturity, perhaps thirty years old, as tall as any other man at Cahir Cullen and with the broadest shoulders and most heavily muscled arms she had ever seen. Even his neck seemed to be carved of iron, the way his stallion's neck rippled with strength.

Yet in spite of all of this power, those were slender and sensitive fingers that held the reins. Donaill's face was shaved clean, and his light brown hair fell past his shoulders, drawn back by a black leather cord.

Above his wide jaw was a curving mouth and a slim, straight nose, and blue eyes that held gentleness and a glint of humor. "Rioghan," he said. "I am so glad I found you. Will you let me and my horse, Cath, take you back to Sion? It is a long walk."

"It is not so long," she argued. "But I thank you." And then, she turned and continued on her way. Her dogs trotted close by her side.

Donaill urged his horse after her. "It is the least I can do after you have come all this way."

"It is no trouble," she said, keeping her eyes on the road. "I have come to Cahir Cullen many times, and always I have walked home."

"But my lady Rioghan . . ." She stopped and waited patiently, still looking straight ahead. "I would enjoy your company," he finished, seeming almost embarrassed.

Rioghan smiled. She had been waiting for that

admission. "Thank you. Then I will accept your offer."

As she had the night before, Rioghan took hold of Donaill's strong wrist and swung up behind him on his black stallion. But this time, instead of making a mad dash through the darkness, the horse walked at a leisurely pace through the cold gray morning, with only Rioghan's two dogs, a few wintering thrushes, and the occasional raven for company. Rioghan held her black leather bag with one hand and allowed the other to rest on her thigh as Donaill's horse carried her home with long, powerful strides.

"I am so glad you accepted my offer," Donaill began, glancing over his shoulder. "For quite some time now I have wanted to get to know you better."

She looked up. "Quite some time? Until last evening you did not even know who I was, king's champion Donaill."

"Well, that may be true. I remember you only as an occasional shadow visiting Cahir Cullen in the night. But now that I have met you face-to-face, I do indeed wish to know more about you."

Rioghan smiled. "There is little to tell—little that would be of interest to you. I have the age of twenty-three years, and for all of those years I have lived at Sion."

He nodded. "Many of us have wondered about that place. We know it only as a place of the Sidhe, where Men trespass at their peril . . . though I will admit, I do not know of anyone who has actually been harmed by any of the Fair Folk. There are only the old stories, which do serve, it would seem, to keep Men away."

"You are right," Rioghan said. "The Sidhe's numbers are few these days. And Sion is indeed a place of the Sidhe, built by the most ancient of them to provide both a ring of standing stones and a safe place to live within the earth for those who would learn to use the ring—and for those who have the greatest power of magic.

"Yet as the years pass, it has become forgotten, as such places often do, as the Sidhe's numbers dwindle. After a time the cave has simply become a home for the Sidhe who remain, and for those who, like me, claim both Sidhe and Man in their ancestry."

Donaill nodded. "I was told that a family once lived there, but that only the midwife has remained for the past several years."

"That is true. My family is not of noble blood. They were farmers all, and some of them, a few generations back, were believed to be of the Sidhe. For countless years they lived side by side with the Fair Folk and made their home in the caves beneath the mound."

"Yet you are the only one left there now. How did that come to pass? Why do you not come to live among us at Cahir Cullen?"

Rioghan paused. "Your fortress is simply not my home. I have never lived there, and I would never really belong."

Donaill shook his head. "King Bran—and everyone there—would surely welcome you and your skills. Would you not like to have other young women to talk to, to work beside, to be with you as companions?"

She smiled. "Do not misunderstand. I have always found Cahir Cullen to be a lively and interesting place. I do enjoy the company of the other women there. But, as I said, it is not my home. I am not like the others."

He grinned. "I can see that you are not. But tell me, please, how it is that you came to live alone at a place like Sion, beautiful though it is."

She looked away, her thoughts drifting back. "My parents went to their rest long ago. After they were gone, my brother became a craftsman and found a bride at the fortress of Dun Orga, where they now live. My two sisters feared to live alone in the woods and also made their way to Dun Orga, where they soon found husbands.

"They are all content, and have invited me to live with them many times . . . yet I find that the only place for me is at Sion. There I can live as I choose, and I have the satisfaction of helping both the people of the Sidhe and the people of Cahir Cullen with the healing skills I learned from my mother and the Fair Folk. It is a very good life."

"I suppose it is," Donaill agreed. "But are you never lonely in that place, Rioghan? Such a beautiful young woman, with only dogs and Little People for companions, so far from the company of men—"

"I often think I prefer the company of dogs to the company of men," she interrupted.

After a brief moment of shocked silence, Donaill laughed. "Now you must tell me why a lovely young woman—one whom many men would like very much to know—would say such a thing."

Rioghan shifted the leather bag under her arm. "It is the same story that many women have. I did go to Dun Orga with my sisters for a time, and I too met a man . . . a man I loved, a man who loved me in return—or so I thought."

"But he betrayed you."

She glanced down at the road. "It is the most common of stories. He was simply another man who thought to acquire a wife for home and take as many women as he wished elsewhere."

She paused, glancing toward the forest as a night-black raven flew off over the pines. "I thought him special. I thought him different. I thought him a hero. But he was just like any other man, and the fact that I loved him could not change what he was."

The stallion's hooves thudded softly on the road as they traveled.

Donaill cleared his throat. "The day will come when you will find the man who is worthy of you. But I am not surprised to hear that you have not yet found that man."

Rioghan rode in silence. She was not quite certain whether she had been insulted. "Why do you say this?" she asked at last, keeping her voice as even as she could.

Again he glanced over his shoulder. She could see him smiling. "Only because you are, as you say, so different from all other women. You are secretive and mysterious, and that is always an attraction to men. You are independent, far more than any woman I have ever known. . . ." He halted the horse and twisted around to look at her. "And you are very beautiful. I only wish I had known who you really were before now, for you have certainly caught the eye of the king's champion."

Donaill's face moved very close to her own. His breath was warm on her face in the cold, damp air. His eyes began to close, and his lips approached hers. . . .

"I may be different from all other women," Rioghan said, sitting very still, with his mouth only a hair breadth from hers, "but I find you are the same as all other men—bragging, boasting, and concerned only with your station in life."

Donaill froze. His blue eyes opened, surprised. Then he drew back from her and turned again to face forward.

Rioghan caught his waist as the horse moved on. She waited for Donaill to respond to her biting comment, but as they continued down the road he said nothing.

Yet she could feel his shoulders shaking. Was he angry? Perhaps she should slide down and continue on alone. She should have known better than to allow this situation—

Then Donaill threw back his head and laughed so loudly that his horse jumped a little and her two dogs looked up in concern. He went on laughing as his stallion stepped up into a trot, even as Rioghan felt the warmth of embarrassment creep over her face. She kept her silence, though, and as much of her dignity as she could.

Let him laugh. He was doing no more than proving her right.

The horse moved more quickly now, and Donaill's laughter finally subsided. It was not long before Rioghan realized they were getting close to Sion. "Stop here, please," she said.

Instantly Donaill reined the stallion to a halt. "Is something wrong?" he asked.

Before the horse could move again, Rioghan quickly slid to the ground. "Not at all," she said. "I thank you for allowing me to ride with you this far. But . . . I would prefer to have no visitors at Sion, unless they have come to ask for my help."

He cocked his head and grinned down at her. "I may well come again to ask you for your help, Lady Rioghan. Perhaps you will look forward to it."

Rioghan stared up at him. "I thank you for bringing me this far. But I assure you, king's champion Donaill, I will not so much as glance back over my shoulder when you ride away."

He laughed again and backed the stallion away from her. "Go in safety, my lady. I can see you are well guarded. I may be back for you sooner than you think."

She raised her chin and then turned to continue on her way, signaling her dogs to come to her side. With a deep breath she walked on down the road, hanging her black leather bag from her shoulder and telling herself that this was no different from any other time when she might have walked home from Cahir Cullen—though she knew he was sitting on his horse and watching as she walked away. . . .

Rioghan smoothed her black cloak, arranged her fall of dark hair by running her fingers through it, and raised her hot face to the cool winter air so that the breeze might take away the heat that coursed through her. In a moment she would be around the next curve and out of his sight. Breathing slowly and deeply, she closed her eyes for a few steps and tried to think of nothing but the feel of the road under her feet and the sound of Scath and Cogar trotting alongside.

Opening her eyes, she felt that her mind was clear once again. There were no more thoughts of Donaill intruding upon her peace of mind, no more images of broad shoulders and blue eyes and laughing smiles, no lingering memories of a hard, smooth waist beneath her arms as she pressed herself close behind a tall, strong man on a galloping stallion. . . .

Horse's hooves sounded on the road once more, though this time they were moving away from her. Then, suddenly, they halted.

Before she could think, Rioghan turned back to look. She had thought to see only the back of Donaill's head and his strong, wide shoulders. But her face grew hot again as she saw, instead, his gleaming blue eyes and wide grin as he caught her gaze.

"Farewell again, Lady Rioghan! Soon you will

not need to look back to see me, for I will be standing at your side!"

With that the stallion galloped away, leaving only the sound of Donaill's laughter floating in the cold winter forest.

Chapter Three

Sabha sat straight and tall on the very edge of her bare sleeping ledge, her hands folded and unmoving in her lap. She remained very still and looked neither right nor left as the door of the house swung slowly open and her husband walked inside.

The afternoon sky was a featureless gray behind him. "Hello, my wife." Airt closed the door and took a step toward her, then another. She continued to gaze straight ahead.

Airt paused, then walked all the way to the ledge and sat down beside her. "I am glad to see you well. I have missed you. I—"

"What do you wish to do?" she asked.

Again Airt paused. He tried to look closely at his wife's face, but she continued to stare at nothing. "I wish to be with you," he whispered, and he reached out to place his hand over one of hers. But she did not respond to his touch; her arm grew rigid the moment he took hold of her, and after a moment he withdrew his hand.

"What do you wish to do?" she asked again.

"Sabha, please do not be angry with me."

"I am not angry with you." Her voice remained as cool and still as the frost that limned the grasses in winter. "I simply need to know what you intend, so that the proper decisions can be made."

He shrugged. "Nothing at all has changed. I intend to be a husband to you, a husband who loves you, as I have always been."

"Yet clearly there is another who also has your love."

Airt sighed, and shifted on the ledge. "It is not like the love I have for you. It is different. It is—"

"Then you do love her."

"Not . . . not the way—" He held up his hand before she could interrupt him again. "Coiteann is not like you. You are a lady who could only be a *cetmuinter*, holding the honored position of a first wife. She is—"

"I know what she is." Sabha breathed deep and refolded her hands. "You intend to bring her into the house. Into *our* house. You intend to take her as a *dormuine*. A second wife. A concubine."

Airt moved a little closer. She held herself very still. "Sabha . . . I am now one of the king's warriors. I may well be chosen as one of his personal retinue, and they are second only to the king's champion himself! Men of such rank often have a chief wife, and then a second or third wife as well. The law has always allowed it. King Bran has three such wives, and Cronan and Fergus, both part of his personal retinue, each have two. You know that it is quite usual for a man of rank to have secondary wives, and now that I am rising into such a level—"

"You wish to have all the symbols of your success for all to see." Sabha turned to look at him. She noted, as though from a great distance, that his face was pale and he seemed to be sweating. His eyes flicked left and right, and he would not meet her gaze.

"We spoke of this very thing before our marriage," she said. "I thought I had made it clear to you that I wished to have no other wife in this house. You said nothing about wanting to do such a thing. Why did you lie to me, Airt?"

"I did not lie to you!" He looked up at her at last. "I simply . . . I just never spoke of it. I did not want to upset you. I do not ever want to argue with you, Sabha."

"And letting me believe the sky is blue, when it is actually red as blood, is not a lie?" Slowly Sabha shook her head, then looked down at the straw. "I see," she whispered. "I see now."

She raised her head, staring across the room, and went on speaking. "You want a second wife. Some women can learn to be content with such an arrangement, but most cannot—no matter what the law allows. I know well that I cannot, and I made certain you understood this before we made the contract for our marriage. Do you not remember?"

He looked down. "I remember. But . . . I feel certain, now, that once you understand that you will always be my beloved first wife . . . that no one will displace you from this honored position . . . that you and no other will be the chief wife . . . you will come to accept this, as the wives of such men always do."

"Airt, you are rising through the ranks of the king's warriors, and you wish all to know of your status. What greater symbol of your status than another wife on your arm—and in your house, and in your bed?"

He tried to look into her eyes, but his gaze wavered and at last he looked toward the fire. "You, too, will benefit from my bettered status. There are advantages for you as well. You could . . ." He turned to look at her again, but the hard mask of her features put a stop to his words.

She said, "You are doing this for yourself alone. Do not insult me by trying to say that it is somehow being done for me. You have found a way to have extra women for yourself while still remaining married. That is for you and you alone."

But Airt held his ground. "Think how nice it would be for you, Sabha," he pressed. "You would have a companion around for the times I am gone in service to the king, which can sometimes stretch into days or fortnights. She would always be here with you, a sister, if you like, to help you with the work."

"Then tell me this, please. If the custom of taking a second or even a third or fourth wife is such a fine thing, why is it only the men who want to continue it? Why does no woman ever ask that another wife be brought into the house alongside her?"

He smiled down at her, and briefly patted her hand. "Sabha, Sabha . . . I know that this is often difficult for the chief wife at first. The other men spoke to me about it. But I want to reassure you that I will be as understanding as any husband could be. And I promise to bring you whatever you like as a special gift, something for you alone."

Sabha felt her face growing hot, even as a cold hand clutched her heart. "A special gift," she murmured, and shifted slightly on their ledge. "I do not know how I can properly thank you."

He grinned. "Just allow me to continue to love you as I always have, and allow Coiteann to join our family."

"Are you so certain she is the right one to be a second wife to you and a sister to me?" she asked, watching his face.

His eyes brightened. "Oh, she will fit in with our family better than any other could. She knows well that she will never displace you as a chief wife, and has agreed to serve us both."

"She is willing to take a place second to me? She would share you with me, freely and without rancor or jealousy?"

"She would, she would! I have spoken to her about it. She—"

"She was here in our home. She was here in our bed. She meant for me to learn of this so that I would divorce you and she could have you all to herself. Do you not see this?"

"Oh, but you are wrong—she wants to be a part of our family, not destroy it!" Airt looked at her and smiled, looking as happy as Sabha had ever seen him. "It will be well, my beloved. It will be very well for all of us. I promise you that."

Again she made herself draw a breath. "I know that you do not intend to hurt me."

"Never, never! I love you, Sabha. That will never change."

"I know that you love me. But love is not enough to make a marriage."

He cocked his head, studying her with a puzzled expression. "What more could any man and woman need to stay together than love for each other?"

"They must have respect. They must have loyalty. When those two things are present, and love is the third part, then they might stay together and be happy for all of their days. But love alone is not enough."

"Oh, but Sabha, I have nothing but respect for you, and my loyalty to you will never waver. You already know that I love you. You need not ever worry about any of those things."

"I know," she whispered, nodding slightly. "I know."

"Then you will accept Coiteann into our home as a sister and second wife?"

Sabha listened to a few beats of her heart, even as she willed herself to remain motionless. "Allow me this," she said at last. "Allow me to stay here alone in our home for a time. Allow me to remain apart from you while you go to live with Coiteann."

His smile faded. "Why . . . why would you want me to do that?"

"Because my position on bringing a second wife into this house has not changed. You must now choose between us, Airt. You must decide whether you want me or you want Coiteann, for you cannot have us both."

Again he reached for her hand, closing his fingers over the fist that rested in her lap. "But I do not want to leave you! That is the last thing I want. I only want to add to our family, not take away from it!"

Sabha moved her hand away. "Go and live with her, and get your fill of her, so that you can never say I tried to stop you. While you are there, you can make your decision. I have already made mine. You cannot, and you will not, have us both."

"Sabha . . ." Airt stood up in the soft straw and faced her. "I will do this. I will go and live with Coiteann for a time, but only because it is what you want. I do this only for you, so that you can think of what I have said and come to understand that it will be good for all of us."

He kissed her gently on the forehead and then walked across the house to go outside, closing the door behind him as he left.

Sabha closed her eyes.

* * *

A heavy, moonless dark surrounded Sion. In the warmth of her cave, Rioghan lit an extra lamp to take away the last of the shadows, and then dropped a few dried flowers into her bronze cup where it rested on the stone edge of her firepit.

Two of her dogs stayed inside the cave with her, but instead of lying down in the comfortable straw they paced about the large space and sniffed the night breeze, occasionally whining or growling low in their throats. And as they paced they would look up at Rioghan and then toward the entrance of the cave, their concern and uneasiness plain in their eyes.

Rioghan, too, found that she could not sit down. She took a ladle and poured a little hot water from her bronze cauldron into her cup, left it to steam on the stone wall of the hearth, and then stepped out into the darkness just beyond the light of the cave.

Mist rolled about her feet. Thick clouds left the sky a featureless black. The only light came from the hearth and lamps behind her, and from the red-gold shine in the eyes of the many dogs trotting back and forth, growling softly, in the open meadow before the cave. A few of the dogs came over to touch her hand with their noses or stand beside her for a moment, always looking out into the darkness, always moving on again to patrol their territory and guard their home.

Then, as one, they stopped and raised their heads. The pack faced the strip of dark forest that separated Sion from the stone circle—and after a heartbeat of standing in complete silence, they shot straight across the meadow.

Rioghan ran after them. The dogs tore through the forest until they reached the clearing where the stone circle stood. Rioghan let them run past her and then crouched down behind the trunks of two pine trees, peering out into the darkness as the dogs began a frenzy of barking.

The ground began to shake with hoofbeats. Across the clearing, a group of men on horseback came crashing out of the forest, riding down the same path Donaill had followed to fetch her the night before—and one of the men Rioghan recognized instantly.

"Beolagh," she whispered, and so it was, the same loud, greedy man who had come here with Donaill, the same man whose small eyes had lit up upon seeing the gold of Sion.

He had brought six other men with him. Their horses' hooves cut and ripped the damp earth as they galloped back and forth across the clearing and in and out of the stones of the circle. The men slashed their swords at the furiously barking dogs as they rode, laughing as they did, and occasionally shouting in triumph whenever one of the dogs shrieked in pain.

Yet a seventh horse had no rider and ran loose, its reins trailing on the ground. Rioghan saw another man move out of the forest until he stood right in the center of the stone circle, facing away from her, held there by several dogs with bared teeth.

Her fear and confusion continued to rise. Why did the dogs not attack the lone man on foot? They could make a quick end to the intruder and then help drive away the others on horseback—but as Rioghan stretched up a little taller, she saw with a shock why the dogs would get no closer.

The man on foot held his sword to the neck of another, smaller figure.

"Kieran!" Rioghan cried, but the Sidhe could not hear her over the baying of her dogs.

How had these men possibly managed to catch Kieran? He was of the Fair Folk! How had he let himself be caught out in the open?

The men on horseback continued to gallop past the other dogs, teasing and striking at them. Then, with a terrible shriek, a huge black hound flipped over in the air amidst a spray of blood. Beolagh galloped past and raised the crimson blade of his sword overhead, shouting wildly as the dog fell heavily to earth and lay motionless.

For Rioghan, shock turned to rage. She stood up, formed her hands into fists as hard as stones, and cried, "*Madra!*"

Instantly the dogs' barking ceased. The pack of black and gray beasts turned away from their tormentors and raced toward her, still growling and whining. In a moment they had her surrounded and milled about in a tight circle.

The marauding men pulled up their horses in the center of the standing stones, surrounding the one who still held Kieran in his grip. All of them kept a wary eye on the dogs, who had suddenly and inexplicably bolted to the edge of the forest.

Rioghan stood very still within her cover of brush and trees. The men would not see her so long as she did not move, but Kieran would surely know she was there and understand why the dogs had dashed away to gather at the edge of the pines.

His captor's sword still at his throat, Kieran raised his head and tried to look over his shoulder at Beolagh. "Leave Sion, and I will bring you other gold," he said to them, in his soft, childlike voice. "I will bring it to you here in the stone circle. Just leave Sion and do not return."

But the men only laughed, though a little nervously, as they continued to watch the strange behavior of the dogs. "Why should we wait for you to bring it?" said the one holding Kieran. "You'll only disappear if we let you go!"

"We want the gold now. We want what is buried inside that mound you call Sion," said Beolagh. "And why shouldn't we have it? What does a woman living alone need with gold? It's a small price to pay for the protection she enjoys from Cahir Cullen!"

"Leave Sion's gold," Kieran said again. "I will bring you—"

A deep rumbling sound rose up from the earth, and then stopped.

The seven men looked at each other. Then, before any of them could speak, the sound began again. It was a low rumble from beneath the enormous brooding stones of the circle.

Their eyes widening in shock, the men watched

as the great stones began to tremble. One of the stones, the largest and tallest of them, actually rocked slightly, as if it would tear itself free of the earth and walk over to crush the intruders.

The men clung to their terrified horses as the animals bolted. The man who held Kieran shoved him violently aside in his panic to get away, and dashed after his comrades in a futile effort to catch up to them, crying out as they galloped off toward the road back to Cahir Cullen.

Peace returned to the clearing. The stones settled back to earth, as silent and still as ever.

Breathing hard, Rioghan bowed her head and shut her eyes. A wave of exhaustion passed over her. She slid her crystal wand back into its slim leather case beneath the sleeve of her left forearm, giving silent thanks once more to her mother for teaching her how to wield the ancient crystal. The wand seemed to be attuned to their family; no one else had ever been able to use it. But it would give Rioghan a brief and frighteningly strong burst of power over natural things made of earth or stone, and it had certainly been effective on this night. She stepped out of the forest and hurried over to Kieran with the pack of dogs close by her side.

The young Sidhe was just getting to his feet. "Are you hurt? Did they hurt you?" she asked, touching his face and his arms and looking closely at him. "What have they done to you?"

Kieran's face was pale and damp, and his dark locks fell down over his eyes, but he drew himself up straight and pushed his hair back with hands that trembled only a little. "I am not hurt," he claimed, after a breath. "They did not want me. I think they're afraid of us, strange as it sounds, as though we had some dire magic we could use to take revenge on them. They wanted the gold in your care but feared to murder one of us to get it."

"Kieran, gold means nothing compared to your life. And the Men are afraid of nothing but old tales and half-remembered wars from long ago. They may fear us, but they do not respect us. Never forget that."

She smiled at him and smoothed his hair. "Come with me back to Sion. There is a little blood at your throat. Let me see to it, while you tell me how this came about."

The Sidhe nodded, and walked with her back to the comforting shelter of the forest. It was only a short distance through the stand of trees to the clearing where Sion stood—but then, to their horror, they realized that once again the forest shook with thundering hooves.

Riders were galloping straight down the road from Cahir Cullen and toward the clearing of Sion.

Chapter Four

Rioghan grabbed Kieran's hand and together they dashed across the clearing to the mound. When they got to the cave, she reached beneath her sleeve and pulled out her crystal wand once more.

"Go and get the others!" she said to Kieran. "Bring all your people's warriors here! Go! Go!" And after only a heartbeat of hesitation, Kieran raced off to bring the men of the Sidhe to defend their land against a second wave of intruders.

Rioghan stood in the clearing at the entrance of her cave. This would leave her backlit by the fire and her lamps, and she hoped that her ominous silhouette would let whoever approached know that the cave was not unguarded.

But the six riders who came thundering into the dark meadow seemed not to care.

The frenzied barking and bared teeth of her leaping, menacing dogs held them just beyond the trees. Their snorting horses shied and swerved and refused to move into the snarling pack—but this time the intruders were ready.

Two of the men pulled wide rope nets, like fishing nets, from behind their saddles. Where had they gotten them? Why had they not used them before? With practiced arms they threw the heavy devices over the dogs—and just that quickly, nearly half of Rioghan's twenty-nine dogs were thoroughly entangled and unable to do anything but snap and snarl in frustration.

While his five companions swung and slashed at the remaining dogs with their swords, Beolagh reined his horse hard around them and galloped to the entrance of the cave.

Rioghan held tight to her crystal wand, keeping it hidden beneath her palm, and went out to face him. She stood tall and bold with her arms held out from her sides, as though shielding the entrance to her home.

"Did you think we would give up so easily?" Beolagh asked, dragging his horse to a stop in front of her. "You may have a few tricks, but these are the king's warriors you're dealing with! You cannot frighten us away as if we were nothing but Little People!" He laughed. "We knew we might have to deal with your dogs, so we were ready for them. And in case you were wondering, we've come for your gold. We know you have no need of it. Give it to us."

Rioghan stared at him, motionless. "It is not mine to give. It is Sidhe gold."

"The Sidhe have no more use for it than you do! We, on the other hand, could do a great deal with it. Give it to us now, and consider it payment for all the goods and protection you have received from Cahir Cullen over the years."

"I will give you nothing," Rioghan answered, and she shut her eyes tight.

Beolagh flinched and raised his arm to his head as a small rock struck him in the shoulder. Then his horse leaped in fright as a second stone landed on its hindquarters. When yet another one struck, the animal spun away and bolted back toward the others before Beolagh could stop it.

"They're slinging rocks from above!" he shouted, rage and frustration clear in his voice. "Flann, Dowan, ride up atop the mound and get them down! The rest of us will finish the dogs and then the gold is ours! Go on now! Go!"

The two men galloped off into the darkness as Beolagh had ordered, heading around to the back of Sion, where they could ride their horses up the smooth, grassy slope of the mound. Rioghan smiled grimly as she watched them go. They would be surprised to find the top of it deserted; there were no Sidhe up there to meet them. Not yet. These stones had come flying only by the limited power that she herself could command with her crystal.

That power was useful, but it was brief. She would not be able to hold these men off for long. The few dogs not entangled in the nets still faced slashing iron swords. Even as she watched the frantic dogs and determined intruders at the forest's edge, there came a heart-rending shriek as another of her dogs met its end. Beolagh yelled in triumph.

Quickly Rioghan stepped out of the light from her cave and into the shadows of the rock face surrounding it. "Scath! Cogar!" she called, her voice a whisper. "Come to me! Come!"

In a moment, to her great relief, the two enormous panting dogs tore themselves away from the pack and came bounding over to her. She grabbed them by their gold and bronze collars and held them close.

"Donaill," she whispered fiercely. "Find Donaill. *Donaill.*" Then she released them, and the pair flew through the night and vanished into the strip of forest, there to race across the stone circle and down the hidden path to Cahir Cullen.

"You're sure you want to bring a second wife into the house? Don't you remember what happened when Bercan did that, a few years ago?"

Donaill leaned back so that his shoulders rested against the curving, grass-covered earthen wall of Cahir Cullen. He and six other warriors—Irial, Lorcan, Niall, Tully, Comyn, and Airt—all sat on thick furs or woolen cloaks tossed on the cold, damp grass, or on one of the several large stones scattered about. Only a few stars showed themselves from time to time through the heavy, slow-moving clouds that shrouded the fortress in darkness.

Yet it was pleasant sitting out here together beneath the flickering torchlight, their breath forming white clouds as they talked and laughed. Donaill and the others often sat out here in the evenings when the weather was not too harsh, enjoying the brisk air of winter as much as they did the soft breezes of summer.

Airt grinned. "I didn't see it, but I heard the stories. And I also heard that Bercan and his two wives are all living peacefully together now."

"When Bercan brought his second wife into his home and introduced her to his first wife, all went well—in the beginning," Donaill said. "The two women were cold, but polite to each other, and it seemed that they would learn to tolerate the situation.

"But then, some four days later, Bercan woke to the sounds of bronze plates and iron tongs smashing against the walls of his house, and of the two women locked in a screaming argument. The new wife had not only rearranged some of the first wife's store of dried flowers and carefully gathered remedies, she had begun to embroider one of Bercan's cloaks—a cloak that the first wife had made for him.

"This was more than enough to send the first wife's cold resentment flaring into violence. She seized the offender by the hair, dragged her out of the house, and threw her face-first into the dirt and rocks in front of the door."

Airt shook his head. "I know that making the adjustment is always the hardest part for the wives. Even the laws understand this. Is not the first wife immune from penalty for three days for any harm she might do the other wives when they first come into the house?"

"She is," Niall answered. "And for any harm she might do the husband as well."

Airt's eyes widened. "Oh," he said. "I had forgotten about that."

"She's only immune for simple assault—not for actual bloodletting or permanent injury," said Comyn helpfully.

"Or murder. She is not exempt for murder, either," added Tully, being equally helpful.

"You're right," said Irial. "And since not many can afford to pay the body price *and* the honor price for murder, it happens only rarely."

"And after three days, the first wife is exempt from only half the penalty, instead of the full penalty," said Lorcan. "That does slow down a few of them after a while . . . but not many."

"Airt, you seem to be forgetting one thing," Irial said. "You must have the first wife's consent, however grudging, before you bring a second wife into the home. Otherwise, the first wife has the right to divorce you and take all of her goods with her—as well as a portion of yours. You would still have only one woman in your house, and you would also have a divorced wife who resents you."

"And it is not just a matter of law," said Donaill. "You cannot do this thing by force. It will never succeed if the first wife will not accept it, and there are many who will not. You cannot ignore the feelings of such a woman. She may do far worse than simply divorce you."

Airt raised his head and tried to look them all in the eye. "I think a man just has to be patient and understanding while the adjustment is being made. It has been successfully done many times. I am sure that Sabha and Coiteann and I will be no different. I look forward to our being a family."

"If you ever see Bercan's wives," said Lorcan, "take a close look at the younger one's face. She still bears the scars from the fall she took that night, thrown down by her sister-wife. Never do the two of them speak unless it is absolutely necessary."

"Bercan's is a very quiet house," said Irial.

"And a peaceful one, too, I should think," said Airt, with a laugh.

"Some might call it peaceful," said Donaill. "But a cold, grim sort of peace it is. Not the sort that I would want in my home."

"I would ask you, though, Donaill," Airt said, "why a man of your status and respect has no wife at all in his house. Surely there are many who would be only too glad to take their places with you there. Surely you, the king's champion, are a man who could have one or two or even three wives, wives who would be pleased to do all they could to gain your attentions—"

Donaill laughed. "I would rather have one woman living in happiness than two or three living in constant jealousy and tension. When I find that one, I will know. You need not worry for me, Airt.

I would rather have true peace in my house, even if I must settle for just one wife."

"Oh, I did not mean to worry for you! I only meant—"

But Donaill suddenly sat up straight and held out his hand for silence. All of them looked at him and quickly glanced at each other—and then the rest of them heard it, too.

There was a scratching, scrambling sound on the outside of the steep grass-covered wall, a wall half again as tall as any man in Cahir Cullen. The seven men leaped to their feet, reaching for the hilts of their swords as they did, and stood tense and waiting.

Something tore at the grass on the other side of the wall—something large and growling and determined. The men each fell back a few paces, braced, and waited for whatever it was to show itself.

Two huge dogs, one gray and one black, leaped up to the top of the wall. The gold and bronze plates on their collars gleamed in the torchlight from the grounds.

Donaill lowered his sword. He took a slow step toward the dogs, and then another. "Rioghan," he whispered.

The two dogs pointed their noses to the dark sky and howled, a pleading, insistent noise that rose up to the clouds and vanished on the wind.

Donaill and his six companions ran to their horses.

Galloping out of the gates and into the night, they followed the narrow path through the dark woods.

Donaill did not need to follow the pair of dogs to know they were going straight to Sion. Only moments before, he and his friends had been relaxing within the safe walls of Cahir Cullen, enjoying a long winter evening with hardly more to worry about than who would fetch their next cup of blackberry wine. But now they rode through the woods at a breakneck pace, for Donaill knew that Rioghan would never have sent her dogs to him unless something was terribly wrong.

It was not long before they heard it.

Beyond the stone circle, on the other side of the strip of forest that separated the stones from Sion, came the sound of rearing horses and shouting men and fiercely barking dogs—and above it all, floating in the cold still air, a steady, hissing chant.

"Leave us!"

"Leave us!"

"Leave us!"

And as Donaill and his men burst out of the woods, he saw Rioghan up on the top of the mound of Sion, lit from below by the fire of the cave and surrounded by the men and women of the Sidhe. She held a bright crystal in her upraised hand and led the Sidhe in their wild, insistent chant.

"Earth, rise up!"

"Earth, rise up!"

Quickly Donaill and his men dragged their horses to a stop and tried to make sense of the wild confusion. Everywhere dogs leaped and snapped as six shouting riders slashed at them with their weapons. Stones flew through the air from the slings of the

Sidhe. And it seemed to Donaill that an ominous shaking and vibration surged through the earth beneath their feet, unnerving the horses and their riders, almost as if the ground itself was about to—

"Earth, rise up!"

The trembling increased. A few rocks tumbled down from above the cave of Sion. All of the horses, including those of Donaill and his men, swung in terror and bolted for the forest, leaping and plunging away no matter what their riders tried to do.

The Sidhe cried out in triumph—but then the shaking stopped.

Donaill turned around. He saw Rioghan's arms drop to her sides. She collapsed to the grass, exhausted. The Sidhe quickly surrounded her, dropping their slings. They all disappeared, then, into the darkness and the night became quiet and still once more.

The invading sextet of riders regrouped. They turned their horses back toward Sion once again, and Donaill's anger flared when he recognized Beolagh as their leader. Forcing his black horse back into the clearing, Donaill shouted out, "Irial! Lorcan! Move now! Get those men away from here! Make them remember why they should not come back!"

The six men who rode with Donaill were among the best of King Bran's warriors, and they made short work of the startled Beolagh and his five companions. Lorcan and Niall cut and pulled the heavy tangled nets off the trapped dogs, leaving the animals free to help.

There was no need to do serious harm to any of these men. The fierce barking and biting of the dogs, combined with the aggressive riding and challenges of Donaill and his men, soon had Beolagh and his followers surrounded. Their nervous horses crowded together as Rioghan's dogs continued to growl and snarl at them, their eyes shining red in the light of the nearby bonfire.

"Beolagh!" shouted Donaill, allowing his horse to trot around the edge of the clearing. "And all the rest of you, the king's own men! What are you doing in this place?" He pointed his sword directly at Beolagh's pale and wide-eyed face. "This is the Lady Rioghan's home! Why do you disturb it in this way? Why have you come here? Answer me!"

Beolagh gaped at him and opened his mouth as if to speak, but said nothing. As silence fell over the clearing, he glanced left and right, and Donaill saw that his own men had all of Beolagh's riders at swordpoint—and none of them seemed any more ready to talk than their leader.

Donaill glanced at them. "I see that not one of you has the courage to answer me. The king will be pleased to know he has such honorable men serving him." He snorted in contempt. "All of you—get off your horses. Now."

Sullen and grim-faced, Beolagh and the other five slid down to the ground. "Move away from there. Stand over here, near the light from the cave, where we can see you."

With the greatest reluctance, the six men let go of their horses and walked in a little group toward the cave. Quickly Airt and Comyn chased away the riderless horses and sent them galloping in a tight herd back down the road to Cahir Cullen. Donaill knew they would not stop until they reached the gates of the fortress.

His warriors surrounded the six men on foot, keeping them at swordpoint in the flickering light of the bonfire. In moments, the sound of their horses' hoofbeats faded away. In the quiet that followed, Donaill could have sworn he heard the faint sound of laughing from somewhere above.

He kept his eyes firmly on his captives, resisting the temptation to look up to see the Sidhe or Rioghan. "I will ask you only once more, Beolagh. Why have you come to this place?"

His anger and frustration beginning to overcome his fear, Beolagh finally looked his captor in the eye. "We have harmed no one here! See for yourself!"

"No one? Were any of these dogs hurt? How many did you kill?"

Beolagh scowled in annoyance. "I don't know. I might have killed one. What else could we do? They attacked us!"

Donaill laughed, though it was filled with contempt. "Oh, of course. You invade their home, so the creatures attack you, and then you have no choice but to kill them. Do you realize what a perfect idiot you resemble?"

Clenching his fists in frustration, Beolagh glared up at Donaill. "None of the Sidhe were harmed. We only want the gold!"

"Gold?" Donaill halted his horse, though he still

kept his sword pointed at Beolagh. "What gold?"

Now it was Beolagh's turn to look disgusted. "You know very well what gold! The gold right there in that cave!"

The man turned and pointed. There in the low light of Rioghan's home, visible along the edges of the black cowhide hangings, were the glints of the gold and bronze and crystal objects that Beolagh had eyed the night before—a beautiful collection of pieces large and small, of rings and armbands and curving torques; of plates and small bowls with magnificent curling and interlocking designs; of stars and crescent moons and horses and dogs and deer and wolves perfectly rendered in gleaming metal and inlaid with sparkling crystals.

Donaill almost laughed. "So instead of serving as King Bran's warriors you have decided to become common thieves? You would rather spend your time stealing the plates and cups of an undefended woman?"

Beolagh scowled and clenched his teeth, but he stayed among his men. "We are not thieves! That is Sidhe gold hidden in that cave. What need does a solitary midwife have for it?"

"Whether she has need of it or not, it's no concern of yours. Anything in that cave is hers and hers alone. Did you not learn that as a child, Beolagh, as the rest of us did? Or were you out stealing the other babes' toys on the day that lesson was taught?"

Donaill's men began to chuckle amongst themselves. Also, he felt sure he could again hear the faint sound of laughing from above, and even from deep within the forest.

But Beolagh only glared hard at his captors; then he turned and spat on the ground. Donaill tightened his grip on his sword and lifted Cath's reins.

"The Sidhe are not our people! They are nothing but animals roaming the woods!" Beolagh shouted. "They live in caves and wear skins and furs! What use do animals have for gold? It will cause them no harm whatever if we take it, no more than if we took a wagonload of rock from their forest! It will cause them no harm. No harm at all!"

Donaill cantered his stallion in a tight circle around the six captured men, forcing them to gather close together and raise their chins to look up at him. "Hear me, all of you!" he cried, pointing his sword directly at them as he rode by. "You are to stay away from this place. You are to leave this midwife and the Sidhe unmolested and in peace. You are to make no attempt to take their gold, or their bronze, or a clod of earth on the forest floor, or anything else that is in their possession. Am I understood?"

Beolagh looked as if he were ready to spit again, but thought better of it. "You are," he muttered, and then elbowed his glowering companions. "Understood," they all said, one after another. "Understood."

Donaill halted Cath. "Good," he said, and gave them all a sincere and pleasant smile. "Then I shall look forward to not seeing you here again. Go on now. You have a bit of a walk ahead of you. I hope you enjoy it."

He backed his horse away from them, and glanced at his men to do the same. Beolagh scowled and looked from Donaill to his own sullen followers. Finally all of them turned and tramped off after their long-gone horses, walking down the dark road that would take them the long but simple way back to the fortress.

When the men were out of sight, Donaill turned to Irial. "All of you—go back to Cahir Cullen. Make sure Beolagh and the others really do return. I must go and find Rioghan."

"You are certain? We will wait—"

"There is no need. It is late enough already. Go and get your rest. I will return by dawn."

Irial grinned, and then turned his horse to go. "If you do find her, it may be later than that. We'll see to Beolagh for you. And I suppose you can always sleep tomorrow."

The six riders cantered across the clearing and then started back down the road to Cahir Cullen, leaving Donaill alone on his horse before the softly glowing cave of Sion.

Chapter Five

Donaill waited, tense, until the other riders had gone. While Cath stepped and snorted beneath him, he listened closely and tried to search the darkness for any sign that Beolagh and his men might have slipped around and come back.

Suddenly Cath jumped forward and the horse's head jerked up. Donaill swung the mount around, his sword raised, and watched as two small shadows moved slowly out from behind the looming dark mound of Sion.

Donaill closed his legs on Cath's sides and reined him back firmly, causing the stallion to half rear. "Stop! You will come no closer to this place until I know who you are. Show yourselves!"

The shadows continued to approach. One leaned upon the other with what seemed to be great weariness, and then the pair moved into the glow of the hearthfire. "Donaill," said a soft voice. "It is Rioghan. Rioghan and Kieran. Please . . . let us pass."

Quickly Donaill backed his horse away and slid down to the ground. To his surprise, another pair of shadows reached out and took the reins: a duo of Sidhe. Cath went with them calmly and disappeared into the darkness.

"They will care for him," whispered Rioghan. "Come inside with us."

She walked out into the clearing, and stopped. Near the entrance to the cave lay the still gray body of one of her dogs.

"I am so sorry," Kieran whispered. "I was not fast enough—or strong enough . . ."

She looked away, then briefly patted his arm. "Do not think of it now. We will do what needs do be done for Garda later. You are safe, and that is most important."

Slowly, still leaning on Kieran, her face pale and her hands trembling, Rioghan walked to the entrance of her home and drew aside the black cowhide curtain. "Come inside," she said again, and Donaill followed her inside the softly lit cave.

"Please, Lord Donaill . . . sit down beside the fire while I see to Kieran." Rioghan led the young Sidhe to the sleeping ledge and made him sit down in the thick straw so she could tend him. Her two dogs Cogar and Scath settled in on either side of the Sidhe, and he leaned his head back against the ledge and rested his arms comfortably on the animals' shoulders.

"I can see that you are very weary, Lady Rioghan," said Donaill, sitting down on a cushion in the straw near the hearth. "Are you all right? What may I do for you?"

She smiled. "I am well, and I thank you for your question. I am always weak when I have been forced to use the magic of the earth, the little that is mine to command. I will soon recover." With a quick glance around the cave, she noted with relief that all was as she had left it. No intruder had set foot inside her home this night.

Rioghan picked up a little stack of firewood and took it to the hearth. "Kieran," she began, as she built up the fire, "you are a young man of the Sidhe, as clever and strong as any in your clan. How is it possible that six loud and clumsy men were able to capture you?"

Kieran said nothing, but his eyes shifted to Donaill sitting by the hearth near the entrance to the cave. In the silence, Rioghan moved to the far end of her little home. There she filled a small bronze cauldron with fresh water, and gathered a few strips of clean white linen.

"Mil and Ceo were walking here to Sion, as they always do each night, to tidy it and bring what might be needed," Kieran said at last. "You care for so many, Rioghan, whether Man or Sidhe, and see to every birth. It seems you scarcely take any time to care for yourself."

Rioghan smiled. "It would seem so. I am grateful

to Mil and Ceo for their constant help."

"I walked with them," Kieran went on, "intending to keep watch and help carry water, when I heard the men riding straight for us through the deepest part of the forest.

"Their voices carried well before them in the woods. It was clear they were determined to get your gold, even if they had to capture you and kill every one of your dogs—and we feared they might do just that, for you know the dogs would never retreat."

She nodded again, glancing at the animals who continued to support Kieran—and thinking of those who now lay unmoving out on the cold, damp earth of the clearing. "Go on. How were you able to keep them away from Sion at first?"

He looked away. "My first thought was for the two women. Mil and Ceo are no longer young, and I feared they could never outrun the men on horseback if they were seen. So I told them to hide in the forest as the men rode past.

"They were safe. They were not seen. But the men rode straight to the stone circle, where the dogs met them, and I knew they would be at Sion as soon as they could get past the dogs. I had to stop them . . . and so I let them see me. I called to them and showed them this."

Kieran reached beneath his moss-green cloak and pulled out a small, bright armband, made from a slender, twisted band of gold. "Oh, their eyes lit up. And they were glad enough to ride away from such troublesome dogs. But I knew that nothing but the promise of the gold I could bring would keep them from Sion. I felt I had no choice but to allow the men to catch me."

Rioghan set her cauldron down onto the coals of the hearth, filled a shallow bronze dish with cool, clean water, and sat down beside Kieran with the dish and the linens. Reaching across her dogs, she tilted Kieran's head back and began cleaning the long, shallow cuts across one side of his neck. "That was a brave thing you did. Brave . . . and terrible. No doubt Mil and Ceo are very grateful to you, as am I. But—as I said—no amount of gold is worth your life."

He winced a little as she cleaned away the last of the blood. "I am glad that the women escaped without being seen. And gold *is* just gold. However, Lady Rioghan, many of these treasures are far more than just ornaments. They are bronze and gold and crystal pieces so ancient they were made by the gods. There was magic worked into those, just as there was power hammered into the stones of the circle . . . magic that helps us all to stay alive here in the forest, even with the coming of men." Kieran looked up at her with enormous dark brown eyes. "I could not let them steal it . . . not any of it."

Rioghan smiled gently and stood up to carry her basin of water and linen back to the hearth. "You are right. Your mother and grandmother have taught you very well. But Kieran . . ." She looked across the room at his young face. "Giving these men a few small things will not appease them. They cannot be bribed to leave us alone. If you give them a little, they will not stop until they get it all. And what will we do when we have no more to give?"

He looked away, but then just as quickly met her gaze again. "You are right. We will have to make sure they can never again get near Sion. Not any of them."

Boldly, Kieran looked straight at Donaill. "Can you not rid us of this evil thieving Man?" he asked, his voice remaining soft. "Can you not put him to the sword and remove this threat to us once and for all?"

Rioghan stopped, almost in mid-step. Her eyes shifted from Kieran to Donaill. Would he agree to such a thing? Would he go so far as to kill one of his own men, simply for the crime of trespassing against the Sidhe?

"Oh . . . well . . . you see . . ." Donaill gave a short laugh and started to get up, then sat back down again. "Much as I might like to—for if ever there was a perfect fool among the king's own men, it is Beolagh—I cannot simply kill someone outright. We at Cahir Cullen live by the laws of the druids. I would be brought before them as a murderer should I kill someone without sufficient cause."

"Sufficient cause?" Rioghan set down her basin. "Our home is overrun with armed trespassers, Kieran's life is threatened, and two of my guard dogs are killed—and your king would not find this to be 'sufficient cause'?"

"My sympathies are with you, my lady. That is

why I am here. But unfortunately, those crimes do not carry the penalty of death."

"It seems they carry little penalty at all," Rioghan murmured, turning to search among the small stone jars on her shelf.

"Beolagh and his cronies might disagree," Donaill said, chuckling again. "They found them to carry a penalty of dog bites and sword slaps and a nice long walk on foot back to Cahir Cullen." He grinned, looking expectantly at Rioghan and Kieran, but at their silence he was at last forced to look away. "I am sorry," he said, his voice serious. "I wish I could do more for you. But I must follow the law even if some do not."

Rioghan went over to Kieran's side. Gently she touched a healing paste to the wounds on his neck and wrapped a long strip of clean linen across them. "There," she said, getting to her feet. "Keep it clean, and let me change the wrappings tomorrow."

The Sidhe stood up, glancing at Donaill, then looked back at Rioghan. "My lady . . ."

She smiled at him. "Go, Kieran. All is well here. I will call if anything is needed."

With one more quick look at Donaill, the youngster turned and left the cave, disappearing into the silence of the winter night. After watching him go, Rioghan folded her hands and sat down on the stones at the edge of the hearth, within an arm's length of the man who sat on the leather cushion in the straw.

"Do not misunderstand me. I thank you for helping us," Rioghan said to him. "I do not know how

I can repay you. I am not certain what would have happened if you and your men had not come."

Donaill smiled, and then he got to his feet, minding his head on the low ceiling of the cave. "I am just glad that you trusted me enough to send for me. I will help you anytime you have need of me, Lady Rioghan. You have only to ask."

She met his gaze for a long moment, but before he could move again she stood up and stepped to the door of her cave. "Walk with me, if you will," she said, brushing aside the black cowhide door. Donaill quickly followed, as did her two dogs, into the quiet of the night.

"Rioghan! Where are you? I cannot see you!"

Rioghan smiled to herself. So quickly had she moved within the deep shadow of Sion that Donaill's brief hesitation had caused him to lose sight of her. "Here, Donaill. The dogs will show you."

She waited a moment, still in the shadows, until at last he walked toward her, feeling his way along the grassy side of the steep mound in near-total blackness. "And just where do you intend to take me, my lady?"

Rioghan smiled again, though she knew he could not see her face. "To a place you have never been, to see something you have never seen. This way." She turned and started up the faint path that tracked back and forth up the far side of the mound. In only a short time she reached the very top, where Donaill and the two dogs quickly joined her.

"Oh," he said, and she stepped back to let him see.

The mound became nearly level at its peak, like a small, grassy meadow floating high above the earth. There was a bare ashy spot near the center where the great fires burned on the appropriate days. Donaill walked forward until he stood near the edge of the mound and then raised both hands, holding them out from his sides, as he simply stood and took it all in.

The ever-moving clouds had thinned enough to finally allow the clear, cold light of the stars to filter through. It cast the faintest glow on the tops of the pine trees, for the top of the mound was high enough to allow Rioghan and Donaill to look down on the forest.

All around them were the endless woods; but to the west, just beyond the narrow strip of trees that separated it from Sion, was the large clearing where the stone circle lay.

The nine stones were only forms distinguishable in the dark at this distance. Even Rioghan was not sure she could actually see them. Yet there was no forgetting their ancient presence in the clearing beyond the trees.

"I have stood upon other hills, and ridden through this forest countless times, but never have I seen the world quite like this," Donaill remarked. "The trees are lined with starlight; the needles have turned to faintest silver. Even the blades of grass ripple and compete to see which will shine the brightest in whatever light there is for them to gather."

He sighed, as Scath and Cogar lay down at his feet. "I thank you for allowing me to come to this place, to see the forest in this way."

Rioghan sat down beside her dogs, throwing the ends of her heavy black wool cloak across her chest and over her shoulder. "This is only the beginning. Watch . . . and listen."

He glanced at her, a gleam of curiosity in his eye, and then sat down in the cold grass beside her. Donaill followed her gaze as he looked out across the clearing to the west, beyond the strip of pine trees where the stone circle stood.

The stones were all but invisible in the deep night. But as the two of them watched, it was not long before they heard it: the faint, sweet notes of a harp, and then the soft beat of a drum, and then high voices singing in harmony with the distant music.

She heard Donaill catch his breath. As the music and the singing continued, the clouds thinned more and more and finally all but vanished, as they did on occasion in the inland forests of Eire. And as the stars shone at their brightest, the nine stones of the circle took shape in the darkness, and shadowy forms began to move among them.

Donaill stretched taller, straining to see. "What is that? No animal moves in such a way, whirling and turning and circling. Who is there?"

"Listen," Rioghan said again. "Listen, and they will tell you."

The music rose and the song grew clearer. It was

a song of ancient days and a long-lost people, of a time when the gods lived and walked in the land of Eire, a time when power existed to make the great stones light as air and move them above the earth . . . when gold lay glittering in the crystal-clear streams and could be made to work itself into the most beautiful of objects.

"Those are the Sidhe themselves, of course," Donaill said. "It is rare for Men to see them. We live within the walls of Cahir Cullen, safe and secure and closed away from the rest of the world. We crash through the forests and thunder down the roads at full gallop, forgetting that the Sidhe live here too, in secret and in silence . . . but I have gotten quite a good reminder of them here tonight."

"They have always been here," said Rioghan, "living in the forest and doing much to maintain and guard it . . . especially from the careless damage done by those men who live in it and ride through it and strip it bare for their pleasure."

"Maintain it? Guard it? How could they do that? It's a very big forest, and the Sidhe are small and few in number."

"Have you never aimed your spear at the largest, strongest stag, only to see it suddenly leap away with no apparent cause? And then, moments later, a smaller, poorer animal charges headlong into you, practically running itself onto your spear point?"

He turned to look at her with an expression of surprise. "Why . . . I do remember—"

"And have none of your farmers ever cleared away the oldest or the rarest trees, only to find themselves plagued with ill luck and thievery for days and weeks thereafter?"

"The farmers often say such things—but I thought them only to be making excuses."

"Yet they learned which trees they could safely take, and which to leave alone." Rioghan smiled in the darkness. "The Sidhe have good reason to carefully guard their treasures, the artifacts I keep, for even now their beautiful pieces retain traces of the most ancient of power. This power helps the Fair Folk to go about unnoticed, helps them to work small feats of magic when they wish."

She glanced at him. "It was not chance that made the stags leap. It was not coincidence that caused the farmer's plows to break or the housewife's cauldrons to go missing."

Donaill turned to her, and in the pale starlight she could see that he was grinning. "I suppose it was not. So, Rioghan, tell me if you will: Who does this treasure belong to? This gold and crystal and bronze which has, unfortunately, caught the eye of Beolagh—does it belong to you? To your family? Or to the Sidhe?"

Rioghan nodded, slowly, and gazed out over the starlit pines. "It does not belong to me, nor to my family. It belongs to the Sidhe, every last piece of it, and I will guard it for them with my life."

"But if it belongs to the Sidhe, why is it all kept here, inside this cave? Would it not be better to hide it among them in the most secret places of the forest?"

"Some of it is with the Sidhe. Each of them wears

at least one piece, or keeps one hanging in their home. You saw Kieran's fine armband when he was here tonight."

"I did."

"As I said, the magic that remains within these pieces can sometimes help the Sidhe with the things that they must do: charm an animal, perhaps, or move about unseen. But the pieces are kept here at Sion—and only passed among the Sidhe from time to time—because Sion is the place that best preserves their power."

"Ah," Donaill said, and she saw his eyes gleam with understanding. "I think I am beginning to see it, now."

"It is not by chance that Sion is formed the way it is. Sion is not a thing of nature. It was built so by the ancients, who made a perfectly curving dome of soil and rock to concentrate the powers of the earth directly into the cave at its base.

"The longer these things of gold and bronze and crystal remain inside, the greater is their power—and so, except for those pieces in use by the Sidhe, that is where they stay. That is where they *must* stay."

"For they will lose their power otherwise," Donaill said. "Yet—why are you the one who lives in the cave? Why not the Sidhe themselves, to guard their own gold?"

"They did live here once . . . generations ago. Sion was a home to them the way Cahir Cullen is to you. But with the coming of Men, it proved to be too vulnerable, too easily found, and so it was abandoned as the Sidhe moved deeper into the forests.

"Then one day it happened that a farmer and his wife found this peaceful place not far from the great fortress. He was of the Men while his wife carried the blood of both Man and Sidhe. They had no doubt they would be safe here, for Men considered them their own and the Sidhe knew their own blood when they saw it.

"The pair did not even need a house, for they had this fine cave to live in . . . and in time, the Sidhe came to know them and to trust them, and even became a part of their family when the first of many marriages took place between them.

"That is how I came to live in this place. I was born here. If I can move well enough between the world of Men and the world of the Sidhe, it is because I am neither and I am both.

"I am happy to have this beautiful treasure of the Sidhe all around me in the cave of Sion, for that is where it belongs—and that is where it must remain, because now, as the Sidhe have always feared, Men have returned to violate their home once again."

"They have done that for the last time, if I have anything to say about it," Donaill said. "That was a lovely story, Rioghan. Now I will ask you another question, if you do not mind: what do you know of the stone circles and its origins? No one at Cahir Cullen knows for sure, and the druids will say nothing; and though I keep it to myself, I think it is because, in truth, they do not know either. I see now that you—and the Sidhe—may be the ones who truly know."

She smoothed her black cloak over her knees. "I will admit that we know little more than you. There are only the oldest stories, which you hear in the songs they sing tonight . . . stories of the ancient gods who could make the great stones hover in the air and arrange themselves into a circle.

"All of us, men and Sidhe alike, have heard those stories, yet no one alive has ever seen such a thing. There are only the ancient tales. And all of us gather at our own stone circles to observe the solstices and equinoxes, the men and their druids at the large circle on the far side of Cahir Cullen and the Sidhe at this one here by Sion.

"Yet the Sidhe know well how special the stone circles are, how powerful, how magical. They are the ones who might gather within them on any night of the year, beneath the light of the stars, to play their harps and sing their songs and dance and make merry and make love—for they know that each time they do so they add to its magic. There is more power here than most men know."

Donaill sat back, resting on one elbow. "I can see how the music and the song might conjure power—but the lovemaking?" She could hear the amusement in his voice. "I did not know that such a thing could raise magic."

Rioghan cast a sideways glance at him. "And yet I cannot think of anything that would increase the magic in a place more than the physical act of love, if it is meant to convey a true feeling of affection between the partners . . . if it is done to preserve the bond between them, done to bring them closer. Nothing is so rare, or so powerful, as love that is true and unshakable."

"Is it so rare? I would have thought—"

"I am speaking of love, true and genuine, which will of course find expression in lovemaking. You are speaking only of sex, which is commonplace and too often carries little meaning. There is a great deal of difference between the two."

"Is there now." He sat up, facing her, and for a moment looked back toward the stone circle. The harp notes came faster now; the drumbeat grew stronger. "I had not thought of it that way before."

Rioghan tried to study his face, but he had turned so that it was in shadow. As before, she began to feel that perhaps he was mocking her—but his tone was so polite that she could not quite be certain. "I can tell you this much, Donaill: women often wish that men would think of it that way. At least, from time to time."

"I thank you for telling me this, then, Lady Rioghan. For, as I often tell the other men, it is not what they think of sex that matters—it is what the women think. Unfortunately, my advice is not often heeded." He sounded wry.

She cocked her head. "You seem to know much about women for a man who has no wife. Surely there must be a woman in your life somewhere."

He continued to gaze out toward the circle. "There is no woman in my house or in my heart. I have no wish to take a wife just for the sake of having one. I am happy as I am, with all that a man could want; I am the king's own champion and a leader of the warriors of Cahir Cullen. I have no wish to cause any woman any unhappiness by making her my wife."

Rioghan sat a little straighter, intrigued by his modesty and confused by how he'd acted earlier, as if wooing her. "You seem to be a kind and honorable man. How could becoming your wife bring unhappiness to a woman?"

He started to answer, but then glanced in her direction. Even in the darkness she could see the gleam in his eyes. "I am so glad that you do not believe it would bring unhappiness, Lady Rioghan. Perhaps you will be the one to become my wife." His white teeth gleamed in the starlight.

She could only blink. She knew he was mocking her now. "Thank you, but I must decline. I had planned to pull the burrs from the dogs' coats tomorrow. I'm sure you understand."

He laughed. "Oh, I understand perfectly." He sat listening to the Sidhe harp and drum for a moment before turning back to her. "I will tell you, though, in seriousness, that I have not yet married for the opposite reason that you have not married: you find all men to be unworthy, while I find all women to be more than worthy. In the end, we have the same dilemma. Neither one of us can choose."

"That may be true," Rioghan said, "but at least neither of us has acted on the fact that we are expected to marry. I live in this place, in part, so I will not have to endure such pressure. And I think you have done the women of Eire a great service by not limiting yourself to only one of them."

"Perhaps." He gave her an intense, piercing look. "But I have not yet given up hope that someday I might find the one who could change my mind."

Rioghan merely smiled, safe within the shadows, and turned away from him to face the stone circle once more.

The starlight seemed brighter than ever now, as though the songs and the music of the Sidhe had opened the earth to receive it in full. Rioghan could not help but feel caught up in the sweet notes of the harp and the insistent pounding of the drum, and in the beautiful singing voices of the Sidhe . . . and it was clear that Donaill was caught up in it, too.

At last he turned back to her, still half listening to the music. "Why?" he asked.

"Why?" She shook her head. "I don't understand. What do you wish to know?"

"I wish to know why you would bring me here with you . . . allow me to sit atop Sion, your home, and listen to the songs and music of the Sidhe as they dance in this magical place. Surely . . . surely you have brought no man up here before."

Rioghan smiled upon hearing the question in his voice, and at seeing the doubt in his face. She looked down and adjusted her cloak yet again. "Only rarely do I bring a man up here, Donaill. Only when I have decided to make him my husband and keep him a prisoner here for the rest of his days."

For a moment he was silent. In the faint light she

could see that his face was serious, no doubt thinking back on the strange tales he had heard of the secretive midwife of the Sidhe who lived alone in a cave in the forest—

"I accept," he said, and reached for her hand.

Rioghan bit her lip so she would not laugh out loud. "That is brave of you," she said, "but I have changed my mind. I shall be kind. I shall let you go after all."

His hand fell back to the grass. "Then . . . if you are not going to keep me, please tell me why you have allowed me to see such beauty in the first place."

She shrugged. "It is simple. I am grateful to you for your help. I thought you should see just what it is you are protecting."

"And if I am impressed by what I see, perhaps I will return to Cahir Cullen and tell the others, so that they might also help you to guard this place."

She sat up a little straighter. "Others?"

"Why, the other warrior men of Cahir Cullen, of course. I have no doubt that they would be very happy to come out here each night and ride through the stone circle and the clearing of Sion, patrolling this area and keeping a close watch on—"

"Thank you, but they would find the dogs inconvenient."

"But . . . I thought you were pleased that I came out to you this night."

"I was. And I thank you for it."

"Yet you do not want my men to give you further help, further protection? Surely a place such as this, a place such as I have been privileged to see and understand, deserves all that Cahir Cullen can—"

"Donaill." She held up her hand, trying to stop his words. "I did not ask for the protection of Cahir Cullen."

"You did not?" He shook his head as though astonished. "Then . . . why did you send for me this night? Am I not Cahir Cullen?"

"You are—but I did not ask for all the men of your fortress. I only asked for . . . for . . ."

"You asked for what, Lady Rioghan?"

She looked away. "I asked for you."

"What was that, my lady? I could not quite hear—"

Rioghan raised her chin and looked directly at him. "I asked for you."

"Ah! I see." He nodded his head, looking pleased. "I think I am beginning to understand now. You were not simply asking for any help. You were asking for *me*."

Rioghan let out her breath. "I believe I said that."

"So you did. And I would ask you this: of all the men who would be pleased to come to your defense, and the defense of this place, you chose me. Why would you do that?"

She was silent, knowing she was being baited, knowing she was being prodded, knowing he was enjoying every minute of it. "Why . . . I asked for you, Donaill, because I felt certain you would have no other task of any importance to occupy you, and that you would be free to come here at any time of the day or night."

He did not answer, but she could see that he was grinning. "I can only tell you, Lady Rioghan, that no matter what I may have been doing, when your dogs appeared to me up on the wall of Cahir Cullen there was no task more important than coming here to you."

"For that, all of us are most grateful."

"For that, all of you are most welcome. But let me ask you this: what will you do the next time someone rides to Sion late one night and demands your gold?"

"I will do what I can—"

"It was not enough tonight."

"The dogs—"

"Cannot withstand mounted foes who carry swords and spears and nets."

She got to her feet and turned away from him. "Why do you care? Those were your own people who came here tonight! What does it matter to you what happens to a midwife who does not even live among men? Why do you not accept my thanks and leave it at that?"

He stood up and walked close behind her. "Rioghan . . . you too are a part of Cahir Cullen, whether you live within its walls or not. You have served it well and you deserve the protection of its king's champion just as much as anyone else."

"I do not need—"

"I ask you again: what will you do when they come back?"

With a little catch in her throat, Rioghan looked out over the silvery black branches of the trees, over the dark stones of the circle, over the little shadows that darted and leaped and danced about the clearings. "I cannot let harm come to any of this," she whispered. "I cannot."

"Then what will you do?"

"I will . . . ask you for your help, king's champion Donaill."

"And nothing would give me greater pleasure than to give you my help, Lady Rioghan of Sion."

She closed her eyes.

"Now that the matter is settled, I will tell you something else. What I said is not quite true. The only thing that would give me greater pleasure would be a chance to know you better."

She drew back and turned to glare at him. "I have already told you all there is to know about me."

He smiled. "That is not what I meant. I would like . . . I want . . ."

"You would like what?" she asked, with all the innocence she could muster.

Donaill laughed. "Ah, I see that you can play the game as well as I. I too have always thought it best to hear the words directly, rather than simply guess at what someone might be thinking." He took a step closer. "I would like very much to know you better—to talk with you, to ride through the forest with you, to walk in the moonlight and sit in this beautiful place with you. That is what I would like."

It was Rioghan's turn to laugh, although she felt a twinge on her heart at his words. A longing. "You have said yourself that you have never found a woman who was unworthy. Why, then, should your interest make me feel special?"

He cocked his head. "Well . . . I cannot apologize for finding something beautiful and good within every woman."

"And I can well imagine what that something is," she murmured.

He seemed not to have heard. "You, Rioghan, are indeed different from any other woman I have met. You are very beautiful, of course, with hair dark as the soft night sky and eyes green as new grass in spring . . . yet you are also solitary and mysterious, and seem to need no man at all. Surely you know that all of this makes you a great prize."

She spun away, her long, heavy cloak swinging about her boots. "Do you think to honor me by calling me a prize? I see your interest in me not as flattery, but purely as arrogance."

"Arrogance? I don't—"

"Simply another conquest for the king's champion. That is all I would be, Donaill. I am under no illusions about that."

Again he moved close to her, this time taking her by one shoulder and gently turning her to face him. "Ah, but you are wrong. You are so different, Rioghan, so very special. . . ." He reached down and took one of her hands in both of his own.

She could only shake her head. The forests and clearings were still and silent now, and a faint light had begun to appear in the east. "You are the last man I would want," she whispered. "Always your status, your position, will be the most important thing to you, and there is nothing more important to the status of a man than the number of women he can draw to him. There will never be enough women for a man who is the king's own champion. One could not even come close."

"One might," Donaill whispered, leaning down close to her. "One might come very close . . ."

Before Rioghan could move, before she could think, his lips were even with hers, and he kissed her, as lightly and as warmly as the dawn sun touches the earth. Then he stepped back and let go of her hand, and when at last she opened her eyes he was gone, leaving her alone atop Sion with her two dogs and the soft gray light of the dawn.

Chapter Six

A few evenings later, Rioghan drew back the black cowhide hanging at the entrance to her home and sat down on the edge of her hearth. She looked out into the clearing, holding and sipping a hot cup of honey-sweetened tea. The cave faced west, and so, sitting as she was, she could see the glow of the setting sun and knew it would not be long before the stars came out.

Each night she had sat here keeping watch, fearing that in spite of Donaill's promises and bold words the others might come back. They still wanted the gold and treasure they had seen, she was sure, and would only laugh at Donaill's claim that the Sidhe, or a midwife, had any right to it.

Rioghan had hardly slept at all these past few nights, certain that Beolagh and his men would return. But at the end of this day, as the sun set, Scath and Cogar—who always remained in the cave with her—lay dozing in the warmth of the fire. The other dogs outside in the clearing sniffed the air and yawned, or rolled in the grass and dry pine needles, or frisked about with each other. They were as calm and relaxed as Rioghan had ever seen them.

She took another sip of her hot sweet tea. She had spent a long day sorting and preparing her different medicines and poultices and infusions, and should be tired and ready for sleep; but instead she felt possessed by a restlessness that was new and strange to her.

She had prepared this calming tea for herself, one that usually helped her sleep after long days of work no matter how tense she may have become, but this time it seemed to have no effect. At last Rioghan set the cup aside and walked outside into the deep gray twilight, into the stand of forest toward the stone circle to the west. Scath and Cogar trotted at her heels.

The path would have been all but invisible to most anyone not of the Sidhe, but to Rioghan it was comfortable and familiar. She walked among the tall pine trees of the twilit woods with long sure strides, breathing in the smell of the cold damp earth and fresh evergreens, happy to be outside after the long day of working in the confines of her home.

There was a rustling in the brush off to one side. Rioghan glanced toward it and smiled. "I merely walk," she said. "I am not going anywhere."

A little distance ahead, a small figure appeared

from behind the black trunk of a pine. "That is a concern, my lady."

She looked toward the figure, but it disappeared as quickly as it had come. She kept walking. "But I do not wish to go anywhere. Do you not want me to stay?"

Another rustling came from off to the side of the path, another soft voice. "We love you like no other," it said.

"Yet you too must make a life for yourself." This time the voice came from the trees on the other side.

"My life is here, as was my family's life," Rioghan said calmly, brushing aside the low, waving branch of a little pine seedling from the hem of her black wool gown. "Again, I would ask you: do you not wish me to stay with you at Sion?"

A shadow darted across her path. "We love you as one of our own," she heard. "Yet you are alone. It is not right that a beautiful young woman should live without a mate."

Rioghan stopped and turned to face the voice. "I am content with my life as it is. Are you so sure that I must bring a husband into it?"

"It is not the way of nature to live so. None should know this better than you, a healer and a midwife."

She whirled to face this new speaker on the other side, but as soon as she turned there were only gently waving branches of pine to be seen. "Perhaps I have simply not found the man with whom I would wish to share my life."

"Yet you believed you found him once before."

She caught her breath, but made herself keep calm. "I did believe that. But I was wrong. He did not love me for myself. He was merely happy to let me care for him and take all I had to give, while he gathered as many other women around him as he could in order to take from them as well.

"This was his way, whenever he thought I was not there—and if I dared to ask, he would only tell me that I should not be distressed. I was the one he wanted for his wife, was I not? The others meant nothing. They were only friends and acquaintances from the fortress. He swore he could not understand how such a silly, harmless thing could cause me pain."

"Yet it was not the mere presence of these women which caused you such pain," Rioghan heard. "He chose to deceive you, so that you would not know and could not interfere. And when you did know, his concern was for them—and for himself—and not for you."

Rioghan closed her eyes as bitter, painful memory swelled up within her. "He *did* deceive me," she whispered. "He deceived me so that he could be with them whenever he wished. And he cared nothing for my pain when I finally got the truth. He could do naught but defend his actions, defend his lies, defend those other women.

"And oh, it did not suit him that I should be offended. This only angered him—and I became the target of his rage. Not the women who had helped him to poison what I thought we had together. His anger was turned on me, and not on them.

"Never would he say that it was wrong for him to do any of these things. Never, never, never would he tell me it was wrong."

She looked into the soft twilight forest again and took a deep and calming breath. "But that is over now. He is free to be with all his many women, with no troublesome mate to interfere with his life and annoy him with her pain. And I am determined that such a thing will never happen to me again. I will be much more careful next time—if there should even be a 'next time.' "

"Why not choose one of us?"

Rioghan smiled, and went on with her walk. "I love you all," she said, "but not like that. As brothers and sisters, even as children. One does not marry within one's own family."

"Perhaps not," said a voice from behind her. She raised her head, but kept on walking. "Perhaps it is true that you should look elsewhere."

There came more rustling, first on one side of the path and then on the other, and then a shadow leaned out from the trees up ahead. "But not too far," said the shadow, before it disappeared once again.

The woods were nearly dark now. The high quarter moon provided little light, and soft clouds covered most of the sky, yet Rioghan walked her familiar path with no difficulty. "I have already said that I could not look for a mate from among the Sidhe."

"Then look to Cahir Cullen."

"Then look to this man, Donaill."

She stopped, her senses searching left and right, but there was only silence. Rioghan laughed a little, and walked on. "Now I know that you are playing a game with me."

"We would not play about this." The shadow walked alongside the path with her for a few steps before vanishing. "Donaill is a fair man. He has never done us ill. Indeed, he has guarded and helped you, and the Sidhe, all of his own accord."

"And for a man, he is not unattractive," added another rustling shadow.

Rioghan continued to walk, but shook her head emphatically at the same time. "Attractive or not, he is not a man who would ever be happy with just one woman. He is a great warrior and takes great pride in displaying his prowess. He is the king's champion and makes sure that all who meet him know this. No doubt he aspires to be king himself one day; no doubt he will do just that. And what king could ever be content with just one woman in his life? It would hardly be fitting for a man of such great stature."

She sighed. "Never, dear ones, never could I go with such a man, for I know that I alone would never be enough for him. No one woman would *ever* be enough."

She listened closely, but the shadows said nothing more. There was only the faint rustling in the brush on either side of her from time to time, and the sounds of Scath and Cogar trotting at her heels, until at last she left the forest and returned to the clearing of Sion, this time walking into it from the other side.

All was silent and still; all was as she had left it. The pack of dogs came to greet her with wagging tails and lowered heads, and then they lay down again just outside the cave. The hearthfire still burned low, and her cup of tea still rested on the stones.

Rioghan sat down beside the hearth and reached for the tea; but when she tasted it, she found that it had grown cold. She set it aside and folded her hands beneath her black cloak, listening to the silence of the starlit forest and thinking of how it had looked from high atop the mound of Sion.

Chapter Seven

Five nights went by, five quiet and uneventful nights that brought little sleep and more long walks for Rioghan . . . and more cold cups of tea.

On the sixth night, by the time the three-quarter moon was high overhead, she thought that perhaps she was ready for sleep. But just as she gathered her soft leather cushions and threw back the furs on her sleeping ledge, her dogs began to growl outside.

Scath and Cogar, always by her side, instantly got to their feet and stalked to the entrance of the cave. Their heads were held low and their hackles were raised. Rioghan followed them out across the darkness of the clearing, her heart pounding, fearing the worst, knowing it could be only one thing.

She went to the strip of woods that separated the clearing of Sion from the clearing of the stone circle, and there she saw six men on their horses ride in from the deep forest path and knew that she was right.

"Midwife!" shouted Beolagh, dragging his horse to a stop. "People of the Sidhe! Listen to me! I know you can hear me!"

"Madra! Madra!" whispered Rioghan urgently, and her snarling dogs turned away from the intruders and crowded back around her in the cover of the brush and towering pines. So far the men had made no move to approach her cave, and she did not want to risk any more of the dogs unless she had no choice.

"I know you can hear me," Beolagh said again, trotting his horse around the stone circle as his five men sat still and watched from the center. "We are not here to harm you. I gave my promise to the king's champion, and we will not attack you—not unless provoked. Neither will we take your gold by force."

Rioghan kept hold of Scath's collar and continued to listen. Though she could not see them, she knew that the Sidhe hid all around her in the forest, waiting, just as she waited.

Beolagh halted his horse. "But hear me well: you, midwife, and all the Sidhe who live here have long enjoyed the protection and bounty of Cahir Cullen—especially the protection of the king's champion, Donaill, who quite recently came to your aid!

"Donaill made us promise not to take your treasure by force—and so we will not. But he did not say we could not accept it if you chose to give it to us!

"It is long past time that you should give something in return. Sharing your gold with us is the least that you can do! We know that you have no use for it! There is no reason why you should not share it with us!"

He rode his horse around the stone circle, trying to peer into the dark woods. The only sounds were the snorting of the horses and the low growling of Rioghan's dogs. No one gave Beolagh any answer.

"All right then!" The warrior pulled his horse around and circled it in the other direction. "Since you choose to be selfish and ungrateful, and take what we so kindly offer while giving nothing in return, we have no choice but to persuade you another way!"

As he rode, he pointed his iron sword at each of the nine standing stones. "We will not take your gold, but we have made no promises about this place. If we do not find our share of the gold waiting for us within this circle by the time of the next new moon, we will pull down this circle stone by stone, and leave each to lie in the mud until the grasses grow over them!"

Rioghan's jaw dropped in horror. Surely they would not do such a thing—they would not dare to touch the ancient stones, this sacred circle, this place that the Sidhe relied upon so much—

"We have our own much larger circle, far to the north of Cahir Cullen! There the stones are tall and straight and perfectly aligned. This small and crudely set place is of no interest and no use to us. It will trouble us not at all to pull it down, not if it will teach a lesson to animals who try to hoard men's gold! I will tell you again: leave the gold for us at the dark of the moon, or this is the last you will see of your circle!"

Beolagh laughed again, looking back at his men, but in an instant was clutching at his horse's mane as the animal whirled in fright. It had been startled by the appearance of a small figure in black right in front of it—a figure with two dogs, one gray and one black, on either side.

"You will never touch this stone circle," Rioghan said to him, her voice low and ominous. Beolagh struggled to right himself in his saddle even as her dogs snarled up at him. "Not now, or in a fortnight from now at the dark of the moon. It has been here as long as—or longer than—the circle that the druids of Cahir Cullen use."

"We care not whether it was built when the world was new, or built the day before yesterday!" Beolagh shouted, now sitting upright on his horse once more.

"This circle is smaller and simpler than your own, it is true," she went on. "Its stones are not so polished, nor so straight, nor so tall. Yet it is perfectly accurate and has helped the Sidhe to survive since, indeed, the world was new. It allows them to know the seasons to the day, and the correct times to plant and to harvest, and better know their place in the natural world. It is like a home to them."

"I do not doubt that it is!" Beolagh laughed. "Animals need no proper homes! They do not need a roof or walls, only a mud floor surrounded by half-fallen stones!" He laughed again, as did all of his men. "If we pull this one down, then you can build another!"

Her dogs snarled and bared their teeth. Rioghan held tight to their gold- and bronze-plated collars. "You know well that it could never be rebuilt. It was built by the people of magic, those from the northern islands now destroyed in the great flood. They alone had the power to move such stones into place, and they are long gone. It could never be rebuilt."

"Then leave the gold, and you will not have to concern yourselves with rebuilding it! Just leave the treasure here, and we will not trouble you again!" As final emphasis to his words, Beolagh cantered his horse to one of the tall standing stones and struck it hard with his iron sword.

The sword shattered.

With a look of surprise, Beolagh forced his horse around and shouted angrily to his men. All them rode back into the forest down the dark and narrow path, and the very stones of the circle seemed to tremble from the thundering hoofbeats of their horses.

When all was quiet again at last, Rioghan sighed and let go of her dogs' collars. They raced about and rejoined their pack, all of them roving back and forth across the stone circle and the strip of forest and the clearing in front of the cave. As the beasts roamed and explored and secured their territory, the Sidhe came out of the shadows to stand beside Rioghan.

"Surely they do not mean to pull down our circle!"

"Would they have such power?"

"Would they dare, even if they did?"

Rioghan shook her head. "Never have I known anyone to bring down any standing stone, yet I suppose it could be done. A few of the most ancient have fallen of their own accord, if the earth has grown too soft and wet to support them. If Beolagh and his men are determined enough, I suppose they could find a way, and not even the dogs could hold them off forever."

"We cannot let them do this!"

"We would die to protect this place!"

"It is our home; it is the sacred circle!"

She looked at them all in the faint moonlight. "I have no wish to let them destroy this place. I have sworn to protect it, for you are my family and this is my home . . . yet I cannot—I will not—see any of you harmed in trying to save it. Perhaps . . . perhaps we should go and search for another place, farther away from the fortresses of men. There are other places, other stone circles—"

"Donaill . . ."

"Donaill . . ."

"Donaill . . ."

Rioghan blinked and looked at the Sidhe's fine faces as they stared at her. "Donaill?" she asked. "Why do you believe Donaill would help us to save this stone circle?"

"He would help you."

"He came to you before."

"He came to you as soon as you asked."

She shook her head and tried to smile. "Dear ones . . . he did come in response to an immediate threat, when I feared our lives might be in danger. I have some value to Cahir Cullen as a midwife and a healer, and so they would send their king's champion to help such a one—and since you are my people, that protection might, at least sometimes, extend to you as well.

"But do not forget: to the Men, Sion is a place of farmers and herdsmen and the Sidhe. These things are simply not the concerns of the great and important warrior men of Cahir Cullen. Indeed, they had never even set foot here before being forced to come on a cold dark night when a servant could not be sent—and they would still have no interest in it whatsoever if they had not caught sight of the gold.

"And this should be no surprise to any of us. Do such men spend their time among the cowsheds of the fortress, or up in the mountaintop pastures with the sheep, or helping to grow the barley in the fields? Of course they do not. And that is all Sion is to them: a place where the Little People live and work, and no concern of theirs.

"The king's champion did come when it appeared that lives might be in danger. But this stone circle means nothing to those who live at the fortress of men. There is no reason why Donaill, or anyone else there, should trouble themselves to help us save it."

"Yet Donaill has seen the view from atop Sion in the starlight."

"And he has seen you for what you are."

"He would help you to preserve your home."

Rioghan hesitated. "If I go and ask him—and he says he cannot help in front of his people, because he does not wish to go against them in public—we will be left more vulnerable than ever."

"We have little left to lose."

"We must have help, for there is no doubt those Men will come again."

"You must ask Donaill for his help."

She looked at them, and smiled in resignation. "Perhaps you are right. I will go to the fortress tomorrow, and I will ask him—but I cannot promise you anything."

At dawn the next day, surrounded by cloudy sky and soft mist from the forest, Rioghan stood before the huge wooden gates of Cahir Cullen with Scath and Cogar by her side and her leather bag hanging from her shoulder. In the surrounding grove of tall holly trees, their glossy green leaves and red berries the only bright spots against the pale morning, were several of the Sidhe. They had accompanied her from the safety of the woods and would await her here until she chose to return.

The watchman on the platform over the gates had seen her approach, and stood watching her now. "Midwife," he said, leaning on the rail with both hands. "Do you wish to enter? I have not been told of your coming. Does someone here have need of you?"

"They do not," she answered, her black cloak drawn up over her head to form a hood. "But I have need of them. I am here to speak to Donaill, the king's champion."

The watchman regarded her a moment longer, then gave her a brief nod. "Wait there," he said. In a moment the enormous gates swung open for her, their iron hinges creaking only a little.

Rioghan walked as quietly as she could across the misty grounds of Cahir Cullen, keeping her two dogs close. There was all the early morning commotion that always happened in such a large settlement—servants heading toward the gates, some with clean empty buckets to fetch water and some with old battered ones filled with refuse; a few winter cows, those spared the slaughter at summer's end, bawling to be milked; other servants shouting out orders to one another; craftsmen hammering metal and wood in the armory; women calling out to each other from the doorways of the round white houses; and children and dogs running and playing in the light of the early morning.

Though she kept her eyes down and looked neither right nor left as she walked, Rioghan was well aware of the curious stares and sudden silences that followed her across the grounds. Most saw her only at night, if they saw her at all, for she preferred to arrive under the cover of darkness and leave again at dawn; but this was not always possible, and since the people of Cahir Cullen normally saw her only in times of childbirth or tragedy, there were whispers along with the stares.

"Why is she here?" they asked one another. "What has happened?" "Why is she here?"

By way of answer, Rioghan walked straight to one of the round houses. In a moment Sabha opened the wooden door to gentle rapping. "Rioghan! Oh, Rioghan, I am so glad to see you, though I fear to ask why you are here. Come inside, come inside. . . ."

Rioghan held up one hand and smiled. "I cannot. At least, not at this moment. Though I am glad to see you looking so well."

Sabha gave her a small, tight smile, then closed her eyes. "I would not say that I am well, though I am better. I walk, and breathe, and even eat occasionally. And I would like very much to speak with you, if you can find a moment for me."

Rioghan nodded. "Of course I will. But first I have a favor to ask of you."

A short time later, Rioghan and Sabha walked together toward one of the largest of the round houses, Scath and Cogar trotting quietly after them. Sabha stopped before the house, and stepped back to let Rioghan walk to the door.

"Please come to me before you leave," Sabha said again. "Ah, I know! Leave your bag at my house, and then you will have to come 'round again to fetch it." She took the heavy bag and then, giving her friend a kiss on the cheek, walked back to her own home and left Rioghan alone to face this great one.

With only a little hesitation, still aware of the many eyes upon her, Rioghan knocked softly on the wooden door. Her dogs sat down close on either side of her and waited.

There was no response. Feeling heat spreading across her face, Rioghan looked down and knocked again, a little harder this time.

After a long while, she heard a few small noises inside the dwelling, as though someone was walking across the rushes and perhaps toppling a plate or cup on the stone hearth along the way. Finally the door opened and Donaill stared down at her, blinking in the new light of the morning.

"Rioghan?" The man pushed his long, light brown hair back from his face, letting it fall in disarray past his shoulders. He tried to straighten the dark wool tunic he wore—the only thing he wore, she realized with a start. "Why have you come? Is something wrong?"

Turning away, Rioghan answered him quickly. "I wish to speak to you, if I may."

"Why, of course, of course! I did not know that you were here! Please come in."

He stepped back to allow her inside, but she remained turned away. "Thank you, but I will wait here for you, if you do not mind."

Donaill seemed to have regained his composure now, after the surprise of finding her on his doorstep, and stood straight and even made her a small bow. "As you wish, my lady. I will not be long."

Then, with a smile, he closed the door again.

Rioghan closed her eyes. It was difficult to think, even to breathe. She could still feel the curious stares of the people upon her as they whispered and laughed at the sight of the strange and mysterious midwife standing outside the house of the king's champion, as though she had nothing better to do.

Even her two dogs seemed to be grinning at her as they yawned and stretched lazily in the faint warmth of the wintertime sun. "You don't have to laugh, you know," she scolded. "I am here on serious business."

Scath yawned again, this time with a little whine as she did, and then rolled on her back in the cool, soft grass. "Thank you for your support," Rioghan said to her, but could not help smiling.

The door of the house opened once again. Rioghan whirled around to look.

"Ah, my lady, I am so glad that you were kind enough to wait for me. Please, will you walk with me?"

Donaill closed the door tight and then walked the few steps to stand right in front of her. He was properly dressed now in a red-and-gold wool tunic and black woolen trousers, with his heavy red cloak fastened by a round gold brooch and thrown back over his shoulder. She looked up at him and started to speak, but the words caught in her throat, and she suddenly felt very vulnerable, very much exposed.

"What is it?" he asked gently.

It was so strange to stand out here alone with

him, visible to all these many people in this busy and bustling place, as though she were just another person who lived here in Cahir Cullen. Always she had preferred the comfort and security of shadows, of darkness, of seclusion, of Sion; but now she felt as alone and unprotected and as careless as a doe who stood alone in an open field in the glaring light of midday.

He reached down and took her hand, tucking it beneath his arm as he turned and led her away. "We will go inside and talk, just you and I. And since I am sure you have not eaten yet today, we will sit down to a good meal and I will listen for as long as you like."

She nodded, and though she walked so close to him that her side was pressed up against his, she felt no need to pull away. His strength, his height, and his broad shoulders shielded her from the outside world in the same way that the stone walls of Sion shielded her. Rioghan began to feel better just walking close beside him, feeling the solid strength in his arms and listening to the faint creak of his black leather sword belt as he walked, and catching a glimpse of his long, light brown hair, tied back with a black leather cord, falling across his shoulders.

"Here we are," he said, stopping as the shadow of a building fell across them. Rioghan looked up, startled. She had almost forgotten why she was here, and told herself that she had most certainly not come here to walk arm in arm with Donaill across the lawn of Cahir Cullen. She withdrew her arm and stepped away from him, folding her hands and drawing a deep breath.

Then she looked up—and again felt like a brazen doe out alone in the clearing. She and Donaill stood in front of another round building with the same white clay walls and steep straw roof bleached gray by sunlight and rain, but this one was perhaps four times as large as even Donaill's large house.

Even from this distance Rioghan could hear, through the very tall pair of doors that stood open, the voices of servants working to prepare food, and the conversation and laughter of the highborn women who gathered here each day to talk and gossip as they worked. It helped them to pass the time as they spun wool into yarn, or wove it into cloth at the looms, or cut and stitched the new cloth into tunics and gowns and long, rectangular cloaks.

This was the great hall, the primary gathering place for the men and women of the fortress. This was where King Bran and his warriors and his druids might hold court, and where the feasts and celebrations were held. And most of the women preferred to go there each day to work at their tasks, so they could enjoy one another's company instead of staying alone in their homes. The great hall was virtually always full of people, even if it was only the servants sleeping there at night in the thick warm straw on the floor.

Donaill started to go inside, but Rioghan remained rooted to the spot. "My lady?" he asked, turning to look at her. "Do you not want to go in? I thought you wanted to have a talk with me."

"I do," she whispered, raising her chin, "but I see that there is little privacy here."

He laughed again. "I see. So there is too much privacy inside my house, and too little inside the hall! Well, then . . ." He paused, looking around, and then he smiled at her again. "Wait here. I think I know exactly what we require."

Chapter Eight

A short time later, Donaill carried a broad wooden plate covered with a square of linen, and Rioghan held two flat wooden cups filled with cold, fresh water. Donaill walked all the way to the back of Cahir Cullen until they stood just beneath the high, curving, grass-covered earthen wall, at a spot where a few large, flat stones lay scattered on the ground.

"Will this do?" he asked, nodding toward the stones. "It is not closed away like my house, nor is it trafficked with people like the hall. A few may see us here, but they have no reason to approach. Will you sit in this place with me?"

She smiled, and then walked to the nearest of the flat stones and sat down on it, still holding the cups filled with water. "I thank you. It is perfect."

He sat down too, and set the wooden plate down

between them. "Please, Lady Rioghan, go ahead and eat, and we will talk when you are ready. I should never have asked you what you wanted when first I saw you this day, as though you were merely a servant or a messenger. I should have seen to your comfort first, offering you food and rest as an honored guest is due, before asking questions. For that I apologize, and I ask you to share this with me now, and then talk to me about whatever you like when you are ready."

Rioghan began to relax. The high, thick walls of Cahir Cullen towered over her on one side, and on the other the scattered houses obscured them from the sight of most of the others. Yet soft winter sunlight and cold air surrounded them, and the two dogs stretched out on the grass between her and the rest of Cahir Cullen. Rioghan smiled at Donaill. "Thank you," she said, and reached down to uncover her wooden plate.

The servants in the hall had heaped it with whatever was at hand, which turned out to be fresh, hot flatbread made with good oats, butter so pale it was almost white from the thin winter milk of the hay-fed cows, a little of the honey saved from the last gathering in the fall, a heap of sliced dried apples boiled in milk, and hard-pressed curds of cheese.

They ate in quiet companionship for a time. Donaill sat back and allowed her to have the first selection at everything, as though she were the most high-ranking of visitors. She glanced at him from time to time, at first still feeling somewhat vulnerable with his gleaming blue eyes gazing down and his ever-present smile always on her.

Yet as she took another piece of oatbread and covered it with hot apples and cool honey, her attention was caught by the ordinary sights and sounds of the morning here at Cahir Cullen. Though she had been here many times and knew the daily life and many of the people, she had always moved among them as a shadow in the background. It had been necessary for her to focus only on whatever birth or injury or tragedy had brought her there in the first place. But now she could sit and watch the people as they went about their normal lives, and she was surprised at what marvelous entertainment it was.

A group of young children raced around the nearest house with slim, long-legged dogs at their heels, chasing an older boy who raised his little wooden sword and shouted out at them as he ran. Rioghan could not help but laugh at the sight of a fat little black-and-white lapdog tearing after them, trying desperately to keep up. Rioghan's own dogs raised their heads as the wild and noisy group rushed by, but not one of the children spared a glance for the king's champion sitting on the rocks or the strange small woman in black who sat across from him.

The children disappeared behind the house, but then came running back again, as though they had gone around and abruptly reversed direction. And then Rioghan smiled behind her hand, hastily swallowing her bite of apples and honey, as she saw the reason why.

Lumbering after the children, shaking her horns at them, was a small black cow with a calf at heel. They were a pair of escapees in search of a few blades of green winter grass, caught now between the shouting, sword-waving children in front of them and the two determined men behind holding wooden pitchforks and coils of rope. The two men began to close in—but just as they dashed around the house, both of them slipped on the damp earth and fell hard on their backsides, sliding in the mud with their feet flying up.

The children scattered, the dogs barked, and the cow shook her horns again and trotted around another house with her little calf bucking and playing behind her. In their wild dash, the children raced past the rocks where Rioghan sat, and one of them tumbled nearly at her feet. As the boy righted himself, he looked up and grinned at her, reaching for his wooden sword, and she realized that his face was very familiar. He was the image of Bevin, who must be his mother.

The children ran away and disappeared once more behind the house. In a moment Rioghan heard a loud bawl from the cow and caught a glimpse of her between the homes, shaking her head and trotting very swiftly as her two masters dragged her back to her pen with ropes caught up in her horns. Behind her the little black calf leaped and played, keeping just one step ahead of the happy mob of children and the boy with the wooden sword.

Rioghan laughed and laughed, even as she kept her hand up to her face, and realized that Donaill's deep laughter joined her own. "I've told those men it's the children who let that cow and calf loose almost daily, just to enjoy the excitement of the chase, but I don't think they believed me! Perhaps they will after today."

And Rioghan laughed until she could eat no more for laughing. She set aside her cup and reached down to pat her anxious dogs, even as Donaill grinned at her.

Finally his face grew serious. He said: "So tell me, Rioghan, what brings you to Cahir Cullen today? And if you say it was only to see those men try to catch that cow and calf, I will be happy, for they must chase her nearly every day, and so I shall see you often!"

"It would almost be worth the walk to see such a funny thing each morning," she said, catching her breath. "And to see the children. The oldest boy, the one who fell at my feet—I feel certain that I must have helped to bring him into the world. He is the image of his mother."

"And no doubt you were there for several of the others, too," Donaill agreed, watching as the children again ran by. He turned and gazed down at Rioghan. "Would you not like to live here at Cahir Cullen, at least during the cold, dark winter months? You could see these children every day and have the companionship of their mothers . . . and not have to travel so far when they need your help."

He clasped his hands together in front of him and leaned forward on the rock. "I would even free those animals myself each morning, if it meant that

I would see you here laughing every day."

Rioghan blinked, entranced by his kind face and blue eyes, and then quickly looked away. She reached for her wooden cup but merely held it, watching the clear water within as it shimmered in the light. "Thank you, but of course I could not think of doing such a thing," she said. "My home is at Sion, where I was born, where I can care for the people of the Sidhe as well as those of Cahir Cullen." She shook her head. "I could never leave Sion."

Donaill smiled sadly, and then he sat back. "Tell me why you have come today, Lady Rioghan . . . and tell me what I can do to help you."

Rioghan set down her cup once more and sat a little straighter, folding her hands on her lap and making herself remember why she was there. "Beolagh and his men came to Sion again last night," she said. "They—"

"Beolagh!" Instantly Donaill's good humor was gone. "Beolagh rode out to Sion last night? They are still trying to take your gold, after I warned them to stay away from you?"

Rioghan held up her hand. "They did not try to *take* the gold."

"They left the gold alone?"

"Well, they did not approach my home."

"I thought you said they were at Sion?"

"They got only as far as the stone circle. And, as they promised you, they did not harm me or any of the Sidhe, or try to take our gold."

He studied her, his face very serious now. "I am

glad to hear that no promises were broken. But what were they doing out there in the dark of night?"

"They . . . made us an offer." Rioghan paused, seeing that Donaill grew increasingly angry. "They said that since they swore they would not take the gold by force, I must give it to them as a gift. And if I refuse, they will destroy something that is of great value to the Sidhe: the stone circle."

"The stone circle!" Donaill stood up, towering over Rioghan, and clenched his fists. "They threaten to destroy the circle? The ancient circle? How could they do such a thing?"

Rioghan shook her head. "It means nothing to them. Your people have their own stone circle, much larger and much more open, far on the other side of this fortress. Your druids have no use for our little circle deep in the forest, nearly lost to the trees and brush. Some people here might be concerned if the Sidhe themselves were threatened—but their stone circle? Never. Beolagh believes that the circle means nothing to them."

"No one here wants to see any of the circles disturbed. They are too valuable and could never be replaced."

"Yet it has been uncounted years since your druids used our small circle, if ever they used it at all. It is of the Sidhe, and therefore of no use or interest to the people here."

Donaill was silent. He gazed out at the laughing, playing children. Rioghan tried to catch his eye, but then looked away.

"I do not expect you to believe or help me," she said. "I had hopes that you might, for you are one man who has seen the world from the top of Sion and who has even sat beside the fire in its cave. But Sion has never been part of the world of Men, and you have no obligation to protect it."

She turned away from him. "I know the things that are said about me . . . the strange woman who does not know if she is human or Sidhe, who has lived too long alone in a cave and whose mind is no doubt touched in some way from such a life." She smiled a little. "Who would believe me? None who live at Cahir Cullen . . . not even the king's own champion."

Rioghan stood up and gathered the folds of her black cloak close around her. "I thank you for the kindness and the hospitality you have shown me this day. But I should have understood that protecting me, and the people of the Sidhe, is one thing; risking your life for a stone circle that is of no use to anyone here is a very different thing. Scath! Cogar!"

She turned to walk away, and the dogs jumped up to follow her.

"Rioghan . . ."

She paused.

"Wait. I am not sure I have heard the whole story. Please come back and sit down, and tell me the rest of it."

"But I have told you all there is to know. The men no longer threaten us directly, thanks to you. They say they will not harm us, and they have not.

But they have also given us the choice of giving them our treasure or seeing our stone circle destroyed."

Donaill placed a gentle hand on her shoulder and walked with her to the rocks. Once she was seated again, he gravely shook his head. "Was there anyone else to hear what Beolagh said to you, anyone else who heard these threats?"

She stared up at him. "If you mean anyone of Cahir Cullen, aside from Beolagh's five dull and grinning followers, there was no one."

Donaill frowned, looking ever more concerned. "No one else?"

Rioghan raised her chin. "You do not believe me."

"Now, now, my lady, I said no such thing! I merely asked if there might be any other witnesses aside from the Sidhe."

"Witnesses."

"Well, it is your word against Beolagh's, of course."

"My word against his."

"So . . . there were no others to hear these words."

"Only my dogs, and the Sidhe hiding in the forest." She paused. "I can see that you do not believe me, and the Sidhe are not here to ask—so perhaps you should ask the dogs. Scath! Cogar!"

The two huge wolfhounds came over, and she gestured toward Donaill. The two animals ran to him and stood up on their hind legs, so tall they could look him right in the eye, and then placed their front paws on his shoulders and eagerly licked his face.

He backed away, raising both hands. "Down! Down!" he cried, laughing as he spoke. "I think that is all the persuasion I need." The two dogs dropped back down to earth, and then walked away to find a warm spot in the grass where they could stretch out once more.

Donaill quickly wiped his face with his sleeve. Then he placed one foot on one of the rocks and gazed down at Rioghan, with his head cocked and his arms folded. "So . . . I must make certain that I understand everything with the utmost clarity. Beolagh and his men have kept their promise not to harm you nor any of the Sidhe."

She nodded slowly. "They have."

"And they have not attempted to take your gold by force, also as promised."

"They have kept that promise as well."

"Yet they say that they will destroy the stone circle of Sion if you do not give them your gold of your own free will."

"That is exactly right."

"And what do you wish me to do about this? I have told you before—I am the king's champion and I must follow the law even if others do not. Do you wish to go before the king and accuse Beolagh yourself, leaving him to the justice of the druids?"

Her eyes widened. "I would have to bring the Sidhe before the king as well, as witnesses—and they would never show themselves there. They would never walk into this fortress and stand in front of everyone in the hall. You may as well ask a wild deer of the forest to do the same.

"You are correct, Donaill. There is nothing here except my word against Beolagh's. No gold has been taken. No Sidhe has been killed. The stone circle remains untouched. And so . . ." Rioghan fell silent again. Donaill's face was serious and still, but she could see the glint in his blue eyes. "I do not wish you to do anything about it, Donaill," she snapped, and got up to leave once again.

He took his foot off of the rock and moved to block her path. "Are you so certain, Lady Rioghan? You will not have the chance to ask me again. Once you say you do not want my help, I will respect your wishes and stay away. Can you and the Sidhe and your dogs keep Beolagh and his men from destroying your stone circle?"

Rioghan tightened her jaw. "I am not certain."

"Then . . . what is it that you would have me do?"

She sighed. As before, he was going to make her ask for what she wanted. She was tempted to simply walk away, but thought again of the invading, intruding men tearing up the earth at Sion, their swords slashing through her beloved dogs, their hands grabbing Kieran and holding him at bay like an animal. . . .

"Lord Donaill."

"Lady Rioghan?"

She took a deep breath. "I would ask you to help me guard the stone circle of Sion, and keep it from destruction by the men of Cahir Cullen."

He studied her closely, first frowning, then looking away, then looking down at the ground while apparently deep in thought. Finally, after much consideration, he took a step toward her. "I will agree to do this for you," he said, "if you will do one thing for me in return."

"What is that?"

"It is very simple," Donaill answered. "Stay here at Cahir Cullen tonight. Stay here with me for a time, and I will do all I can to help you."

Chapter Nine

Rioghan sat very still. For a moment she could only blink and open her mouth to try to form words, but none came. She was not yet certain whether she felt the greatest insult or the first stirrings of excitement.

Perhaps it was a combination of both.

At last she rose slowly to her feet and looked him directly in the eye. "You will help me . . . if I stay the night with you?" She tucked her hands beneath her cloak so he would not see them trembling.

He looked entirely astonished. "You wish to stay the night with *me,* Lady Rioghan?" Donaill shook his head and stepped back. "Why, I could not think of anything I would like better, though it seems to me a bit soon. . . . I am not accustomed to women inviting themselves into my bed so quickly, but perhaps this is the way of the Sidhe. Ah, I understand now." He grinned broadly. "All right, then! I accept your offer. If you would like to stay with me in my house, in my bed, I will bring out my finest, softest furs, put up the newest leather screens for privacy, and accept most enthusiastically. When would you like to come? It is a long while until nightfall, but I suppose we could find something to do to pass the time until—"

"I have said nothing at all about agreeing to stay the night with you!"

"But—you did indeed! I heard you! You said, 'You will help me if I stay the night with you.' You are right: I will help you. And you are most welcome to stay the night with me."

He started to walk toward his house. Rioghan quickly followed, struggling to find her voice.

"I did not say that I would stay this night or any other with you! I was simply repeating what I thought you had said to me!"

He stopped. "You thought I was inviting you to spend the night with me, in my home, in my bed?"

"You said—"

"I simply invited you to stay here at Cahir Cullen—as my guest, of course."

She raised her hand to her neck, but said nothing, so he continued. "I had thought that you might stay with Sabha. I am sure she would be happy to have you sleep at her home."

Rioghan began to breathe again.

"There is to be something of a feast tonight," Donaill continued. "My brothers, Irial and Lorcan, went out with a hunting party yesterday, and they brought back a pair of wild boars. Everyone will gather in the hall tonight to enjoy them to the fullest, since there will be more than enough dried meat and smoked fish in the months to come. And the feast would be even livelier if we had a guest—especially such a lovely and charming guest as you."

He moved closer, until he stood right in front of her. "Stay, Lady Rioghan, as my guest. Beolagh's men will not ride out tonight. They'll be here, eating and drinking along with everyone else." Gently he reached out and touched her cheek, brushing away a strand of her long dark hair.

She closed her eyes.

"Stay and enjoy the hospitality of Cahir Cullen for just one night," he repeated. "Surely you have earned a rest, if anyone has."

Rioghan reached up and took hold of his fingers where they continued to gently stroke her cheek. She lowered her hand, still holding his fingers, and looked into his eyes again. "Thank you, Donaill," she heard herself say. "I would like very much to stay at Cahir Cullen tonight, as your guest."

"Sabha, truly—you need not go to all this trouble for me."

Sabha closed the door and hurried across the straw-covered floor of her house. "You do not know how glad I am to see you, and to have something to occupy my mind this day. Rioghan, you have never been to a feast here at Cahir Cullen, is this true? Ah, I thought not! Here—I will start the water to boil right now!"

The woman lifted the biggest bronze cauldron she could manage, set it on an iron tripod over the fire, and then filled it with all the drinking water in the house. Again she hurried across the straw to the door. "Wait here. I will go and fetch Bevin and Aideen and borrow a new gown and a mantle and—"

"Sabha!" Rioghan had to call out her name just to get her attention, but then smiled when at last the young woman stopped and turned to look at her. "I am so glad to see that you are feeling better. You have never been far from my thoughts. I know that even the strongest of women can be broken by such a thing."

Sabha pushed a strand of soft brown hair from her face, and tried to smile a little. "Better?" she whispered. "I would not say that I am better . . . only, perhaps, that I am not yet broken. Not yet."

Rioghan nodded. "That is enough for now. And if it will help you to comb my hair and dress me like a little girl's play-dolly, then I am happy to let you do it."

Sabha smiled again, a little brighter this time. "Oh, we will do much more than that, I can assure you! Wait here." She hurried out the door and slammed it shut behind her.

In a few moments, Sabha returned to the house. With her were Bevin and Aideen, two women whom Rioghan knew from the times she had helped them with illnesses and births. Bevin, she believed, was the mother of the sword-swinging boy she had seen earlier today, the one leading all the other children in the merry chase for the cow and calf.

All three women carried stacks of fabrics, armloads of small, flat pottery jars, and little wooden boxes. Rioghan smiled at them as they approached, beginning to relax in spite of herself.

"Ah, Rioghan, what fun we will have with you today!" said Aideen.

"We have always wondered how you might look with your hair braided, and dressed in something other than black," added Bevin.

"We'll know soon," said Sabha, a little breathless. "Servants are on their way with more water." She dropped her bundle of bright green and soft gray fabrics onto the new furs on the sleeping ledge, and handed Rioghan a length of plain linen. "The water is almost ready. Now, off with your clothes, my lady. Your bath awaits!"

Sabha walked around the house and closed all the wooden shutters on the small, high windows, then lowered the deep bronze tub from where it rested on its edge against the stone hearth. It was far larger than the small, shallow basin that was all Rioghan had at Sion. This was large enough to sit in and even lean back against the sides.

Bevin opened the door to take bucket after bucket of fresh, cold water from the servants, and all three women picked them up and poured them one by one into the bronze tub. Then, as Rioghan stood watching, wrapped only in the linen, the three of them lifted the cauldron from the hearth and poured its boiling contents into the ice-cold water of the basin.

Great clouds of stream rose up into the house. The bronze basin groaned and clanged and contorted itself as sudden heat struck cold metal. "Get in, get in!" said Aideen. "It is perfect. Here is some new soap, and, oh, you will want to try this! It is wonderful for bathing."

Rioghan took the soap from her, and also a small linen bag filled to bursting with oatmeal and tied off at one end. "Use that for scrubbing, along with a little soap," said Aideen. "It will set your skin to glowing."

"Sit back, Rioghan. I will wash your hair while you relax," said Bevin.

"And I will have your new clothes and a few other things waiting for you when you get out," said Sabha.

Quickly Rioghan walked to the bronze tub, dropped the linen sheet to the straw, and stepped into the water. "Oh," she said, sitting down. "Oh . . ."

"Lovely, isn't it?" said Bevin. "I am sure it must be difficult for you to arrange for such a bath at Sion. We thought you might enjoy this."

Rioghan could only nod. "I have only a shallow basin for bathing. I can heat only a little water at a time. It serves to keep one clean, of course, but this . . ."

She sat back against the side of the deep tub. Its sides were so high they came up past her waist. The steam continued to rise as she took the soap and the linen bag of oatmeal and began scrubbing away, enjoying every moment.

When she was finished, she leaned back to let Bevin pour warm water over her hair and wash it gently but thoroughly with soap. "Ah, it is tangled, Rioghan," the woman said, patiently picking out the knots with a wooden comb and working the lather all the way through to the ends.

"Oh, I do not doubt that it is," Rioghan said, feeling embarrassed. "It is so heavy, so thick. . . . It is not like yours." She looked up at the other women with their long, neatly braided plaits of hair, so lovely and smooth compared to her own wild and windblown mass. She had never worried about her hair, always content to simply twist it so that it hung down her back and did not interfere as she worked.

"We can show you a few things about your hair, if you like," said Bevin. "Do you think that Sabha's beautiful plaits simply braid themselves before she gets out of bed in the morning?"

"I can assure you that they do not," Sabha said with a laugh, and Rioghan quickly shut her eyes tight as Bevin dumped a final bucket of warm water over her hair to rinse the last of the soap from it.

"Ah, I could stay here all day," Rioghan said with a sigh, sinking down once more as the steam continued to play about the surface of the water.

"I know how you feel, but it's best to get out before the warmth begins to fade." Sabha stepped to the side of the basin and held up a rectangular cloak of thick wool. "Here you are. Step out and wrap up in this—that's it—come now, over to the ledge. The furs will keep you warm while you dry off, and then we will try you in your new clothes."

Rioghan sat down on the edge of the ledge, quickly drying off with the heavy wool. It was a bit rough and scratchy, but warm even when it was wet.

She looked up at the three women who had been so kind, feeling almost as if she had emerged from her marvelous bath reborn. "Thank you," she said, with all sincerity. "Bevin, Aideen, and, oh, Sabha—thank you."

All three turned to her and smiled back with nothing but happiness and merriment in their eyes. "You are most welcome," Bevin said. "No one deserves such kindness more than you."

"Come, come now!" Sabha said, quickly turning and busying herself with something at the hearth. "Do not make me weep. We have work to do yet, Lady Rioghan!"

"That we do," said Aideen. "And we'll start with this."

Aideen placed a small, plain pottery jar on the furs beside Rioghan and opened the lid. Inside was a soft white cream, fragrant with the sweet, delicate scent of violets.

"This is my favorite," said the woman, touching a little of the cream to her finger. "Made from beeswax, white violets, and a few other fine things. Now, while you are still warm and damp from the bath, work it into every part of your skin that you can reach. It feels wonderful!"

"It does, it does," murmured Rioghan, smoothing it along her arms and into the parched skin of her elbows and fingers. "And the scent is lovely. I may have to beg you for a little of this to take back with me."

"Do you not know how to make such things, Rioghan?" asked Sabha, who was unfolding and smoothing out the fabrics she had brought. "You are so good at preparing medicines and poultices and teas. Surely a soothing cream would be simple for you to make."

Rioghan continued to work the cream into her skin, moving to her knees and roughened heels. "I probably could learn—I believe my mother used to make things such as this—but it seemed that my time was better spent on the medicines that everyone needs, that could even save a life. Things like this just seemed a bit . . . a bit frivolous, I suppose."

"It is not frivolous to take care of oneself," argued Bevin. "How can you help others if you yourself are neglected and uncared for?"

"I made this cream myself, and I will send some back with you—along with the recipe to make it," said Aideen.

"And if you are finished with the cream," said Sabha, "try this." She held up a long linen gown in a subtle shade of silvery gray. "I think it will fit you. Let's see!"

Rioghan let the wool cloak fall from her shoulders and quickly pulled the linen undergown over her head. Standing up, she let it settle into place, delighting in the lightweight feel of the fine new fabric.

"It's lovely," she said, looking down at herself,

"but not nearly warm enough! Sabha, what have you done with the rest of my clothes?"

"Rioghan, my dear friend, there will be no dreary black for you tonight! We have brought you all that you will need. This is next—and this—you will not be cold!"

Sabha dropped a mass of dark green wool over Rioghan's head and carefully adjusted the long gown as it dropped into place. It reached just past the knees and was cut lower at the neck than the undergown, and so showed off the fine silver-gray linen, which reached to the floor and came up higher at the neck.

"Perfect, as I thought," Sabha crowed. "And if by chance you are still cold, let me assure you that the way you are going to look when you walk into the hall will attract all the warmth you need. You will turn the head of every man there!"

All the women laughed, including Rioghan, though she held up her hands in protest at the same time. "Men never look at me. I am nothing for them to look at. They always think I am one of the Sidhe, small and dark-haired as I am. Always they look at the tall and beautiful women of Cahir Cullen, with their blue eyes and golden hair—"

"But on this night, we will show them just how lovely black hair and green eyes can be. Sit down again now—sit down; we are not finished with you yet!"

Rioghan sat down once more on the edge of the fur-covered sleeping ledge.

"Turn this way—"

"This way!"

"Hold still now—"

While Aideen and Bevin turned her head this way and that, until one could reach her hair and the other could work on her face, Rioghan closed her eyes and went along with whatever they wished to do with her. In a moment Bevin was tugging at her long wet hair with a wooden comb, while Aideen began dabbing at her cheeks and lips with something cool and wet.

"Bevin, I fear to ask what you are doing to my hair, and so I will not—but Aideen, what do you have planned for my face?"

Through half-closed eyes Rioghan could see Aideen smile. "It does not need much. Your green eyes are already set off by brows and lashes dark as night. I have here some blackberry juice and water, to add a little color to your cheeks and to your lips. Never have I seen skin so fair. . . . There!"

Rioghan blinked and opened her eyes. But she dared not move, for Bevin still had her hair firmly in her grasp, combing and tugging and twisting it.

Sabha returned and held out a handful of objects to Rioghan. "These are mine," she said, "and I would be so happy if you would wear them tonight. They would look beautiful on you."

In Sabha's hands lay a glittering collection of delicate gold. She set it all down on the soft white furs and began by lifting out two small identical pieces. They looked like a pair of teardrops woven of shining gold wire, with a long loop at the end. Sabha placed the loops over each of Rioghan's ears so that the gold teardrops swung just below her ears on either side of her face.

"Hold out your arms," commanded Sabha, and when Rioghan did so she placed a slender, twisted ribbon of gold around each wrist—bands left open in one spot so that they could be pulled slightly apart and slipped onto the wearer's arm. Each end of the band was capped with a small sphere of brilliant, heavy gold.

"Stand up," said Sabha, and Rioghan cautiously slid her feet to the floor, for Bevin still had a firm grip on her hair. "Raise your arms," Sabha told her, and this time she wrapped a slender belt around Rioghan's waist—a belt made entirely of delicate gold links. When it was hooked together, the end of it trailed almost to her ankles.

"Hold this, now, while I get the mantle," Sabha commanded, and gave Rioghan a circular golden brooch beautifully decorated with polished black jet.

Rioghan smiled when she saw the brooch. Dark and gleaming jet was one of her favorite things to wear, for it was a substance of the forest itself, made from the most ancient of trees after a long, long sleep within the earth. Her own bronze brooch, given to her by her mother, was itself inlaid with the stone.

Sabha added a woolen mantle to the outfit. It was a rectangle of soft new wool, woven in a plaid of dark green and silvery gray with just a few lines of red as bright as holly berries. She took the golden brooch from Rioghan and fastened the mantle with it at the left shoulder.

"Am I finished?" Rioghan asked.

"Just one more thing," said Bevin. She lifted Rioghan's hair from beneath the green-and-gray mantle and took all the remaining gold ornaments from the pile on the white furs. These were four lightweight, hollow golden spheres, dotted with a delicate pattern of holes and with a larger hole at the top. With just a little more tugging Bevin fastened them in Rioghan's hair, then stepped back at last. "I think we are through with you. Here . . . look at yourself!"

Bevin held up a polished bronze mirror in front of Rioghan, turning it so that it would catch the fire's light.

"Oh . . ."

Rioghan lifted up one hand to touch her face, her hair, her shoulder. In the hazy reflection of the bronze mirror she could see her own features, but in a way she had never seen them before.

Always, it seemed, she went about with her black cloak pulled up over her head or with her long, heavy black hair falling around her face to hide it. But in the bronze mirror she saw a young green-eyed woman with her face open to the world, her skin fair and flushed and touched with deep color at the cheeks and lips.

Her glossy black hair had been tightly and neatly braided straight back along the top of her head, on either side of the center part, with the ends hanging down behind her shoulders in two long streams reaching nearly as far as the golden belt at her waist. The rest of her hair was in two long braids on either side of her face and fell down in front of her shoulders to the belt. Attached to the end of each of the four braids were the delicate golden spheres.

The gold-wire earrings framed her face. The twisted golden bands gleamed at her wrists. The belt of gold links hung low on her hips, bright against the dark green wool of her gown, and outlined a slender figure usually hidden beneath her heavy black garb.

Rioghan lowered the mirror as her heart began to pound. Again she felt exposed and vulnerable and entirely out in the open, standing here with her smooth braided hair revealing her color-stained face, and a tight-fitting gown and gold belt showing off her body. For a moment she wanted to tell Sabha to bring back her clothes so she could retreat to the safety of black wool and solitude . . . but then the image of Donaill came into her mind.

He would be waiting for her in the flickering lights and merry company of the king's hall. Waiting for *her*.

Rioghan turned to the three women. "I cannot thank you enough."

"There is no need to thank us," said Sabha. "It is our pleasure."

"Though I think it will be Donaill's pleasure when he sees her!"

"Bevin! Do not embarrass Rioghan," said Aideen

with a laugh. "Though I must say that I agree with you!"

Rioghan, too, laughed out loud, and handed the bronze mirror back to Bevin. "Ladies, you have indeed worked magic this night. At this moment I am feeling bold enough to walk into the hall and sit down at the feast. Please, let's go now, before I change my mind!"

Chapter Ten

In the deep blue twilight, with the stars just beginning to appear near the horizon, the four women walked together across the quiet grounds of Cahir Cullen. Just ahead was the enormous round building that was the king's hall. Light shone from its high windows, and smoke poured through the hole cut in the very center of its conical thatched roof. As the four of them approached, the good smell of wood smoke reached them along with the delicious aroma of roasting meat.

They started toward the door, but then Sabha stopped and placed her hand on Rioghan's arm. "I cannot go in," the woman said. "He will be there . . . he will be there with her. I cannot go in. He would expect to sit with me on one side of him and her on the other." She shook her head. "I would have done anything else for him, anything at all . . . but not that. Never that."

Rioghan smiled gently at her, forgetting her own nerves for the moment. "I am so sorry. You must remember that the choice was Airt's, not yours. The choice and the loss are both his. There was nothing you could have done to change his thoughts on this. Or his actions."

"I understand that now." Sabha took a deep breath. "Go now. Enjoy yourselves, and tell me about it later!"

The four of them hugged each other, and then Bevin, Aideen, and Rioghan all walked through the doors of the king's hall.

Never did Rioghan recall seeing so many people crowded together in one place at one time. The conversation and laughter rang almost painfully loud. In the center of the enormous hall the stone-walled circular firepit blazed with bright yellow light, sending clouds of smoke and the occasional spray of sparks up toward the hole in the roof.

Forming a circle around the firepit was a row of beautifully dressed men and women. They were seated on leather cushions placed on the thick, dry straw of the floor, and faced each other across polished squares and rectangles of wood. Before them on the wood rested golden plates, each one with two golden cups beside it.

Above each plate was a small flat stone holding a fine white beeswax candle. Pressed into the base of each was a decorative cutting of holly, the glossy green leaves and bright red berries setting off the brilliant gold of the plates and adding bright spots of color to the winter gathering.

Over the firepit, two wild boars turned on iron spits above the crackling flames, and at the edges bronze cauldrons rested on iron tripods set over the coals. An army of servants turned the spits and stirred the cauldrons, hurrying back and forth with bowls and plates between the firepit and the long, rough wooden slabs laden with food across one section of the rear wall.

Rioghan glanced quickly about but for a panicked moment saw not one familiar face—not even among the women. She stayed close to Bevin and Aideen as they peered through the smoky candlelit haze, looking for their husbands. "Ah! There he is—and Bevin, there is Niall. Rioghan, I know that you are Donaill's guest, but I do not see him. Would you care to sit beside me and Tully until he arrives?"

"Thank you, but . . . I will—I will just wait." Donaill had not come. Or he might yet come. Rioghan wasn't sure which she feared more. She turned and hurried back toward the door, intending to go back to Sabha's house and get her own clothes and—

"Why, good evening to you, Lady Rioghan."

Rioghan stopped and stepped back a pace. Donaill stood in the doorway, framed by darkness and flickering torchlight. He smiled down at her and reached for her hand.

He seemed even taller than she remembered, his shoulders broader and his cloak wider. Perhaps it was just the heavy leather boots he wore with his smooth black leather breeches that added to his height. It must have been the new wool tunic in a beautiful plaid of red and gold and cream that made his shoulders seem even larger and stronger, as did the heavy red cloak pinned over his left shoulder with a large golden brooch.

And it must have been his hair, now long and loose and flowing down to his shoulders, that made his skin seem even smoother and his blue eyes even brighter—the soft, light brown hair that set off his powerful neck and wide jaw.

It was as if she had never seen him before, yet knew him very well at the same time. And as she stood staring at him, the noise of the many shouting, laughing people began to fade. All she heard was the sound of Donaill's voice saying, "You look so beautiful this night. Will you come inside with me?"

"Thank you. I will," she replied, and stepped back to let him walk through the doors. She turned to move beside him as he went to find his place beside the king.

"I will sit beside King Bran, of course, said Donaill, surveying the people as they walked past, "since I am king's champion. But first I must find him. . . ."

"Do you not know the king's place in the hall?" Rioghan asked, carefully looking straight ahead as she walked. "How could that be, if you always sit beside him at a feast?"

"Well, you can see that there is no beginning and

no end to the places where we sit, since our hall is round. And so the king moves among the people each time there is a gathering and chooses a different place to sit."

Rioghan nodded as they walked over the thick carpet of straw, stepping aside once to let the servants pass with plates stacked high with hot oatbread and wooden bowls heaped with butter. "Ah! Here we are."

She found herself standing beside Donaill in the warmth of the blazing fire, looking down at King Bran. He nodded to her in greeting as she presented herself to him. "Thank you for coming, Lady Rioghan. You have been a great help to us, and you are always welcome here . . . though I must say I am not sure I would have known you tonight, had Donaill not told me your name just now. Sit down, please, and enjoy this night among my people."

She smiled, feeling her spirits rise. "I thank you for your hospitality, King Bran," she said, and together she and Donaill sat down on the smooth leather cushions in the straw.

As Donaill turned to her, she became aware that the noise of conversation had faded somewhat. She looked up and realized that Donaill was not the only one looking at her. Half the people of the gathering were looking and pointing at her, whispering and glancing at each other.

Once again she was acutely aware of her uncovered face, of the bright lights upon her, of her braided hair and dark-stained lips, and the colorful clothes and gleaming gold that so boldly invited everyone to look at her.

She tried to ignore the curious stares, but knew they must all be wondering who she was and why she was there. Then Donaill turned to look at the staring men and women, smiled and nodded pleasantly at them all, and turned back to Rioghan.

"Rioghan, look at me." He reached out and touched the side of her cheek, his fingers gently asking her to turn her head. As she faced him, raising her chin, he drew his fingertips down the side of her neck and brushed back a strand of dark hair that had somehow escaped her braids.

"They are only curious. I don't believe they recognize you . . . and I must tell you, I am not sure I would have recognized you, either. Your hair is so beautiful, for now it reveals your face, and the color of the gown and mantle sets off your eyes and your fair skin. Rioghan, you must never again wear dull black gowns or hooded cloaks."

She bit her lip. "It is not just that I look different. They do not *expect* to see me here. They are wondering why someone like me—a midwife, a servant, one of the Little People—should be present at a gathering of kings and warriors and noble ladies."

Donaill shrugged. "It does not matter whether they expect you or not. All that matters is that you have honored me by being my guest tonight, and that you eat and drink and listen to the music and enjoy yourself as you never have before, here in King Bran's hall."

Rioghan could not help smiling at him. "Thank you. Perhaps I will."

Donaill lifted his gold cup of wine, like a small bowl, in both hands, and offered her a drink. After a brief hesitation she accepted, taking a small sip and looking at his glinting blue eyes over the rim. As the wine spread its warmth through her chest, Donaill too drank from the cup, and his eyes never left hers.

The other people soon turned back to their own conversations and laughter, for now the meat was being served—great slabs and joints of the roasted boars that Donaill's two brothers had hunted.

With his jet-handled dagger, Donaill took two large slices from the wooden tray that the servants brought around and placed them on the gold plate between him and Rioghan. Using the dagger, he cut the pieces into neat strips and offered the first to her.

She accepted, reaching across the polished boards for a little gold dish of salt. As she did so she glanced down the curving row at the other people—and there she saw Airt and Coiteann sitting together. Like herself and Donaill, they shared a plate between them.

Rioghan's hand stopped halfway to the salt. The strip of meat she held fell to the boards as she slowly withdrew her hand, staring at the other couple all the while.

Coiteann had eyes for nothing and no one but Airt. She kept his cup filled with blackberry wine and his plate heaped with oatbread and butter and honey and roasted boar, stopping the servants as they passed by and watching to see when the next course was brought out so that he might have the choicest serving.

Airt, however, sat quietly, mostly watching the others or gazing down into the burning candle as though he did not see it. He seemed to have eaten only a little bread and a few bites of meat, and touched the wine not at all.

Rioghan sat back. She continued to watch them. Donaill followed her gaze, and his mouth twisted in a wry grin when he realized who she was staring at.

"Ah, Coiteann and her newest conquest," he said.

Rioghan began to feel cold. "You know her?"

He nodded. "Everyone knows her. She is certainly working her way up through the ranks. She began with farmers' sons, and then moved to craftsmen and armorers, and now has caught her first warrior—at least, the first who will be seen openly with her. She must be quite pleased with herself this night."

"I did not think that a woman like her would be of interest to a man like you."

Donaill gave her a sideways look; then he laughed. "Half the men of this fortress have had Coiteann, but I am not one of them." When Rioghan frowned ever so slightly and looked away, he cocked his head and touched the side of her face.

"Truly, I am not," he said, moving his hand away as she looked up at him once more. "Why eat from the same plate as every other? I prefer my own plate, thank you very much . . . and I do not share it except on the most special of occasions."

With that, he lifted their golden plate, turned it so that the newly cut pieces of roasted boar were nearest to Rioghan, and offered it to her again. She hesitated only a moment before smiling up at him and accepting another slice.

"Airt is both young and a fool," continued Donaill. "He thinks to find importance for himself by having more than one wife, even when that one wife has made it clear to him that she will never accept another woman in her house."

Rioghan nodded. "I know Sabha well. I know that she and Airt spoke of this before they contracted their marriage, but Airt is certain he can persuade her."

"He is almost too certain." He looked down the row at the other couple again, and seemed to be deep in thought. "Rioghan . . . I want to ask you this, for you are one who might know. Do you think that Coiteann has used more than just her own freely offered gifts to capture Airt so completely?"

Rioghan paused. "It is possible," she answered. "I myself believed I saw the touch of dark magic on him. She may well have tried some sort of unnatural charm to hold him at her side."

Donaill finished the piece of meat he had selected and tossed the bone back behind him into the straw. "Is she so powerful? It seems that if she had such magic she would have done more with it up to now—more than just persuade a foolish young man to take her to his bed."

"She may well have had a little magic, but you are right—it is not enough to force his will. He could easily break free of her if he truly wished to."

Donaill grinned. "Ah, that is what I thought! No woman's love charm is *that* strong." He offered Rioghan the wine cup again, and this time she readily accepted.

The warmth of the hall, and of the food, and of the wine, crept over Rioghan like the softest and warmest of furs, and left her feeling more relaxed than she had in a very long time. "Rioghan, I am so glad to see that you are enjoying yourself," Donaill said. "I know that you are not accustomed to being at a large and noisy gathering such as this. If there is anything else that you might like, you have only to ask."

She smiled at him. "I thank you for your hospitality. There is far more here tonight than I myself would need in five years at Sion . . . more wood thrown on the fire, more food on the tables, more wine. . . ."

"And more conversation?"

Rioghan looked down at their shining gold plate. "The Sidhe are good companions."

"Yet they do not share your home. Save for the dogs, you are alone much of the time, are you not?"

"Alone is not always the same as lonely. I have the Sidhe for company, as I said, and the dogs are loyal guardians. Even the wild creatures of the forest are ever present. I am never truly alone."

"But you must be lonely sometimes."

"It is a good and satisfying life. I have been of help to the people of Cahir Cullen, especially the women here, have I not?"

"You have indeed. And we are grateful to you. But . . . could you not do as well living here, living among us?"

She hesitated, looking around the hall once more at the beautifully dressed people and the shining gold before them, at the huge fire and the endless quantities of good food and wine. She thought of what it would be like to live here in this lively, busy place, with the sisterlike companionship of Sabha and Bevin and Aideen . . . and the presence of one such as Donaill.

"King's champion Donaill! I want to thank your brothers for this feast. Something to remember during the months to come when we're all chewing dried beef!"

Rioghan looked up and felt a sudden chill, as if the huge fire in the center of the hall had gone out. Standing over them was the rough bearded form of Beolagh.

"You are welcome," said Donaill, after a brief glance up at the other man. "But surely you're not finished eating already. Shouldn't you go back to your place so that you don't miss the final course? I hear they've got apples boiled in milk and honey and covered with hazelnuts. You will not want to miss that."

"Actually, it's watercress with fat-hen leaves first, and then the apples. And you're right, I don't want to miss it. But even more than that, I don't want to miss finding out who this new woman is, sitting beside you tonight. Might I know her name?"

"You might, if she wishes to tell you. What say you, my lady?"

Rioghan drew a breath and started to answer; but as she looked up into Beolagh's face and saw not the first sign of recognition in his eyes, she looked away again and took another sip of wine.

Instantly a gleam came into Donaill's eye. "Do you not recognize this lady, Beolagh? I assure you, you have seen her before."

A deep frown came over the other man's face. "You are not very funny, Donaill. I am quite certain I have never seen this young woman before. I would not forget so pretty a face—serious though it is—or such radiant black hair, or such a fair form.

"Oh . . . wait!" He started to laugh. "You're going to tell me I saw her when she was a child, or some such! Well, that would explain why I may have seen her before but do not recognize her now."

"It has not been that long since you have seen her," said Donaill. "But if you do not remember, then I suppose she will have to remain a mystery to you."

Rioghan set down the wine cup and nibbled daintily at a bit of buttered oatbread.

"Well, she must be from Dun Orga, then, or perhaps she is the pretty daughter of one of the farmers or herdsmen." Beolagh shook his head. "I will admit, when I first saw her I thought you had brought in one of the Sidhe! She is so small, and has hair as black as jet, as most of them do. Though I should have known, Donaill, that the king's champion would not be sitting with one of the Little People at the king's own feast."

With that, Beolagh nodded to Donaill and wandered off to speak to someone farther down the row.

Chapter Eleven

Rioghan set down the last of her bread. Donaill leaned down to look at her, trying to catch her eye, but she only glared down at the candles and tapped her finger impatiently on the boards.

"I am sorry," Donaill said. "He will never be more than a rough, crude man, no matter that he was born into the high ranks. Though I certainly enjoyed the little joke you played on him . . . keeping him ignorant of who you are."

"Beolagh thinks to insult me by calling me one of the Little People. I know the opinion which all Men have of the Sidhe—that they are nothing but primitive and inferior versions of Men, small and dark instead of tall and fair, little more than animals living wild in the woods—"

"Not all Men think so, Lady Rioghan. I hope you understand that I do not."

She gave him a quick glance, then went on tapping her finger. "I am proud to have the Sidhe accept me as one of their own. Indeed, at this moment I would rather be the poorest of the Fair Folk than the wealthiest of Men."

"I hope you will never have to make that choice, my lady."

Her mouth tightened. "And I would like to show him more than a joke. I would like to show him—and the others of his kind—what one of the Little People can do."

"Rioghan, it does not matter. Men like Beolagh are impressed by nothing but a forceful blow. Except for Beolagh and the ones foolish enough to follow him, the people here have always treated the Sidhe well—or at least left them in peace—have they not?"

"They have."

"Then, please—do not give him another thought. Just stay here and enjoy the rest of the evening with me. Look, I will give you this, to help you remember this night."

He reached out and took the bright sprig of holly from the white candle, and brushed away the bits of wax that clung to it. Carefully, frowning a bit in concentration, Donaill tucked the holly into the gold-and-jet brooch Rioghan wore at her shoulder, weaving the woody stem in and out of the gold circle and arranging it this way and that until it was to his liking.

"There," he said, sitting back. "The holly leaves are as green as your eyes. It's a perfect match." He reached out to stroke the hair at the base of her neck again, and she could not help but look up at him. His eyes reflected the soft glow of the candles as he smiled down at her, and then his eyes began to close as he leaned down—

There was a short cry behind them. Rioghan sat up and turned toward it. One of the serving women stood close beside the firepit, clutching her wrist and wincing in pain. Rioghan scrambled to her feet and hurried over to her.

"What has happened?" she asked, trying to get a look at the woman's arm.

"Oh, it's nothing, nothing at all. Please don't trouble yourself, lady."

"It is no trouble. Let me see." The woman moved her hand to show a bright red mark on the underside of her wrist, already shiny and blistering. "I tried to move the rocks from the firepit to the cauldron to bring the water to a boil. The rock fell."

The firepit was so crowded with spits and cauldrons and rocks that an extra pair of water-filled cauldrons had been set down on the bare earth beside the pit wall. The servants had been trying to place fire-heated rocks into them to bring the water to boil. "Where is your shovel? Here, I will help you move the rocks. You must take care of your arm."

"I had no shovel. Only crossed sticks."

Rioghan frowned. "It is dangerous to try to lift heated rocks with only sticks. Such injuries are too common. Why do you not have an iron shovel?"

The servant shut her eyes in pain. "I don't know. Some say that one of the warrior men demanded a new sword, and that the armorers came and took some of our tools."

Rioghan's mouth tightened. "I can well imagine which man would demand a new weapon without a care for the needs of servants." She patted the woman's shoulder. "Wait here. I brought a few things with me. I can give you a clean wrapping for the burn and something to ease the pain."

Just then another of the serving women hurried up, holding a dripping wet cloth. "Here, Ita, wrap this around it. We must get back to work; the water is not boiling fast enough to steam the honey and the milk! They are all waiting for their apples and honey—look, even the king is beginning to frown! Hurry, hurry!"

The two women brushed past Rioghan as if nothing had happened and went back to the precarious work of trying to lift the hot stones from the coals with flimsy crossed sticks, and get them into the water-filled cauldrons.

"Wait," Rioghan ordered, moving close beside them.

From beneath her sleeve she took her crystal wand from its leather case and held it flat against the inside of her arm, holding the end in the tips of her fingers. She turned a steady gaze on the rocks among the smoldering coals, pointed the concealed wand at them, and whispered a word under her breath.

One of the rocks lifted itself slowly from the coals. Rioghan kept her hand pointed at it, and as she moved her hand toward the waiting cauldron, the stone moved with it. When it hovered over the clear water, Rioghan whispered another word, and the stone dropped with a hissing splash into the water. A little cloud of steam rose in its wake.

The two servants jumped in surprise. Rioghan moved her arm again and moved a second, third, and fourth stone into the cauldron. "Now it is done," she said, "and there will be no more burns. I will ask that the armorers replace the tools you need without delay."

"Thank you, lady," said Ita. "Oh, thank you."

"I don't know how it was done, but we're grateful to you," said the other serving woman.

"You are most welcome. I will leave you something to treat the burn. Good night to you both."

"Good night to you, Lady Rioghan," they said, before disappearing again into the crowd of bustling servants. "Bring the honey and milk!" she heard one of them say, and two more servants set down flat bronze pans sloshing with honey and fresh milk over the now-steaming cauldrons on the dirt floor. "The water boils now, thanks to the Lady Rioghan. Hurry, now, hurry!"

Smiling to herself, Rioghan carefully slid her wand back into its case and returned to her place beside Donaill. "That was well done," he said with a grin. "Though I would not have thought you to

be quite so bold about letting everyone here see what powers you have."

She glanced down. "Ordinarily that is true. That sort of magic is not to be used to boast about one's powers, or to entertain men with an evening's worth of wine in them."

"Then . . . why were you so bold with it this night?"

His voice was gentle. He was not mocking her. He seemed to genuinely want to know. "The serving woman badly burned her arm," Rioghan answered. "They are lacking the proper tools to do their work. I could not make an iron shovel, but I knew I could move the rocks. I did not want to see another of them injured."

Donaill nodded. "That was kind of you." He glanced down at her wrist, hidden now by the long sleeves of the silver-gray undergown. "I ask about your magic only because I am concerned about you. Think of this: if Beolagh wants your gold, what interest might he take in a wand of the sort you have, if indeed he knows you have it?"

She looked toward Beolagh. He sat beside Airt and Coiteann, and all three of them stared at her in silence. Clearly they had witnessed her small trick of levitating the rocks.

Rioghan turned back to Donaill. "If anyone else took this wand, they would find it only a sparkling toy. Nothing more. It was my mother's, and her mother's before her, and has been passed down through my family for too long a time for anyone to remember. We are the only ones who have ever been able to wield it. Perhaps the Sidhe could use it, but they have never tried, as far as is known. The women of my family are the only ones to have the power—and the knowledge of the proper words—to use this wand."

"I see. But . . . I have heard no stories of the midwife shooting great bolts of lightning from her wand, or raising a flood, or stirring a wild windstorm, or any other such thing. Is it a wand of levitation only?"

"Most of the time it is. It is attuned to the earth, and especially to rock, though at times I can use it to manipulate wood as well, since trees are earthbound things." She smiled. "You need not worry, Donaill. I have no great powers. I am no threat to anyone here. I have only an ancient wand and a few old crystals, and they allow me to do some small things. That is all."

"That is all? I think it's more than enough!"

They looked up over their shoulders. Beolagh stood over them once more, but this time he glared down at Rioghan.

Instantly Donaill was on his feet. "You've not had enough to drink yet, Beolagh. You're still standing. Go and join your men and continue with the wine until you're too drunk to walk. Then you'll be much better company."

"That's the midwife!" Beolagh said, pointing at Rioghan. "That's the midwife who lives with the dogs in the cave! Why didn't you tell me who she was?"

"If you could not see who she was, after invading

her home and demanding her gold and threatening to destroy that stone circle, we felt no need to go to the trouble of telling you."

"Coiteann told me who she was, or I might never have known! Look at her! She looks so different with decent clothes and her hair properly arranged! She's trying to hide the fact that she's really one of the Little People!"

Rioghan got up. Her fear was rising but her anger flared right along with it.

Donaill moved to stand between her and Beolagh. "She is my honored guest, and that is all you need to know," he said, his voice low and dangerous. "If you so much as cast another glance in her direction or dare to trespass at her home ever again, you will answer to the king's champion. And if anything should happen to that stone circle, I will come looking for you."

Beolagh ignored him and tried to push his way past Donaill to glare at Rioghan again. "She hides her identity the way she hides her gold! Those things are meant to be shared, but she keeps them all to herself!"

Donaill shoved him back a step. The hall had fallen silent, and everyone sat watching them. Beolagh refused to be deterred. "I know her trick with the wand and the rocks just now. And that's not all I've seen her do! When once my men and I rode past that mound where she lives, she made the stones of the circle shake and move! We thought they were going to walk right out of the earth and crush us all!"

Donaill's mouth began to twist. From all around them came ripples of laughter. Beolagh's face began to flush red beneath his dark beard. "I think it was your own shaking that you saw, and nothing more," Donaill said, chuckling.

The others at the boards laughed even louder—but Rioghan did not join them. She was horrified by the situation in which she found herself. She'd been having such a fine time, lulled by the wine and the food and the warmth and the company, and most of all by Donaill and his flattery. Now here she was, trapped and exposed by an enemy, with noplace to hide and no way to defend herself.

What had she been thinking?

Beolagh was not finished yet. He pointed at Rioghan yet again and roared, "Such power belongs to the druids, not to a madwoman like her! Not to one of the Little People! You are the king's champion, Donaill. What were you thinking when you brought one of them here to the king's hall to sit among us?"

Donaill said nothing . . . and neither did Beolagh, for he was occupied with the process of toppling over like a tree, struck a tremendous blow by Donaill's right fist. His eyes glazed and he staggered a step, and then another, and then he went crashing down into the straw right beside the cauldrons on the floor. His flailing hand struck one of the flat bronze pans, flipped it over, and sent its steaming contents flying straight into his face.

He did not notice the thick coat of milk and honey sticking to his face and beard, for he was quite unconscious. The last thing Rioghan heard as she fled the hall was the uproarious laughter of everyone there.

Donaill left Beolagh lying in the straw, made a brief apology to his king for spoiling the last course of the feast, and hurried out into the cold night to search for Rioghan.

He had thought she would return to Sabha's house, but the place was dark and no one answered his knock on the door. Then he heard a man's voice calling his name.

"Donaill! Here!"

It was Lorcan, his brother, waving to him to come toward the front of the fortress. "She's leaving," Lorcan said, and pointed at the gates.

Donaill saw a small figure making its determined way across the darkness of the grounds, with two huge dogs following on either side. He smiled. Apparently she'd stopped only long enough to grab her own black clothes and ever-present leather bag from Sabha's house and toss them over her arm, for she still wore the fine new attire the other women had given her. Her gray mantle was easily seen in the light of the torches.

"Rioghan!"

She paused . . . then kept going without looking back—but it was enough to let him catch up to her. "Rioghan, please," he said, just as one of the front gates swung partly open to let her through. "Will you not stay among us tonight?"

She shook her head, staring at the ground and

refusing to look at him. "I cannot," she whispered.

He reached for her shoulder. "I am so sorry. One day I will have to teach Beolagh a lesson he will not forget. But until then—"

She whirled around the instant his hand touched her mantle, and now she looked straight at him. "You tell me I should live here among you. You would have me live among men such as that?" Her green eyes flashed with anger and distress. "The Sidhe are kind and the dogs are loyal. I can think of no better place to live than the one that I have now."

Donaill was pleased to see that the small sprig of holly from their place at the feast was still caught in the gold brooch that fastened her mantle, though undoubtedly it was the farthest thing from her mind. "Someday I hope you will want to live here," he said gently, but she only tightened her jaw and raised her chin.

"To your folk, I will always be one of the Little People—and it is clear they have no place among the noble men and women of Cahir Cullen."

She took a deep breath and struggled to regain her composure. "Again, I thank you for your hospitality. But it will not be this night that I stay among you." She turned and slipped out through the gate, which closed again as soon as she and her dogs had gone.

Lorcan walked up to stand beside Donaill. "You could not persuade her to stay?" he asked.

"Not this time. This is more than she is accustomed to."

"Pity. She did look quite lovely tonight. Perhaps you should have tried a bit harder."

Donaill grinned, then turned to walk back toward the hall. "Oh, I will not stop trying," he said. "But it's like taming a wild creature. You must be prepared to let it run free when it wishes, so that it does not feel trapped. She'll be back. I'll make sure of it."

Chapter Twelve

A few more days went by, gray and quiet days that Rioghan spent working as busily and intensely as she ever had. On one long afternoon when a cold, misty rain kept her inside her cave, sorting and patiently crushing and preparing her many herbs and remedies, she looked up to see the faces of Mil and Ceo at the entrance to the cave.

"Come in, come in!" she said, cleaning her hands with a linen rag and walking over to greet the two Sidhe women. "Is everything well with you?"

"It is," said Mil. She was the older of the two visitors, a little bent with age and with hair almost white. "We just wanted to see you and perhaps pass the afternoon with you."

"In truth," said Ceo, smoothing back her own dark hair, which had only a little gray in it, "my mother is worried for you after your adventure at Cahir Cullen. You were a guest there at the feast a few nights ago, were you not?"

Rioghan smiled, and walked back to the bench where she had been working. "I was. And though the day started out well, it did not end so, I am afraid."

"We know." The two Sidhe came over and sat down in the straw beside her low bench, watching as Rioghan continued her careful sorting of a great stack of plants. "You work so hard, dear Rioghan," said Mil. "Winter is meant to be a time of rest after all the work of the harvest."

"To say nothing of the time spent preparing and storing food and firewood and warm clothes and furs to last until the spring," added Ceo.

Rioghan shook her head, gazing down at her herbs and flowers. "I have no time at all for rest. Indeed, I fear it, for these days I have far too much to occupy my mind."

Her guests waited patiently, expectantly, sympathetically, so after a moment Rioghan went on. "It seems that if I stop working for more than a moment, I think first of Donaill and the feast and the time I spent as a friend—not just a servant—of the women of Cahir Cullen. Then, in a heartbeat, I swing instantly to the same helpless anger I felt at being insulted and threatened by a drunken lout like Beolagh."

"Did Donaill not defend you?" asked Ceo.

"Oh, he did. He did. He dropped Beolagh unconscious to the floor at the first hint of an insult."

Mil gave her a slow smile, her eyes twinkling. "No harm will ever come to you so long as he is near. Of that I am quite sure."

Rioghan smiled back at her, but her mouth was tight. "I am sure of it, too. But there is something else about him that concerns me far more."

Ceo frowned. "What troubles you, lady? Do you not like him?"

"He likes you very much," opened Mil.

Rioghan came out from behind her bench and sat down across from them in the clean, warm straw. "I *do* like him," she began. "And yet it is impossible for me to believe that I could ever be more to him than a temporary prize to be shown off at a feast."

She shook her head. "To a man like him, I am but a mysterious woman whom he, the charming and irresistible Donaill, has managed to win where all the other men have failed . . . and, once conquered, I will only find myself set aside and forgotten as he moves on to his next pretty challenge. . . . Or it could be far worse."

She gazed off into the distance as her visitors remained silent, and after a moment made herself go on: "He might well be content to let me stay with him, and we might marry and be happy together . . . but then one day I would begin to realize that I was not the only woman in his life.

"I would find that he was perfectly happy to have me as a wife, but that he also saw no reason why he should not keep company with any other woman he chose when I did not happen to be around . . . and that he would see no reason to share this small and unimportant part of his life with me."

"Ah, Rioghan, I understand your fears," said Mil. "But such things happen to many women, and you must simply—"

"It happened to one of my sisters. It happened to Sabha. It happens to women every day." Rioghan got to her feet and resumed her work at the bench. "But it will never happen to me."

Mil and Ceo looked at each other. Rioghan knew they would try to persuade her that Donaill was not such a man, and that she should—

There was a noise near the entrance to the cave. Rioghan looked up just in time to see Scath and Cogar fly out of the straw and bolt outside.

She hurried over to peer worriedly out past the cowhide hangings on her door. All of her dogs had gathered on the far side of the clearing, at the strip of forest between Sion and the stone circle, but they were all quietly eager in their watch of whatever held their attention in the trees. They frisked and whined and trotted back and forth, and a few even wagged their tails.

"Rioghan!"

The call reached her across the rain-damp ground of the clearing. It was only a single word, but she knew instantly the voice. "Donaill," she whispered.

Though he could not possibly have heard her, the king's champion rode into the clearing as if she'd invited him, and her dogs fell back from the feet of his black stallion to let him pass. Rioghan pulled on her heavy black cloak and stepped out into the rain.

Cath trotted up to her, his broad hooves splashing on the sodden earth of the clearing. Donaill looked down at Rioghan and gave her a smile as bright as the sunniest summer day, though the rainwater dripped from his light brown hair and soaked his dark red cloak. "Good day to you, Lady Rioghan! It is lovely weather, would you not agree?"

"It is what one might expect, some twenty days before midwinter," she answered, wondering what he could possibly want, and why he was so happy on such a dreary day. "Is there someone at Cahir Cullen who needs my help?"

"At Cahir Cullen? All is well there, my lady. You are not needed today—or rather, I should say that your midwifery is not needed. You, Rioghan, are always welcome there . . . and needed, as well."

She raised her chin to look at him, and stepped close enough to place her hand on Cath's wet black shoulder. "I will come if my help is needed, but that is all. I have no reason to go there otherwise. So Donaill, please tell me why you have come to Sion this day."

He grinned down at her again. "Only to bring you a message. I will be gone from Cahir Cullen for a few days, and I wanted you to know this before I left."

Rioghan withdrew her hand. "Gone?"

"Only for a few days . . . three, perhaps four. I, and a few other men, are riding to Dun Orga at the request of King Bran."

She frowned. "Why would the king order you to travel there now? The days are short and gray and wet. The nights are long and cold and filled with winter-hungry wolves. What is at Dun Orga that cannot wait for spring?"

He laughed. "I agree with you: the spring would be far better—but there is a new king's champion at Dun Orga, and our king wishes to have his own champion there to remind Dun Orga of who truly has the greatest warriors."

He sat back on his horse, beaming, to let her admire him. No doubt he thought she would be impressed by the sight of his iron sword and the jet-handled dagger fastened to his belt, by the heavy gold bands around his wrists and the twisted gold torque at his throat; but she could only stare up at him in disbelief. "You would make such a journey in the cold and wet of winter, just to impress another warrior with your prowess?"

"Why, I am not just a warrior, Lady Rioghan. I am the king's own champion! And I mean to impress not just the champion of Dun Orga, but their king and all their warriors as well. There is not one of them who can stand up to me, and I intend to remind this new warrior of that. There is no better way to keep the peace than a perfectly timed show of prowess."

Rioghan sighed, then caught hold of Donaill's stallion's reins just behind its chin. "In that case, leave Cath here with me. I will see that he is kept warm and fed and protected from wolves, as all horses should be in winter." Cath swung his great head around to lip at her black cloak, as if in agreement with her, but Donaill only laughed again.

"That is very kind of you, but I assure you that Cath will get the best of care and no wolf will ever get near him. And how would I get to Dun Orga, then?"

She let go of the reins. "You say this is the king's request?"

"It is." His voice became gentler. "Do not worry, Rioghan. Beolagh and his men will not disturb you again. I showed him his place in front of everyone at the feast, did I not?"

"You made him a joke. An object of ridicule. But that is all."

"That is all? Why, short of killing him, there is no better way to defeat a man than to humiliate him. And that I did quite well!" Donaill looked convinced.

But Rioghan only clenched her fingers beneath the cloak. "If they are truly no danger to Sion, why did you have to ride all the way out here to warn me that you would be gone?"

His face grew serious, though she noted that his blue eyes still sparkled. He leaned down alongside his horse's neck so that his face was nearly level with hers. "I came for just one reason," he said.

His voice was so soft that she had to lean forward to hear him over the dripping of the rain at the entrance to her cave. "I came because I wanted to," he said. Then he stretched out to steal a quick kiss from her lips. Sitting up straight, not giving her time to react, he rode away again across the wet and muddy clearing.

* * *

Bowing her head against the cold and steady rain, Sabha walked with some determination across the wet grounds of Cahir Cullen. She threw the ends of her blue-and-green plaid cloak over her shoulder as the wind picked up. But she would not be out in the cold for very long, for she knew exactly where to find what she was looking for.

A fire burned low in the central pit of the great round hall. Servants worked at the boards along the rear section, grinding wheat in rotary querns and cleaning watercress and clover for boiling later on. A few men sat on cushions in the straw, playing at chance or at fidchell. The women, who often gathered in the hall to work together at their weaving or spinning or sewing, had already gone back to their homes to prepare the evening meal for their families. Sabha walked quietly across the straw until she stood over one of the men at the fidchell boards, and her shadow caused him to look up.

"Sabha!" Airt scrambled to his feet, jarring the game board so that some of its gold-capped pegs fell over. "Sabha, I am so glad to see you! Come over here; come sit with me by the fire where we can talk."

He took her by the arm and hurried her over to the hearth. With a careful but deliberate move she withdrew her arm from his grip and stood quietly beside the stone wall of the firepit, folding her hands and taking a deep breath.

"This will not take long," she said. "I know you must be returning home soon. Coiteann will be waiting for you."

He seemed not to have heard. "It is good to see you," he said, looking as happy as she had ever seen him. "I have missed you. I have been—"

"There is no need to tell me what you have been doing. You have spent your days and nights with *her*, and that is enough."

Her husband shrugged and looked down at the straw. "It's true, I have, but—"

"Listen to me, please. I have come here to tell you . . . to tell you that I forgive you."

"You forgive me?" He looked up again, and reached for her hand.

"I do. And I still love you." She closed her eyes as he held tight to her hand, but did not move.

"Oh, Sabha, I have never stopped loving you . . . never, never . . ." Airt moved close, and she thought he would try to kiss her. Quickly she turned her face away.

"I have come to remind you that if you wish to return to our home—and do not require me to accept another woman there—then it can be your home once again."

He pressed her hand gently between both of his own. "You would take me back again? You are saying you want me to come home?"

"I am saying that, if you love only me, and need no other woman in your life, then I would indeed take you back into my life and into my home."

Airt paused, and though he still smiled down at her, Sabha could see the sudden faraway look in his dark eyes . . . and she knew very well who was foremost in his thoughts.

Even now, he could only think of Coiteann. Even now, he was still looking for some way of convincing his wife to allow another woman in their house. And she knew he would never give up hope that this would happen.

Sabha turned away. "This choice must be yours and yours alone," she said, walking toward the door of the hall. "Please think on this, and do not make me wait much longer."

"I will think on it," he called from beside the fire. "I love you, Sabha! I love you!"

Sabha hurried out into the cold gray afternoon.

The end of the day approached. With increasing anxiety Rioghan and ten men of the Sidhe made their preparations for the night to come and for the invasion it would surely bring.

It was not yet the dark of the moon, but Rioghan was certain that with Donaill away, Beolagh and his men would not hesitate to return to Sion and demand that she hand over the gold—and destroy the stone circle if she refused.

Already she and the others had hidden away all of the gold and bronze and crystal treasures stored in Sion. Rioghan was exhausted from dragging in load after load of deadwood from the forest, so that they might keep the fire going in the pit and have torches burning all through the night. Five of the Sidhe stayed with her in her cave to stack the wood and prepare grease-soaked woolen rags to make the torches, while the other five collected stones for their slings and ran them up to the top of Sion to await whoever might intrude on them now that Donaill was away. Everywhere the dogs roved back and forth, watching and waiting, caught up in the tension as all of them were.

"Kieran," Rioghan said, ripping up the last of an old wool cloth to make rags. "I want all of you to stay atop the mound when they get here."

"Atop the mound? Sion? But why?" He walked toward her with an armload of heavy torch sticks. "It's the circle they want. We should wait for them in the trees."

Rioghan shook her head. "As much as I want to save the circle, I cannot have any of you lose your lives over it. Not even that ancient stone circle is worth your life."

"But this is not only about the stone circle being threatened. If not the circle, it will be something else."

The other Sidhe looked up at Kieran's words. "These men are determined to have our gold."

"They will destroy us all to get it if they must."

"We must not give in to them!"

Rioghan knew they were right—yet she did not want to ask them to risk their lives. She could only hope that perhaps Donaill was right, that Beolagh and his men would think better than to bother them here again. But Donaill was gone—gone on a meaningless errand to impress some other king, some other champion, some other warriors—and she and the Sidhe were left here all alone to defend themselves as best they could from the outlaw warriors of Cahir Cullen.

"Kieran, we should bring more water inside. We may have to defend this place for a long while. And perhaps one of you should run back to your homes and bring more cloaks and furs; it will be very cold tonight—"

"Too late," said a breathless voice at the entrance to the cave.

All of them turned to look. Luath pushed back the hangings and stepped inside, staring back at them with wide but determined eyes. "They're coming."

Chapter Thirteen

Instantly the Sidhe inside the cave bolted outside to race up to the top of the mound. "Did you see them?" cried Rioghan, as Luath followed the others.

"I did!" he called over his shoulder. "Two groups of riders—one on the road, one on the forest path!" And he disappeared around the back of the mound, leaving Rioghan alone with her dogs at the entrance to her home.

Two groups. Two groups of riders! Beolagh must mean to surround them this time, to distract and confuse and overwhelm them. Rioghan pulled her crystal wand from its case at her wrist and stood in the fading light to await the enemy. She tried to focus on the battle to come, but foremost in her thoughts was Donaill—Donaill and her rising anger toward him.

She had asked him for his protection, not just for herself but for the Sidhe and their stone circle. Asked him for protection from his own people, and he had promised to give it to her. Yet while the threat was at its greatest—just three nights after the two of them had publicly humiliated the man who was her enemy—Donaill had ridden away to do nothing more important than prove his status to another king's champion, leaving her and the Sidhe alone to face the threat that his own people brought them.

Her dogs turned as one to face the main road where it ended at the clearing. But before they could charge, Rioghan ordered them back. "*Madra. Madra!*" she said in a hiss, and reluctantly the pack returned to surround her, still facing the road and growling with their hackles raised.

She held tight to Scath's collar with her left hand and raised the crystal wand in her right, remembering the slashing swords of the men who had already taken two of her dogs. In the silence, she looked back and forth from the road to the strip of forest surrounding the stone circle.

Luath had seen two groups of riders coming. He'd said there was one on the road and one in the forest. Two groups—but the dogs looked only to the road.

The pounding hoofbeats grew closer.

And then both groups of riders burst out into the

clearing and charged toward each other. The dogs erupted in a frenzy of barking and tore back and forth at Rioghan's feet, desperate to charge the intruders but held back by their mistress's command.

Rioghan forced the dogs to stay with her and braced herself for the attack to come, confused by what she was seeing. She had expected Beolagh's men to come late in the night, but Sion had been invaded by two bands of marauders, and they had come so early that the western sky still glowed gray with daylight.

Had Beolagh brought more men this time, in hopes of surrounding and crushing them once and for all while Donaill was gone? Why did they not turn toward the cave and try to take the gold they had come for? Or go to the stone circle and destroy it as they'd threatened? What were they waiting for? Why did they regroup in the clearing and charge and shout at each other, instead of heading toward the cave?

Chaos reigned in the clearing, which had now become a battlefield. It became apparent that if the two groups did not charge Sion, it was because they were fighting each other. Or perhaps they were just fighting for control of their horses, which were leaping and bucking and slipping on the muddy ground in their frantic efforts to escape the rain of stones falling down on them from high atop the mound.

Rioghan saw the dark flash of iron swords in the twilight—and then she saw—and heard—something else.

One man wrestled his great black horse away

from the mob and sent it galloping toward her—a man with broad shoulders and upraised sword and flying red cloak.

"Rioghan! Call off the stone throwers and go inside! Go inside the cave and be safe. We will make short work of this!" And Donaill turned and galloped off again, swinging his sword and roaring in rage at those who had dared to invade her home.

Rioghan let go of Scath's collar and lowered her crystal wand. "Kieran," she said to Scath, and the dog raced away. For a moment she could only stand and watch as the unexpected battle raged in her normally quiet clearing—and she realized, now, that she was watching a clash between Donaill's ten men and Beolagh's five—and that Beolagh, caught by surprise and overconfident to start with, was definitely getting the worst of it.

No more stones flew down from the top of the mound. As Rioghan watched, Donaill's men teamed up to pull each of Beolagh's from his horse and slap him down hard with the flat of an iron sword. Rioghan found herself wishing they would use something more that just the flat so that this lot would never again trouble the peace of Sion—but stopped herself from entertaining such bloodthirsty thoughts.

As Donaill had said, they must follow the laws even if others did not. But if Donaill could not or would not put a stop to this once and for all, then Rioghan—and the Sidhe—would have no choice but to find another way.

It was not long before Donaill once again had

Beolagh and all his men on the ground at swordpoint while their horses galloped riderless down the road for Cahir Cullen. There had surprisingly been no deaths, but all six of the invading men were on their hands and knees, if they could struggle to get up that far, for this time Donaill and his men had left them unable to stand on their feet.

As darkness descended, Rioghan lit one of the torches she and the Sidhe had prepared and walked out to the battlefield with her dogs. She was not ashamed to feel some degree of satisfaction at the sight of Donaill's captives, with their faces bruised and swollen, and all of them covered in mud and filth. They cowered from her dogs as she approached, blinking and squinting and trying to shield their eyes from the glare of her torch.

Donaill slid down from Cath as she came to stand beside him. "Lady Rioghan. I have again brought to their knees those who would try to trouble you, just as I promised you I would. And I say this to you now"—he pointed his sword at his captives—"if ever again these men dare set foot within this clearing, or your stone circle, or indeed come anywhere near you or your dogs or any of the Sidhe, I will have them dragged before the king as criminals. After the king's justice they can look forward to lives as slaves . . . or exiles."

He moved his sword so that its bloodstained iron point passed right in front of their faces. *"Do you understand me this time?"*

All of them nodded, too beaten and breathless to speak, and climbed slowly to their feet.

"Then go, and do not dare to ignore my warning again. I will not be so gentle with you ever again."

The six men limped away, leaning upon each other, clearly beaten almost too sore to move. It would be a long walk for them back to Cahir Cullen.

The light had no sooner faded from the sky when Sabha heard a knock at her door. Opening it just a little, she saw what she needed. She closed it quickly and reached for her cloak.

In a moment she was outside and closing the door behind her. "Walk with me, Airt," she said. After a brief look of disappointment—had he really thought she would invite him alone into the house?—he followed her across the quiet grounds of Cahir Cullen.

"Why have you come?" Sabha asked. "Is something wrong?"

"Nothing. And everything," her husband answered. They walked until they were nearly to the surrounding earthen wall of the keep, and Airt paused beside one of the cattle pens built against it. He turned to his wife and took hold of both her hands before she could react. "Nothing, because at this moment I am here alone with you . . . and everything, because we are otherwise apart."

"It was not my choice for us to be apart," she said, struggling to keep the catch out of her voice. "The choice was yours alone."

He looked down. "It was. But I know now that it was the worst choice I could have made."

Sabha raised an eyebrow. "It has hardly been a fortnight. Can you be so sure of that so quickly?"

"I can," he said, looking up at her again. "It is . . . nothing like living with you. She demands my full attention every moment. She insists I do not love her if I do not compliment her often enough, or bring her some gift each evening when I arrive home. She cries often, over such small things . . . and when she heard this day that I had spoken with you in the hall . . ." He sighed and looked away, staring at nothing, and shook his head. "I want to come home," he said.

Sabha gazed at him, folding her hands to keep herself still. "You could have come home at any time, yet you stayed with her all these many nights."

He smiled a little, still looking away. "You know it would not be true if I told you I had no affection for her at all. I wanted to make her a second wife, and that alone would tell you that there must have been a certain bond between us. The times were not always bad. And sometimes I still think . . . I still wish . . ."

A cold wind seemed to blow over Sabha. Airt seemed to catch himself, and he turned to look straight at her. "I wish to come home."

Sabha looked up at the rising moon, just as the clouds parted and allowed the full white light to shine down upon her. "Then come home tomorrow," she said. "The house will be waiting for you in the morning. All will be just as you left it."

He stepped close, reaching out to put his arms

around her, and tried to draw her close. "Could I not come home to you tonight, right now? I have missed you so very much. It was you I thought of, even when—"

Sabha held herself very still and did not return his embrace. "In the morning, Airt. You may come as soon as the sun is fully risen, but you must bring Coiteann with you."

For a moment she saw a glimmer of hope in his eyes. "You want me to bring Coiteann to our home?"

"She must hear you say that you have chosen me, and only me, and that you want no other woman in your house. She must see for herself that you are happy to walk into our home with me and shut the door in her face. It must be done this way so that there can be no doubt of your choice. Do you agree to this?"

Sabha did not fail to see disappointment flit across his face. "Of course I do. Of course! I will be there waiting tomorrow when the sun rises—waiting for you, waiting for the moment when we can once again-"

"Just bring her with you. She must be here, too."

"I will bring her. I promise. Ah, Sabha, the sun cannot rise soon enough for me!"

"Nor for me," she answered, and quickly walked away. Airt was left standing alone among the shadows and the moonlight.

Donaill and Rioghan stood in the torchlit dark of the clearing, holding Cath's reins and watching as

Donaill's men again followed their beaten foes back down the road. "They will make certain these men do not come back and try to finish what they started," Donaill said.

"There seems little danger of that this time," Rioghan said, looking after them down the road.

Donaill grinned. "We did do a better job of giving them something to remember us by this time, didn't we? But it is more than that. Irial and Lorcan will inform the king, and the druids, and indeed the entire fortress, of what Beolagh and his followers have done."

Rioghan nodded. "The story that six armed men tried to steal from a lone woman and a handful of Sidhe will not win them much respect, I think."

"It will bring them nothing but ridicule. And they've earned it."

She looked up at him, intending to thank him for driving away the intruders yet again—but in the light of her torch, she saw that he was blinking and wiping away blood from a cut above his eye. "Here, I will see to that for you," Rioghan said. "Come with me."

"Truly, there is no need. None of these six could do any harm to me. I would be too ashamed to show my face if they could!"

"It will be a scarred face, or worse, if you do not let me clean and dress that cut. Please . . . come with me."

He said nothing, but only smiled. A pair of shadows reached out of the darkness to take Cath and lead him away, to care for the horse, and together Rioghan and Donaill walked to her home.

Chapter Fourteen

With the men gone from the clearing and the tension eased, Rioghan's dogs trotted off into the night. Some continued their patrol around Sion, while others lay down to keep watch from the shadows. They were quite unconcerned about the presence of Donaill, and a few of them even greeted him with wagging tails and friendly sniffs. Rioghan glanced at them with a slight frown and then walked into the cave ahead of Donaill, tying back the black cowhide hanging and forcing herself to think only of the business at hand.

"Truly, you need not go to any trouble for me. I can take care of this when I return home." Donaill bent low to walk inside the cave, and then stood near the entrance with the top of his head nearly touching the ceiling.

Rioghan placed her torch down in the hearth and then moved to the workbench to find her small bronze cauldron and some fresh water. "You came here, as promised, to defend me and my own, and you were injured in carrying out that defense. It is my duty to care for you as I would care for anyone else at Cahir Cullen."

"Is that all?" he asked.

She paused, but did not look at him, concentrating instead on pouring clean water from a wooden bucket into her waiting cauldron. "What else might there be?"

She knew without having to look that he was grinning at her, and that his blue eyes shone with good humor. Then suddenly his voice was serious. "Where is your gold, where are your beautiful things? The Sidhe's things? The cave is bare! Did they take them? Surely we caught them in time, before they could get inside this place!"

Rioghan laughed. "They took nothing, Donaill. The Sidhe have hidden away their ancient gold and the beautiful things. No one will ever find them now."

Donaill nodded, and sat back down again. "I am glad to know that these things were not stolen."

"They were not." Rioghan set down her bucket of water. "I thank you for coming here this night," she said, as she carried the cauldron to the fire. "Though I will tell you, I was surprised to see you. I thought you said you would be gone for some days."

Donaill sat down on the low stone wall surrounding the firepit and grinned at her, looking immensely pleased with himself. "Beolagh was surprised too, wasn't he?"

He was all but laughing now, his eyes sparkling and his teeth white in the soft light of the fire. She had expected to see the swaggering king's champion boasting of his bravery, but Donaill instead reminded her of a small boy who had just played the most marvelous prank. "I knew that something had to be done about him, and quickly. So I made up the story about my leaving for a few days, and sure enough, he took the bait like a hare whose mother never taught it any better."

Rioghan could not help smiling back at him as she walked to the wooden shelves mounted across the far side of the cave. "It was a good trick, I will admit. And an effective one. Though I am sorry you were hurt in the process."

He shrugged his broad shoulders. "I have taken far worse than this, and would have taken worse this night if need be." He looked a bit solemn now, but still his eyes shone, and he got up and walked slowly across the deep straw carpet toward Rioghan. "When we sat together at the feast, I told you that I wanted very much for you to come and live at Cahir Cullen—live among our people and truly be a part of them."

She turned to stare back at him, almost glowering, but he kept talking before she could interrupt. "Yet I know very well that ignorant men such as Beolagh have treated you very badly. I know you would never come to live at Cahir Cullen so long as anyone is there who would dare to treat you with contempt or disrespect."

"It is not just I who was so treated. I was also thinking of the Sidhe."

"The Sidhe have also been ill-used by some from Cahir Cullen."

"And my dogs."

He smiled gently. "And your dogs. I do not make a joke of it, Rioghan. I know that two of your magnificent companions met their deaths on the swords of Beolagh and his men. It should never have happened."

Rioghan took down a little bundle of dried herbs from the many on the shelves along the cave wall. "You are right. It should not."

He took a step closer, watching as she placed the leaves inside a small wooden cup and began to crush them with the rounded end of a smooth, slender bone. "There is something else that you did not hear," he said, "something that I want to tell you now."

She continued to work, making herself look only at the leaves as she ground them to powder, and after a moment he went on. "Just as you walked out through the gates that night, I spoke with one of my brothers. I told him that though I knew I had no choice but to let you go back to Sion that night, I would make certain you would return to Cahir Cullen. That is why I set this little snare for Beolagh, so that I could both put an end to his threats and show you, beyond any doubt, that I do indeed keep my promises."

Rioghan set down the bone and looked up at him. There was nothing but sincerity in his eyes. She could not help but smile at him, could not help but feel the same warmth and gentleness around her heart that his presence always seemed to bring. "None can say that you do not keep a promise, Donaill."

"Not even you?"

"Not even me." Rioghan took the cup of crushed leaves and walked back to the hearth. "Sit down, please, Donaill. It will not be long before this is ready."

She sat down on the firepit wall, facing the cave's entrance and the quiet darkness of the clearing. Donaill took his place an arm's length from her, watching intently as she lifted her small bronze cauldron and poured its steaming contents over the leaves in the wooden cup. "Cahir Cullen is fortunate to have you," he said. "Many there have had their suffering eased—and, I daresay, their lives saved—because you were willing to come to them."

Rioghan held the cup by its rim and swirled it gently, letting the hot water mix well with the crushed leaves. "It is no trouble. A healer is of little use if she has no one to heal."

"But a healer would be of even greater use if she lived among the people whom she served."

Rioghan set down the cup. "I do live among them. Making my home at Sion allows me to live among both Cahir Cullen and the Sidhe." She smiled a bit. "And I am not sure that your people would welcome my twenty-eight dogs."

"Some arrangement could be made for your dogs. Rioghan—"

"Hold still now. This is ready. Let me clean the wound." She stood over him and dipped a linen cloth into the cup, then reached out to steady Donaill's head with one hand and clean the cut above his eye with the other.

"Close your eye now . . . and I warn you, this may sting a little."

She saw him wince, but went on working diligently to clean the deep gash. "There," she said, lowering the cloth. "It is well that we got to it quickly. Such a cut can easily fester and grow poisonous . . . but this one will not, I think."

He sighed as she finally drew back from him and set down her wet cloth. "My lady, your potion burned worse than fire, but if you say it will keep me well then I am grateful to you."

"And you are welcome."

Donaill sat quietly, watching as Rioghan poured the remains of her potion on the edge of the fire and cleared away the cup and linen. She stood at the far end of the cave and waited for him to get up, expecting to hear that he must be leaving soon and returning home.

He did get up, but he walked to the back of the cave and stood beside her sleeping ledge. As she watched, he reached down to gently stroke the soft furs that covered it . . . the gray-black of the badger, the lighter gray of the wolf, the tan and white of the hare. She stiffened a bit at the sight, feeling as if she herself had been touched, and took a step toward him—but stopped when he looked up at her.

"This is a warm and comfortable home you have made here," he said. "It was your family's home, and now it is yours. I can understand why you would not want to leave it. But . . . I want to ask you again, Rioghan, to make your home at Cahir Cullen, where you can be welcomed and protected and live among those who need you."

She stood in silence again, all but mesmerized by the sight of him absently stroking the soft furs on the place where she slept. "Again, I thank you for your offer," she said faintly, still watching his hand. "But I prefer to remain here where I can serve both man and Sidhe."

He smiled at her, and to her discomfiture sat down on the edge of her sleeping ledge right on top of the furs. "Yet I have another offer to make to you. Perhaps you would come to Cahir Cullen if you knew you would not be there alone. Perhaps you would come . . . if you were coming as my wife."

Wife . . .

Rioghan blinked. She ventured one step forward, and another, until she stood at the other end of the fur-covered ledge. "Did I hear you correctly? You are asking me to make a contract of marriage with you?"

"I am." Donaill turned sideways on the ledge,

one leg propped up against it with both hands resting on his knee.

It seemed strange to Rioghan to see his large, masculine, broad-shouldered presence in the close quarters of her home, with its low ceiling and delicate furnishings. Yet it was also strange, as she looked at his face in the flickering hearthlight, how all else around him seemed to vanish into the darkness. She saw only his shadowed form, now almost near enough to touch.

"I am very different from the other women of Cahir Cullen, or of Dun Orga, or of any of the other fortresses of Eire. I have no doubt that any one of them would be happy to become your wife. Perhaps even more than one. Why would you want to marry one as strange and different as I?"

She could see him smile in the darkness. "I have told you before that I enjoyed finding how different you are . . . and I do not find you strange. Different, perhaps, but not strange. You are wise and strong and kind, and I admire those things in both women and men. And I know that under your somber black cloak you are a young and beautiful woman who must surely desire a man in her life, and in those things you are not different after all."

"If I desired a man in my life, do you not think I would have brought one into it before now?"

"Perhaps you have, Lady Rioghan. Perhaps you have." Again he simply smiled at her, waiting for her reply.

Rioghan considered. She could turn her back on him at this moment and not speak another word:

she could order him to leave her home, and she knew that he would do so. Instead, she sat down on the very edge of her sleeping ledge, folded her hands, and faced him.

"I had an offer of marriage once before, some years ago," she said. "I believe I may have told you of it."

"You did. And as I recall, he betrayed you."

"He did."

"Yet, Rioghan, I can tell you that I have no intention of betraying you. It is a source of pride to me that no woman has ever been distressed by the way I have treated her. I do not want that to change."

"Yet, Donaill, you have never been married. I might ask if you loved any of the women you have known up to now."

He smiled, though there was no mockery in it. "If I did, it was only the affection all young people feel for each other when they run carefree through the woods on a summer's night—no more and no less. Each of us felt the same, and there was no confusion or injured feelings."

"I see." Rioghan nodded. "Do you not feel such lusty affection for me?"

He sat back a little, but then grinned. "Indeed I do feel it, my lady. I simply did not want you to believe it was my only interest in you, for it is not. . . . And, I will confess, I do not know if you have any such affection for me."

She continued to gaze steadily at him. "I will not deny my attraction to you," she said. "You have been kind to me, and made me feel safe in your presence. You are a strong and handsome man. It would be strange if I felt no attraction to you at all."

He leaned toward her, looking carefully at her face. "I am glad to hear all of this. Does it mean you are thinking of accepting my offer?"

"I am afraid it does not."

He gave her a sly look, filled with amusement. "Are you saying you would prefer only the casual interaction that many men and women enjoy with each other, with no marriage and no other commitment?"

She continued to gaze at him, beginning to enjoy his banter. "I am not saying that at all. I am saying that the attraction I feel for you is simply nature, and nothing more. It has not much to do with love, or respect, or loyalty, for I do not love you. It is not enough for marriage. And though my attraction for you is strong, it is no different from the doe in her season, who stands for the largest and most aggressive stag and then walks away again without another thought for him. But I will not indulge myself like a doe."

Donaill tilted his head. "I thought I might have more to offer than merely being the largest of the stags—gratified as I am to know that that is how you see me."

She smiled. "I have said, have I not, that I do indeed feel safe in your presence? That you kept your word about protecting Sion from Beolagh and his men?"

"You have. But—"

She cut him off. "You have not told me why you believe that we should marry."

He frowned. "I believe I did tell you. I find you beautiful and learned and wise, and unlike all other women. You say that you find me handsome and honest and kind. And strong, like a stag." Donaill grinned again. "Surely you can see that neither of us is growing younger. Perhaps it is time for us to live in the warmth of another's company, instead of apart, each in our own lonely cave."

"No doubt the men at Cahir Cullen would surely think it strange that Donaill, who could have almost any woman he wanted, would choose Rioghan, who is nearly one of the Sidhe, to be his wife."

"The women there would not think it strange, for they are the ones who know you best. They are each a friend to you and would welcome you, just as they did at the feast."

"And the men?" She did not underestimate the importance of his peers.

He snorted. "The men will learn. The men know that I am the king's own champion and not to be shown disrespect. And neither is my wife."

"The king's own champion," she whispered, "who always gets what he wants."

He frowned. "Indeed I am the champion, sworn to be the sword-arm of the king. I will not hide the pride I feel at that. I gave much to reach that, the most accomplished and prized of positions, and it is a great part of who and what I am."

She nodded gravely. "I do not believe it is possible to separate the man who is Donaill from the man who is the king's champion."

He shook his head, obviously frustrated. "I do not understand. How can anyone separate themselves from their accomplishments? Could you separate Rioghan the woman from Rioghan the healer?"

"That is a good point you make. But I can tell you that my status among your people will never be the most important thing to me."

"As you believe mine is to me. But Rioghan, that status you disdain is the very thing that allowed me to save this place where you live, and defend you and the Sidhe on this night—and it will also allow me to share a very good life with you as your husband. You will never want for anything, Lady Rioghan, and neither will your children . . . *our* children."

He smiled gently at her, his hands still folded. "I have no wish to watch you marry some other. Or to watch you grow old out here alone. Please . . . will you not consider my offer?"

Slowly she shook her head. "I cannot. I could never be the wife of a king's champion, or of any other high-ranking man."

He kept very still. "And will you tell me why you cannot?"

"Because . . . because I do not believe that any man of your status could ever be content with just one woman. Indeed, you have not been thus far; it is why you are not wed. I fear that I am simply a different sort of woman for you to conquer, simply another challenge for the king's champion. I am one who may well be placed in the honored position of the king's champion's wife, but I could not ever keep him from all those other women who are always in his life . . . and who will always be there for him whenever his wife is not."

He started to speak, but she went on too quickly. "Far better, for me, to have an honest man of the land who has little more to offer me but loyalty and love. If it should come to it, I would rather stay alone here, and live in peace, than make a home with the finest of men and live each day in torment and uncertainty."

"Never would I allow you live in torment, Lady Rioghan," Donaill vowed quietly.

She looked away. "That is true . . . for *I* would never allow it, either."

"If it is loyalty and love that you value most, I assure you, you would have all you could wish for of both."

She raised an eyebrow. "You do offer me respect, Donaill, but I dare not count on loyalty, and I have heard nothing at all of love from you."

He smiled, trying to keep his words light. "Yet perhaps there *is* love in my heart for you, and I simply wish to keep it safely there until I know whether you might return it. And . . . perhaps you do the same."

He got to his feet and closed the distance between them, then stood towering over her. Before she could react, he took both of her small hands between his own and held them gently, warmly. "Ah, beautiful doe," he said softly, "will you at least agree to let the stag pay you court? To walk with you, and protect your flank, and shield you with his size and his weight and the sharp horns that are his weapons . . . and stroke your sides with the softness of his muzzle until you no longer wish him to leave?"

She closed her eyes as his fingers moved slowly down her cheek; then she reached up and caught them. "I cannot ever agree to a marriage with you," she whispered.

His face was very close to hers. "But to a courtship?"

With each breath her chin rose a little, until her mouth was nearly touching his. Her desire was so great. "A courtship . . . I will accept," she whispered at last, against all her best judgment. And then the softness of his mouth reached hers at last.

For many heartbeats, Rioghan was conscious only of his lips, and his warm breath, and the size and heat of his body shielding her from all else in the world. She began to reach up to him, to place her hands on those strong, wide shoulders and cling to them and draw him closer, closer . . . but he caught her wrists in a gentle hold and pressed them together in front of her.

"A courtship it will be, then, Lady Rioghan," he said; and he drew back from her.

She blinked as light from the hearth flickered over her again, as the cold, damp air of the cave was all that remained to surround her.

"And I will do all I can to prove I am not a man who will betray you," he added.

"I do not know how anyone could ever prove such a thing," she whispered.

He smiled and walked toward the entrance of the cave. "I do not know either," he said. "But I will do my best to find a way."

Then Donaill stepped outside into the darkness. A moment later, Rioghan heard the sound of hoof-beats galloping away.

Chapter Fifteen

In the gray morning light, Sabha stood behind one of the small, high windows of her house and watched her husband walk across the grass toward her door. He moved rather slowly, for he had a heavy stack of tunics and cloaks thrown over his shoulder. She recognized them as being most of the clothes he owned, for he had taken them to the house where Coiteann lived with six other unattached women and servants.

Before he could touch the door, Sabha opened it. "Good morning to you, Airt," she said. "You have chosen to return to our home?"

"I have," he said, looking up at her and smiling. He shifted the load of clothing on his back. "May I come inside? I am so anxious to—"

"Where is Coiteann?"

He paused, beginning to sweat under the load he was carrying. "She is still at her home and has started her dye work already. I have left her, Sabha. I have no wish to see her again. I have come home to you."

A few of the other people of Cahir Cullen, catching on to what was happening, had stopped to watch. Sabha glanced at them and then looked back at Airt. "Leave your things in front of the door. Go and get Coiteann and bring her here. And bring anyone else who wishes to hear what you have to say to me."

Airt stood and stared at her. The clothes seemed to grow heavier by the moment, but he made no move to drop them. "You want me to bring Coiteann here? And . . . others?"

"There must be no question of what your choice has been. It must be perfectly clear to all, especially to Coiteann. Bring her here, and say your piece, and then you may return to your home."

At last he set down his clothes, letting them fall to the grass near the door. "I will be back very soon," he said, turning to go.

"Very soon," she called after him, knowing that all of the spectators would hear.

It was not long before Sabha again opened the front door of her house. This time there was a fair crowd of people standing in little groups between her dwelling and the others. Shouldering his way through the gathering to stand in the grass before her was Airt, and hurrying after him was an increasingly frantic Coiteann.

The thin blond woman halted wide-eyed in the middle of the yard, her long pale hair flying as she looked wildly from the crowd to the stack of Airt's clothes to Sabha standing coolly in the doorway. "Airt!" she demanded, with a look of real fear and confusion in her pale blue eyes. "Airt, what is this about?"

He tried to speak, and tried to look at Coiteann, but instead simply looked down at the cold, damp ground.

In that instant Coiteann turned and tried to flee. "Coiteann!" Sabha cried. The woman stopped as if seized. "This is something you must hear. Look at Airt. He will tell you what he has chosen to do."

Slowly, her hair falling down over her eyes, Coiteann looked up at Airt. Again he searched for words, glancing at the crowd and finally meeting his blond lover's shocked gaze. He took a deep breath but returned his vision firmly to the ground.

"I have . . ." he whispered. "I have decided to . . . to . . ."

"Please speak louder," Sabha said, as the crowd watched and Coiteann began to shake. "We cannot hear you."

He sucked in his breath and looked up at Sabha. "I have decided to return home to you, my wife," he said.

Sabha nodded slowly and thoughtfully. "And you do this by your own choice?"

"I do," he answered, looking neither right nor left.

"And you wish to have no other woman but me? You wish to take no other wife but me?"

"I wish to have none but you. I want to come home to you, Sabha."

"What of this other woman you have loved? What of Coiteann?"

"I have no wish to see her ever again. I love only you, Sabha, and I want to come home."

Taking her time, Sabha looked from face to staring face in the gathered crowd of Cahir Cullen's inhabitants, and then at Coiteann's pale skin and open mouth as the woman struggled to breathe. "You did not know of this, Coiteann?"

"He has said nothing!" she managed to say in a gasp. "He said he would make me his wife! His second wife! He said he could persuade you to accept me!"

"Then he has lied to you as well as to me," said Sabha. "Or perhaps I should correct myself. Airt says it is not a lie if he simply does not tell you about a thing. So I suppose you will be glad to know he did not lie."

Sabha turned her gaze on Airt. "And so, my husband, you are ready now to walk away from her forever and stay only with me?"

He looked steadily at her, ignoring the staring crowd, ignoring Coiteann's quiet sobbing. "I am ready to do that, my wife."

"I have waited long to hear you say these words.

But I will tell you now, Airt, that there was no need for you to say them."

His face grew even more serious. Coiteann's sob caught in her throat. "What do you mean?" he asked in genuine confusion.

Still facing them, Sabha pushed the door open behind her and stepped aside. Airt's eyes widened at the sight. Just inside the house were neatly stacked bundles of clothes, furs, cauldrons, tools, wineskins, and small wooden boxes. "Everything I brought with me to the marriage sits here now at the door. My father will be here later today, with a wagon and a riding pony, to take me and all of my possessions back to my home at Dun Orga. Never again will I live in Cahir Cullen as your wife."

Airt swallowed. "You are . . . leaving?"

"I am."

"Do you . . . mean for me to go with you?"

She smiled a little. "I do not mean for you to go anywhere with me. You made it clear that you would never give up the hope of having both me and Coiteann in whatever way you could.

"I never agreed to having another wife in our house. You knew my feelings on this long before we were married. But I know that even now, you are still determined to find a way to have your second woman. I can see it in your eyes and hear it in your voice. You will never cease from your quest to gather as many women around yourself as you possibly can, and if that causes me pain, well, that is insignificant, for you are certain I will adjust if I am forced to.

"Never would I have thought you capable of such cruelty towards me. But that is what happens when men are guided only by their sex and not their hearts."

Then the crowd gasped. Coiteann clutched at Airt and huddled close to him, for Sabha had turned so that her left side faced them. She looked straight ahead and then slowly raised her left arm straight out from her shoulder, so that her finger was aimed directly at the two of them.

All they could see of her was one foot, one arm, and one eye. The crowd murmured among themselves and fell back a step or two, for Sabha stood in the position of cursing.

No longer was this just an entertaining squabble on a cold winter morning.

"I am not your wife, Airt of Cahir Cullen," Sabha began, still looking straight ahead. "You kept the truth of your feelings from me. You took another woman when you promised you would not. You brought her into my bed and home without my knowledge or consent. For that alone I could divorce you.

"I have decided that I do not want a man who could do such a thing to me. Coiteann, if you want him, you may have him. But you will live with knowing that he meant to set you aside and return to me—at least for a while. I have no other hold on him. There are no children. He came back for me alone, but he will not have me. Enjoy your life together. I will someday make a new life with one who is not faithless. Each of you can make your future with one who is. That is the curse I place upon you both."

Slowly Sabha lowered her arm, and then turned to her right until she faced them once more. Coiteann cried out in anger and frustration, while Airt could only stand red-faced and clench his fists, staring at the ground. The crowd around them first murmured to one another, and then began to chuckle, and finally laughed and laughed out loud at the perfect vengeance Airt's young wife had thrown upon his head.

Rioghan sat beside her hearth in the predawn darkness, eating a few pieces of barley flatbread and butter and drinking a hot cup of yellow-flower tea with a little honey. Cogar and Scath lay in the warm straw at her feet, while the other dogs walked their never-ending rounds of the clearing as they watched for any and all intruders.

The sky was just beginning to turn gray when the dogs in the clearing stood very still, raised their heads, and raced off toward the road.

Scath and Cogar stayed inside the cave, watching with hackles raised but making no move to leave. The rest of the pack remained silent. Rioghan set down her cup and got to her feet.

The dogs were behaving the way they did whenever servants from Cahir Cullen traveled up the road to fetch her. She wrapped her black cloak closely around around her and fastened it with her bronze-and-jet pin. Picking up her black leather bag filled with medicines and clean wraps and dried herbs, she walked out into the cold, damp dawn to see who had need of her now.

The mist was heavy this morning. It hid the road from her; all she could see was dogs moving in and out of the grayness, which parted like a veil as she walked through it. Then suddenly she was at the edge of the road and could see two figures standing on it, trying to stay calm while surrounded by silent, menacing dogs.

She saw one man—young and dark-haired—and a young blond woman whose hands were stained from dye. Rioghan stopped short as she recognized Airt and Coiteann.

What would bring them here? Where was . . . *Sabha. Oh, Sabha.*

Rioghan remembered what she and Sabha had spoken of so that an injured wife might have justice, and knew what Sabha must have done.

"*Madra,*" she said quietly. Her dogs trotted back past her toward the clearing and disappeared into the mist behind her. She stood and waited alone at the edge of the road, allowing her visitors to approach and speak first.

"Lady Rioghan," said Airt, taking a step toward her. "This is Coiteann, my—"

"I know you both," Rioghan said. "Is there someone at Cahir Cullen who has need of me?"

"There is not," Airt said, "but Coiteann asked to come here and speak to you, for she believes you might be of help to her."

Rioghan's eyes flicked to the small blond woman. Looking at that pale and slender face, she saw cold blue eyes trying to appear warm and friendly. Eyes filled with pain, fear, and anger.

Rioghan knew what must have happened. Sabha had indeed gotten her justice and must have gone back to her own family at Dun Orga. This, the aftermath, remained to be dealt with, and the task of dealing with it was hers.

"Come with me," she said, and the three of them walked across the clearing to Sion.

With her two dogs keeping a wary eye on the strangers, Rioghan invited Airt and Coiteann into her home and did her best to make them comfortable. When they were seated on black cowhides tossed onto the straw, she herself sat down on the low stone wall of the hearth and folded her hands. "Why have you come here?" she asked, looking at Coiteann.

The other woman glanced at Airt, and for a moment Rioghan saw again a sharp, cold look in her eyes. Then she looked at Rioghan and tried to smile.

"Perhaps you have not yet heard," Coiteann began, "but Sabha has left her husband and gone back to her people at Dun Orga."

Rioghan nodded. "I supposed as much, when I saw you on the road." She turned to Airt. "You understand what she has done?"

His mouth tightened and his face flushed red. "She was very cruel to me. She allowed me to think that we would once again live together as man and wife, but when I returned—"

"She told you she had already decided to leave you."

Both of them stared at her. "Then you did know," whispered Coiteann. "Did you put her up to it?"

Rioghan matched her gaze. "I spoke with her of what she might do, after she learned that her husband had been with you. But the choice, and the doing, was hers and hers alone."

Coiteann nodded, her face grim, and finally looked away.

"I would ask you again," Rioghan said, "why have you come here?"

Coiteann drew a deep breath, and a look of sadness crossed her face. "I have come—or rather, we have come—to ask you for your help."

Rioghan said nothing, but merely waited for Coiteann to go on, studying her face all the while.

"I know what Sabha said. I was there, for she insisted that I be there to hear it all."

"Then you heard Airt say that he had chosen Sabha over you?"

Coiteann swallowed and raised her chin. "I did."

Rioghan was confused. "Why would you wish to stay with a man who would publicly choose another over you?"

"Because . . . because I believe that Airt and Sabha were never really suited to each other. He remained with her out of duty and because he felt sorry for her, while she stayed with him because of his position as one of King Bran's warriors." Her eyes narrowed again. "And, of course, she stayed with him to torment him. To do the sort of thing she did this morning."

"I see," Rioghan whispered. "You believe he truly has feelings of love for you."

Coiteann glanced at Airt, and he gave her a tight smile. "I do believe that," she said, and turned back to Rioghan. "I am not proud of the things I have done in the past. I have long feared that one day I may find myself alone, with no husband and no children. If Airt is willing, and he says he is, then I want nothing more than to try to make a life with him."

"Most women want a husband and children. But . . . why do you need my help to find yours?"

Coiteann hesitated, and looked again at Airt. Rioghan caught his eye before he could speak. "Perhaps you would like to walk up to the top of Sion," she said to him. "It is quite beautiful up there, watching the morning mist as it burns away and unveils the countryside."

He glanced at Coiteann and then back to Rioghan. "Go, Airt," Rioghan said gently. "The dogs will not trouble you. We will simply stay here and talk for a time."

He nodded at the two of them, then hurried outside and disappeared into the fog.

Chapter Sixteen

When he had gone, Rioghan faced Coiteann again. "Tell me. What do you want me to do for you?"

Coiteann stood up and paced across the straw, looking up at the many bundles of dried herbs and plants and flowers that hung on the cave walls and lined the wooden shelves. "I must be sure it will work this time," she said. "I cannot go through a humiliation like this morning's again. Not ever again."

She shut her eyes and crossed her arms tightly over her chest. "And neither can Airt. Already his honor among the king's warriors is gone. Yesterday they treated him worse than the youngest and newest of them, treated him worse than a servant. And there is no doubt that he will be the butt of every satire told at every feast and gathering for countless years to come.

"The only way that I can see–the only thing that could help us both—is for us to make a respected marriage to each other. Then we might have a chance at being accepted among the other families of Cahir Cullen. But that can happen only if the marriage lasts. If it is not strained. If there are children."

"In short," Rioghan said, "it can happen only if the two of you remain faithful to each other."

Coiteann nodded. "You understand."

"I do. But no one can ever guarantee such a thing. Many have tried, but such a thing cannot ever be promised for certain."

"Yet you could help. There are things that can be done—charms of binding. . . ." The woman threw up her dye-stained hands and then ran them through her long blond hair, clutching the sides of her head. "You must help me, Rioghan! I cannot fail this time. It is as much for Airt—whose wife has abandoned him and left him with nothing, as you well know—as it is for myself."

Rioghan stood up, and now it was her turn to pace across the cave. Scath followed her as she went and stood beneath the bundles of herbs on the far wall. "Many folk have managed to make good marriages, and they have not needed the help of one such as I. Do you hope to make the work simpler for yourself by relying on magic instead of love and care?"

"I do not," Coiteann said. "You did not hear all

that Sabha said. She placed us both under a curse."

Rioghan slowly turned. "A curse."

Again the anger was clear in Coiteann's eyes. "She cursed us both to live with faithless partners—with each other. Surely you knew that she would do this."

"I knew the strength of her anger. I knew the depth of her pain."

"She has left us without the hope of a real life together! She has gone now; she does not want Airt any longer. I am willing to build a life with him, and he would do the same with me. Can you let us walk away from here still carrying the weight of a scornful wife's curse?"

Rioghan stood in silence for a time; then she sighed. "It is my wish to help all who ask it of me . . . all those in need, all those who suffer. That is what I did for Sabha. Now that that task is completed, I can do no less for you." She looked up into Coiteann's angry blue eyes. "Tell me. What exactly do you want from me?"

"I want you to make for me a charm of binding," the blond girl said quickly, walking over to stand nearer Rioghan. "One which will keep my love only for the man who places it around my neck—and that man will be Airt. That will help us both to overcome Sabha's curse."

Rioghan's eyes narrowed. "You yourself have some knowledge of magic. Why not make your own charm?"

"You are far more powerful than I. Your knowledge is far greater. And it does not seem to me that

I could break a curse that I myself carry." Her expression softened. "Please help me, Lady Rioghan. Help both of us. I ask for Airt's sake as much as for my own."

Rioghan studied her. A charm of binding, was it? Her first thought was that there was nothing she would like more than to bind a woman like Coiteann to Airt.

"I do not like selfishness," Rioghan said after a moment, pacing slowly across the straw, "especially when it comes at the clear expense of others. You have behaved as a selfish young female who saw nothing wrong in going from man to man to man and taking from each whatever you could persuade him to give you. It did not matter that his wife might be expecting to have all of her husband's heart, and not have him secretly sharing bits and pieces of it with whatever pretty face and attractive backside might happen to come along.

"You saw no harm in poisoning the marriage of another with your secret attentions and flatteries. It caused you no harm, so you believed it must not have harmed anyone else . . . and even if it did cause harm it was simply none of your concern. Is this not true, Coiteann?"

Rioghan watched the blonde from across the cave, waiting for the outburst sure to follow such criticism. But the woman only looked down at the straw and fidgeted with the ends of her plain leather belt. "It is true," she whispered. "I have learned, now, what can happen. And I do not ever want it to happen again."

"Yet you have lived this way since you were barely out of your childhood. Why should you suddenly change your ways now?"

"Rioghan," the woman said, still looking down, "you did not see the shame of it yesterday. You did not see Sabha's face as she cursed us, nor hear the crowd's laughter when they realized what she had done. I cannot ever let that happen again."

Slowly Rioghan nodded. "It seems to me that nothing but good can come from keeping the two of you together. If it means you and Airt can make a life together—and stay together—then I will help you."

Coiteann closed her eyes and breathed a great sigh of relief. "I thank you. We both thank you."

Rioghan moved to the far end of the cave, where she kept wooden boxes and leather bags filled with many fine and rare things, and began to search through them to see what might suggest itself for this task.

She began with a length of slender iron chain, but knew that this charm would require far more. Binding. That was the thing needed here. The binding and confining of the wearer of the charm, holding and preventing her from reaching out to any other man, and keeping her love only for one.

Binding required weight and power and impenetrability. It would require things of the earth, the heaviest and strongest of the four natural elements. Water and air had force, but could contain nothing on their own. Fire would only destroy anything it tried to hold. This task needed the power of the earth.

She found a box of small stones. Some were shining crystals of startling beauty, clear and glittering even in the low light of the cave. Some were duller and heavier, some were rounded and others flat on one side . . . but all still seemed too light, too ordinary.

Beneath it was another box, this one containing odd, small shapes of various metals. There were little lumps of shining gold and larger pieces of green-tinged copper and rusty-black iron.

Rioghan took out one of the pieces of iron, but quickly put it back. She had never much liked iron; it always felt cold and dead and surprisingly brittle, even for all its weight and supposed strength. And if left alone for only a season or two, it would turn to rust and dissolve into nothing.

What was this?

In with the pieces of gold and copper and iron was a large lump of smooth metal with a silvery black finish. Rioghan lifted it out and instantly thought back to the day the Sidhe had brought it to her, as they often brought odd or interesting things they came across that they had no immediate use for. It seemed that she might very well have a use for this now.

It was the metal called *luaidhe*, heavier than any other, yet soft enough to be easily pressed into whatever shape might be desired. It was perfect.

"Give me three long strands of your hair," Rioghan said. Coiteann walked close, ran her fingers through her blond mane, and handed over the strands of hair. Rioghan lifted out the *luaidhe* piece and carried it, along with the iron chain and the strands of Coiteann's hair, to the entrance of the cave. Brushing aside a little of the straw on the floor, she took one of the loose, flat stones from the hearth, set it on the bare earth of the cave floor, and placed the heavy piece of metal on the stone.

Now the soft, silvery black rock was in direct contact with the earth. Pressing down on it with another hearthstone, Rioghan began to whisper, under her breath, words in the oldest of languages . . . words that only the Sidhe, and a few others, still knew.

Soon the piece was smoothed and flattened into shape. It was of a size to cover the palm of her hand, and its silvery black finish was attractive; yet it was heavier than any stone or any piece of metal she had held.

Rioghan wrapped the strands of Coiteann's blond hair around the flat, heavy piece, and then wound the slim iron chain over and around it all. As she did the winding she continued to whisper softly, eyes half-closed, working by feel, her hands slowly moving lower and lower to the earth as she did, as though the *luaidhe* piece were becoming too heavy to hold.

At last, using both hands, she raised it up and looked at it. The soft, glowing, heavy lump of metal, dug from the heart of the earth and shaped to Rioghan's will, was now itself bound up with Coiteann's hair and iron chain. Slowly she got to her feet, feeling weighed down simply by holding the thing in her hands.

She held it out to Coiteann, who took it without hesitation and then held it up, eyeing it closely.

"Give it to Airt," Rioghan said. "Tell him to hold it close between his hands, place a kiss upon its surface, and then place it around your neck so that it rests over your heart. Once he does this, he should then give you a kiss with all the sincerity he possesses—and you must do the same for him. Once you have both done this, you will be bound to him for as long as you live."

"Thank you, thank you," Coiteann said softly, tucking the amulet and chain into a bag she carried at her belt. "You have done more for me this day than you know."

"Go in peace, Coiteann," Rioghan said, stepping back to let her pass. The woman hurried outside and ran with light footsteps to search for Airt.

The afternoon was cold and gray and still. Donaill, restless with the short days of winter, walked with his brothers, Irial and Lorcan, across the quiet grounds of the fortress toward the gates. All around them, gray-white smoke from the hearth fires of the houses rose up to join the cold sky, as did the white clouds of their breath on this unusually cold day.

"Donaill," called a young feminine voice from behind them. "Donaill!"

The three men turned to see Coiteann hurrying over to them. "Well, now," said Irial, leaning over to Donaill. "You are the one in her favor today?"

"I suppose it is time for her to move on to a new man," added Lorcan. "After what happened this morning with Airt."

Donaill laughed. "I can tell you only one thing about Coiteann's next conquest: it will not be me. I have decided to look elsewhere."

"Oh, just as we thought! Well, that lady is a strange one, but I cannot say she was not a pretty sight at the feast. Maybe you—"

"Donaill, I am so glad I caught you before you left!" said Coiteann, running breathlessly up to him. She seemed not to notice that two other men stood beside him.

"We are just going out for a bit of hunting before dark," Donaill answered patiently, with a polite smile. "What can we do for you?"

She walked up close in front of him and smiled brightly, as if she had never been so pleased to see any man. "I have something to ask only of you, not of your brothers," she said softly, and reached out to smooth and straighten the edge of his heavy red cloak where it lay over his chest.

Donaill stood motionless. At last she withdrew her hands, and spoke again. "I do not need to tell you that I have not held a place of high honor among the people of Cahir Cullen," she began. "Everyone knows what happened yesterday between Airt and Sabha and myself. I can never let such a thing happen again." She sighed. "Airt and I hope to make a life together. I wish to be respected as his wife, not laughed at as a . . . a . . ."

She looked up Donaill, and tried to smile. "I wish

to make peace with all those whom I might have offended. I wish to start with you."

"With me?" He shrugged, and laughed a little. "Why with me? You have not offended me, Coiteann."

She hung her head again. "I believe I have offended everyone here, at one time or another. And I wish to start with you because you are the highest-ranking man here, save the king, and I fear to approach him."

Donaill smiled. "Again, I will ask you: what can I do for you?"

Her face lit up. "Oh . . . you can let me perform some humble service for you. Let me change the straw on the floor of your house. Let me sweep the ashes from your hearth. This will let you see that my intentions are real, and are not just words. You will see that I mean to follow them up with actions."

Donaill glanced at Irial and Lorcan. "I would have to ask my brothers. The three of us share the house."

"Oh, but that is good; that is even better! I could do this for all three of you while you are out hunting. When you return, you will find that all is done, and maybe a little extra, too."

His brothers shrugged. "This is for you to decide, Donaill," Lorcan said. "You are the one who was asked."

Donaill could only laugh. "Coiteann, if this will help you, then go ahead and sweep my hearth if you wish," he said. "We will be away until dark. If changing the straw on the floor of my house will help you to be a respected wife, then I am pleased to let you do it."

"Oh, thank you, thank you," she said fervently, looking straight into his eyes. For a moment Donaill looked back at her, and saw in her eyes a kind of coldness and determination that was somehow disquieting.

But he assumed it was merely the determination of a long-scorned woman who had finally decided to raise her station in life. "You are welcome," he said. "We will be back at dark."

He and his brothers turned and continued on their way to the gate, leaving behind a smiling Coiteann.

Chapter Seventeen

As night fell, Donaill and his two siblings walked slowly back across the grounds of Cahir Cullen. All of them were wet and muddy from the afternoon's hunt through the cold rainy woods, but quite satisfied with their catch of five hares. The beasts dangled from a leather cord thrown over Irial's shoulder.

They left four of the hares with the servants, to be prepared for the king and his family, and took the last one back to their house. They pushed the door open, and the three of them paused. "Well, Donaill," Irial said, "perhaps you should let Coiteann offend you more often."

They walked inside. A fire glowed in the newly swept hearth. A single beeswax candle had been lit in a stone dish over each sleeping ledge. The floor was thick with fresh, clean straw. And lined up on the hearthstones were three large wooden plates filled with hot wheaten flatbread with butter, chunks of boiled beef with salt, and watercress in hot meat drippings. Three cups of heated honey wine, each with a little wisp of steam rising up into the cold air, rested beside each plate.

"Well, I'm not going to complain about it," said Lorcan. "I think our brother was most kind to allow Coiteann to do this for us."

"I was just trying to help the lady by giving her what she asked for," said Donaill. "Maybe she is not as shallow as we thought."

"Either way, the food looks good," said Lorcan, and all of them laughed and set down their weapons. They picked up their plates and cups and sat down together in the fresh straw to eat the hot food and drink down the delicious steaming honey wine.

At last, when he could eat no more, Donaill set aside his plate and stood up. Taking the still-warm cup of wine, now half full, he moved to his sleeping ledge. There he found that the furs had all been smartly shaken out and neatly placed, and the straw-stuffed leather cushions beaten into fresh shapes and invitingly arranged on the furs. And there was one more thing laid out on the ledge—a new linen tunic, dyed to a deep shade of black.

He lifted it up and looked at it by the candlelight. The dye work was quite good and even, he noted, but the thread itself had been spun a little coarsely. The weave was loose here and there, the stitching rather uneven.

He guessed that Coiteann must have made the tunic herself. She was the one whose task it was to make the dyes and add the color to newly spun wool and linen yarn before it was woven into cloth, so perhaps she was a bit awkward with the unaccustomed weaving and sewing. She had certainly gone to a lot of trouble just to impress him, he thought with a little grin. Had she even woven it in one day?

Well, a little unevenness did not trouble him. He was glad enough to strip off his wet and dirty hunting tunic and wet leather breeches and boots, and put on the fresh, dry tunic—though he reminded himself that he must not wear this tunic when next he saw Rioghan. It might upset her to know that he had done a kindness for Coiteann, that he had allowed her into his house and accepted a gift from her. Women often found it difficult to understand such things and thought that any little gesture meant far more than it actually did. Things were going very well between him and Rioghan, and he wanted to make sure they stayed that way.

Donaill drank down the rest of the wine and then lay back on the cushions with a sigh, pulling the fur covers up over his shoulders. It had been a long day. The warmth and the food and hot honey wine worked together to bring fatigue rolling over him. The last thing he remembered was the empty cup of wine falling from his hand to the clean straw below.

* * *

The moon was nearly full this winter night, but fortunately for Coiteann its light was hidden by low, thick clouds. No one noticed her in the darkness as she walked across the yard and slipped into Donaill's house, carrying a pair of leather bags—one large and one small.

The beeswax candles had long since burned out. The hearthfire burned low. And on the sleeping ledges, three men snored deeply, each one with an empty wine cup lying below him in the straw where he had dropped it.

She smiled in the darkness. The wine she had prepared especially for them had done its work . . . and now she would finish hers.

Near the fallen cup, also carelessly dropped to the straw, were Donaill's clothes—and his sword belt. Tracing along the length of the belt, she came to his jet-handled dagger and pulled it out of its thick leather sheath.

She stood over him with the dagger in her hand. "Now you will become mine, and not hers. Never hers," Coiteann whispered, and moved toward the sleeping man in the darkness.

At dawn the next morning, two servants trudged across the cold, misty grounds of Cahir Cullen and called up to the watchman over the gate, "Let us pass!"

Slowly one of the tall, heavy gates moved open enough to let the two men slip out. "What is your task?" asked the watchman, closing the gate again behind them.

"We've been sent to bring Rioghan," the first servant said.

"One of the king's men requires her attention," said the second.

"What's wrong with him? Which one is it?"

The first one shrugged. "We were not told," he said. "We know only that we are to bring her, because she will want to see what has happened to this man—even though there is nothing she can do to help him."

Coiteann watched the servants go out through the gate, and smiled to herself. She looked forward with vast enjoyment to Rioghan's arrival. There was quite a surprise waiting for her at Cahir Cullen this day.

Rioghan ran down the tangled path to Cahir Cullen faster than she ever had before. Her black cloak flew out behind her, the leather bag bounced on her shoulder, and her two dogs trotted steadily by her side. The servants had long since been left behind to travel along the road instead of on the difficult forest path.

You will want to see what has happened to this man . . . though there is nothing you can do to help him.

They would not tell her who it was. They said they did not know. And perhaps they didn't. At any rate, it did not matter now. Rioghan knew it could be only one man.

What did they mean, there was nothing she could do to help him?

The path flew by beneath her feet. At last she pushed her way through the final barrier of brush and saw the gates of Cahir Cullen.

Gasping for breath, her heart pounding from more than just the run, Rioghan shifted her leather bag from her shoulder to underneath her arm and walked through the open gates. And there before her, walking calmly and looking as smug as Rioghan had ever seen a woman look, was Coiteann.

"Who has sent for me?" Rioghan whispered, as her dogs stood silent and glaring by her side.

"Why, I sent for you," Coiteann answered. Her voice was sweet as honey, but Rioghan saw that now she made no effort to hide the coldness in her eyes. "There is one here whom you will wish to see. Come with me." She started to take Rioghan by the arm, but when the dogs growled and raised their hackles she let go. "Come with me," she said again, beckoning to Rioghan and still smiling, and Rioghan followed her toward the houses.

Servants walked the grounds, going about their usual tasks in the faint late-morning warmth. It seemed to be a day like any other at the fortress. But Rioghan's anxiety only increased with every step she took, as she realized where Coiteann was leading her.

"Why do you walk to Donaill's house?" Rioghan asked, her heart still hammering. "Who is there who needs my help?"

"I told you," Coiteann answered, walking along as lightly as if she were on her way to the king's own feast, "there is no one here who needs your help. Merely one for you to see." She pushed open the door of Donaill's house. "And here he is."

Slowly, pushing her cloak back from her head and brushing her damp hair away from her face, Rioghan stepped inside the house. A quick glance around the shadowed room showed her that the king's champion's brothers still slept—though Donaill sat up on the furs on the edge of the sleeping ledge, his head down, his feet in the clean new straw.

"Here is your morning meal, just as I promised," Coiteann said with a bright smile, reaching for the plate of bread and honey and boiled apples on the stones of the hearth. "Are you feeling well this morning, my lord Donaill?"

He looked at Coiteann for a long time, and then slowly smiled at her. "I seem to still be feeling the effects of your very good wine," he said, rubbing his head. "But I can say that it is very good to see you, Coiteann."

He did not notice Rioghan at all. She could only stand and stare at the two, barely able to breathe, stand just a few steps away and be no closer to Donaill than if she were still at Sion.

"Oh, it's just the food I have brought that you are glad to see," Coiteann protested with a little laugh, giving his thigh a pat even as she watched him carefully.

"But it is true. I am glad to see *you*." Donaill still stared at the other woman, and even through her anguish Rioghan saw that he kept himself always facing Coiteann. He was even beginning to lean toward her. "It is always good to see you."

Coiteann smiled in great satisfaction. "Here," she said, handing him the wooden plate. "Take this, and while you eat I will ease the tension in your shoulders. It will take away any pain from your head that the wine may have left, I promise you. Turn around now—that's it, turn around—"

Slowly, reluctantly, he shifted around on the ledge until he faced away from her, and took the plate she held out to him. Coiteann reached up for his shoulders, running her hands up his back and caressing him as she did so.

"There," she said, patting his shoulders and then beginning to knead them with her hands. "That's better, isn't it?"

"It is." He set the plate aside and turned to face her again, staring and silent, as if he had something to say to her but could not recall what it was.

Rioghan looked away—and got another shock. Piled up in the straw near the far end of Donaill's sleeping ledge were a stack of gowns and cloaks and household things: Coiteann's things. Coiteann's clothes.

She was moving in. Moving in with Donaill, to live with him in his house.

There was a knock at the door. With a haughty look at Rioghan, Coiteann walked across the room to answer it, as though she were already the lady of the house. And there in the doorway, with cold gray light behind him, was Airt.

For a moment he stood very still, blinking, as

though he could not believe what he was seeing. "Coiteann!" he said at last. "I thought . . . I thought you must have left our home early to begin your work! Why are you here?"

"I am where I wish to be," she said, her voice cool and superior. "Come inside. We will explain it to you."

Slowly, with confusion clear in his wide eyes, Airt walked inside and saw Rioghan there. *We wear the same face this day, you and I,* she thought, looking up at him. *Both of us wear our shock and pain and confusion for all to see . . . and we both know that it will only get worse.*

Over on the sleeping ledges, Irial and Lorcan were finally beginning to stir. Rioghan glanced again at the cups that lay in the straw beside each man's sleeping ledge. It did not seem normal that they should continue to snore past dawn when there were visitors coming and going in their house. There had been no late-night feast the evening before to keep them up late . . . but perhaps there had been specially prepared wine for these three men.

Donaill sat on the edge of his bed, again holding his head. His two brothers slowly sat up on their own beds and did the same. Airt and Rioghan stood beside the stone wall of the hearth, unable to do more than simply watch the bizarre scene unfold before them.

Coiteann returned to the sleeping ledge to sit close beside Donaill on the furs, sliding her arm through his as though they had always been together. It was clear that she loved being the center of attention, loved having all eyes on her . . . especially the eyes of Rioghan and Airt.

"Tell them, Donaill," Coiteann prompted. "Tell Rioghan and Airt and your brothers what we have decided."

Again, he looked at the smiling blond woman for a long time. "Coiteann and I are to be married," he said at last, and smiled back at her.

Rioghan felt both hot and cold all at once, felt as though the pit of her stomach were dropping into the earth. She could barely get her breath. This was not real. This could not be happening. Just two days before, he had come to her and promised her a courtship . . . and she had accepted.

Was she caught up in some terrible dream from which she could not awaken? If she was, then Airt was trapped there with her, for he clearly felt the same horror and disbelief at Donaill's words that she did.

Had it been only yesterday that he and Coiteann had come to Sion, where Coiteann had hung her head and vowed that she wished to become the respected wife of Airt, where she had begged for a charm of binding to keep her forever bound to him?

There was no sign of the amulet now. Not on Coiteann, not on—

Another blow seemed to hit Rioghan and take the breath from her. Had Coiteann tried to use the charm of binding on Donaill? Rioghan did not see it on him, but even if Coiteann had tried such a thing it would not have been strong enough to force him into forgetting all else but her. It could not have done this! And neither could the poorly made but newly dyed black tunic that Donaill wore. It seemed just like the one Airt had worn, which had been just enough to nudge him into Coiteann's waiting arms . . . a place where Airt had already been inclined to go.

But what had happened here?

Lorcan stood up and walked across the room, wrapping a cloak around himself. He seemed shocked, too. "Donaill," he said, trying to get his brother's attention. "I thought you said yesterday that you were looking to the Lady Rioghan."

Donaill gazed off into the distance for a time, then shook his head. "I may have said that once, but it was very long ago."

"It was yesterday," Lorcan said.

Donaill tilted his head and blinked, then gazed at his brother. "I may well be hungover this morning, but I can only tell you that I am driven to Coiteann as I have never been driven to any other woman."

Driven . . .

No one in the room could fail to see the smirk of victory on Coiteann's face. Rioghan began to feel cold again as she wondered just what this woman could have done to so thoroughly control a powerful man like Donaill, to play with his will the way a child played with a toy.

Irial, too, came to stand beside the hearth and look closely at his brother. "If no one else will say it, I will. Coiteann has been through half the men of this fortress, and now, it seems, she has started on the other half. She is not—"

Donaill leaped to his feet, knocking the plate of food on his bed to the straw. "You will not speak of her in such a way! Those tales are only malicious gossip spread by a few jealous women. Coiteann has told me so herself!"

"Donaill—"

"It is true that she was greatly popular among the men here, and how could it be otherwise? She is wise. She is lovely. She is skilled. She is wonderful. And I will defend her with all the power of the king's own champion against any who would dare to speak ill of her!"

"You intend to marry her?" Airt whispered.

"I do! And I will consider myself a fortunate man to have been the one to win her!"

Silence fell on the gathering, as cold and ominous as a winter wind. "Then I will leave you to her," said Airt, and he turned and left the house without a single glance back.

Irial and Lorcan stood across from their brother and shook their heads. "I think you made the better choice yesterday," said Lorcan.

"But if this is your wish, then I wish you joy of it," said Irial. "Perhaps we can all go hunting later . . . if you still want to go." Then, with an apologetic yet resigned glance at Rioghan, the two brothers also left the house, leaving Rioghan alone with Donaill and Coiteann.

The slamming of the door echoed in the cold silence. Rioghan flinched at the sound. And as she looked at Donaill, who still seemed not to notice her, the darkness that surrounded him seemed real enough to taste.

This could not have been his choice alone. She could never believe that. But perhaps she was simply denying the hard reality of it all. So many men seemed to consider it their primary goal in life to collect as many women for themselves as they possibly could, in any way they could. Rioghan was under no illusion about that—but perhaps, in her growing desire for Donaill, she had closed her eyes to the fact that he was in truth no different from any other man.

It seemed now that he had merely been trying to add her to his own group of women, intending to keep her out at Sion while having Coiteann—and any other woman he wanted—here at Cahir Cullen.

Perhaps the darkness she felt was only the reflection of her own despair.

Rioghan closed her eyes and thought of how easily she had allowed all this to happen. She had been the one who fled the fortress on the night of the feast. She had shown Donaill that she preferred the isolation of Sion. She had made it oh, so easy for him to keep her apart from all his other women here at Cahir Cullen, for she had stayed out at Sion, where she would never know what he did while he was here.

So easy.

Rioghan made herself take a step forward. She could not let it end this way. If she had been wrong about Donaill and his intentions toward her, she wanted to hear it directly from him.

But Coiteann stood up and faced her with a cold glare. "You will not touch him," she said in a hiss.

"I am not asking you for your permission," Rioghan whispered, still watching Donaill.

"Very well, then! Ask *him.* Ask Donaill if he wants you to touch him!"

Rioghan struggled to draw breath. "Donaill," she said, trying to get his attention. "Donaill . . . you told me that you cared for me. You offered me a courtship, and I accepted. Have you changed your mind? Or was there never any truth in any of it?"

Very slowly, he turned in her direction, meeting her gaze at last. "There was truth," he said. "I did not lie to you, Rioghan."

"Then why . . . How is this possible?"

He looked away again. "I do not know," he said, shaking his head. "I do not remember. I only know that Coiteann is here, and she is my partner, and she is very special to me."

"And is she the only one who may touch you?"

"Why . . . of course she is," he answered, looking back at Coiteann again. "I do not want her to think I am giving my attention to some other and am not here for her. She is the only one who may touch me, or do whatever else she wills with me. She and no other."

Rioghan closed her eyes as pain and despair did their best to overwhelm her. As she turned to go, all she could hear was Coiteann's cold laughter calling after her.

"Feel free to visit us whenever you like!" the woman said, as Rioghan stumbled toward the door. "He will take no notice of you. Please do visit us often!"

Chapter Eighteen

Rioghan again fled the fortress of Cahir Cullen, her dogs running by her side through the open gates. She intended to run all the way back to Sion and never look on the place again—but she got only a short way down the forest path before dropping to the earth beneath the glossy green leaves and bright red berries of the holly trees.

She held her head in her hands and waited for the tears to come . . . but though her eyes burned and her chest was locked up tight, she did not weep. Instead of grief, she found there was only anger—anger that threatened to grow into rage, anger at both Coiteann and at Donaill.

Coiteann had done this thing. There was no doubt of that. She had somehow been able to force Donaill's will and bring him under her control, but first she would have had to get close to him—closer than he should ever have allowed her to get. He had just made an offer of marriage to Rioghan. What was such a man doing with another woman in his home?

She shook her head. If Donaill had not wanted Coiteann to be there with him, she could never have placed her charm or enchantment or curse upon him in the first place. None of this would have happened.

Rioghan clenched her fists and slammed them into the earth. Then her wailing filled the wintry forest, the terrible lament of one who has loved and trusted . . . and been betrayed.

Coiteann lifted up the last of the leather bags filled with her possessions and left her house one final time. It was certainly going to be nice to live in the large, fine house of the king's champion instead of in these cramped quarters with five other women. Pulling the door shut after her, she was mildly surprised to see Airt standing there waiting.

"Good afternoon to you," she said coolly, walking past him. But he reached out to catch her arm and forced her to face him.

She thought he would be angry—but all she saw in his eyes was pain. "You must explain yourself to me," he whispered. "You owe me that, if nothing else."

She jerked her arm away. "I owe you nothing," she said with a sneer. Then, after smoothing the sleeve of her gown where he had grabbed it, she smiled. "But I will tell you, since you are so sure you want to hear. Come with me."

Coiteann walked across the very center of the fortress, through the scattering of houses, walking proudly with her head held high while Airt hurried after her and everyone in Cahir Cullen saw them. At last they reached the cattle pens, where the five black winter cows and their calves lay resting in the straw beneath the sheds. Coiteann stood next to the wooden rails, set down her leather bags, and looked up at Airt.

Airt shook his head, searching for the words. "Why?" he asked again. "Why have you done this?"

She folded her hands atop the fence rails and smiled sweetly at him, unable to conceal how pleased she was with herself. "You are the reason why," she began. "It should be crystal-clear to you. You told me you wanted a life with me. You told me you would take me as a wife. You even moved into my house so that I would believe you were serious."

"I was serious. I was—"

"Yet when your beloved Sabha told you she would take you back if you got rid of me, you wasted no time accepting her very kind offer. But you, one of the king's bold warriors, did not have the courage to tell me what you had decided to do."

He hung his head. "I thought I could still make it work. I thought I could still persuade her to accept you as my second wife, once she took me back."

"I am sure you did," said Coiteann, brushing a strand of pale blond hair from her face. "You lied to both of us. And now you have neither one."

Airt closed his eyes. "But yesterday . . . yesterday you went with me to Sion, and you told me, you told Rioghan, that you wished to build a life with me and be respected as my wife."

Coiteann laughed. "So, Airt, it is well if *you* deceive a woman with your promises and lies, but you are shocked when a woman dares deceive you in return? I said what was necessary so that Rioghan would give me what I required: a charm of binding."

"Binding," he whispered, his eyes growing large. "Did you . . . did you use such a thing on me? Is that how—"

She only laughed again. "Oh, Airt, there was no need for any such thing with you. It was clear to everyone—especially to me—that you had an appetite for the company of other women whenever your dear wife was not present. It took hardly any effort at all to turn your attention to me . . . and only the smallest amount of dark magic to convince you to take me inside your very own house."

"Dark magic?"

She raised her both hands, showing him their dark-stained palms. "I am the one who makes the dyes," she said. "The reeking, bitter dyes that ruin my hands but add such beauty and color to everyday life here.

"I spun thread to make a tunic especially for you, and when I prepared the black dye for this thread it was no trouble to add a few special things to it . . . dark, cold things to encourage dark, cold actions.

"I used the burned ashes of my hair and the dust and earth from my boots at the end of the day. I used red heather, for that is the shrub of unbridled greed and of passion that knows no boundaries. And, of course, I used a drop of my own blood, drawn with no pain and no sorrow."

"Then you took me from Sabha with dark magic," Airt said, his voice beginning to shake. "You forced me to—"

But Coiteann only laughed as she put down her hands. "There was no need for force," she said in a sneer. "It was like forcing a dog to fresh meat. The magic that I wove into your black tunic merely gave you the courage to do what you wanted to do all along, which was take me into your house and into your bed."

"Donaill, too, wore a new black tunic this day." Airt's face was gray as ash. "Is that how you turned his attention to you?"

"In part. But there was more, for he is not like you. He had indeed set his sights on Rioghan alone and intended to make her his one and only wife. I knew this task would be more difficult, so I gave him my very personal attention." She fixed Airt with a smug look, as if daring him to ask any more.

"I fear to ask you what else you might have done. But . . . why Donaill? You had never shown interest in him before. Why did you try to take Donaill?"

Her eyes narrowed, and a slow, grim smile spread

across her face. "I know very well who was behind Sabha's revenge. Rioghan was here to tend her on the night you left her for me. It is no coincidence that Sabha tricked you and lied to you and then cursed us both. She did not have knowledge of how to do such things. She had help, and she got it from Rioghan."

Coiteann's face grew dark. "It was Rioghan who ruined our relationship and who tried to ruin my life. She tried to destroy me when I had done nothing to her, and now I will have my revenge.

"She took you from me, when you were the man I wanted. Now I will take her man away from her, using some of her very own magic . . . and a little more, as well."

"You must undo it," Airt said urgently. "You must let him go! You must undo whatever it is you have done to him!"

Again, the laughter. "I cannot hold him by force. I can encourage him, but he will do what he wants. He can leave me, if that is truly his wish—but is Rioghan so much better a woman than I am? Can that cold and lonely midwife do the things for him that I can do so well? We will see which he prefers."

She ran her fingers down Airt's chest. "Do not worry for Donaill," she said. "He will have a good life with me. A very good life. You, of all men, should know that."

With that, Coiteann turned and walked away, leaving Airt standing alone with his despair to watch her as she returned to Donaill's house.

* * *

They had been watching her for quite some time now. They always accompanied her whenever she left Sion, and they would have come running when she cried out. They were there in the trees now, and in the brush, keeping watch over her. The Sidhe.

Scath and Cogar lay on either side of Rioghan to guard her and keep her warm. She raised her head and peered into the soft twilight that filled the forest.

"What will I do?" she asked, knowing they would hear. "How could he have done this?"

A shadow moved behind one of the trees. "Those things are for you to say, and no other."

She got to her feet, unable to sit still any longer, and found that she was cold and stiff from sitting so long in spite of the dogs' best efforts. She began to pace, walking with slow steps from tree to tree, thinking aloud and hoping the Fair Folk could offer her some comfort.

"Was it all a lie?" Rioghan's voice shook and her breath came fast—too fast. "Was his courtship of me, his protection of Sion, merely a game—a bit of harmless fun with the strange, reclusive woman of the cave? Perhaps he made a bet with a few of the other men. Perhaps they were all amused at the idea of he and I—"

Another shadow moved in the twilight. "Donaill has never behaved in such a way before."

"He has never been cruel."

"What you describe would be a terrible cruelty."

"Yet he has gone, in the span of two days, from offering me a courtship to wanting to marry Coiteann." She tried to make herself think calmly, analytically, to soothe her raging emotions and use reason instead—but still her voice shook, and her heart pounded and raced, and she struggled to draw breath even though she had been sitting still for a long time.

"He could have gotten away from her, had he truly wished to! He must have had no such wish, at least, not last night! He has chosen her, that I have plainly seen, and I can only wish them the greatest of happiness together!

"What else can I do?" she whispered, stumbling to a stop. "What else can I do if he prefers another? What else . . ." She dropped her head into her hands, fearing she would cry out again, and that this time it would tear out her very heart.

Then, just as the darkness fell, the shadows moved out of the forest to surround her. Soon she was safe within the soft touches and gentle embraces of the Sidhe, and their whispered words and soothing presence eased her pain somewhat and reminded her, again, that she was not alone, and would never be alone so long as she lived among them.

After a time they withdrew, leaving her again standing by the trees in the dark and misty forest with her two dogs calmly standing beside her. Rioghan drew a deep breath, realizing that now she could breathe slowly and easily as she had always done before, and that her heart was quiet and steady once again. Even her hands had lost most of their trembling.

"I agree with what you say," she began, folding her hands and pacing slowly among the trees. "Donaill has never been a cruel man. Nor has he been a liar. Always his actions have matched his words. Always—until now."

She stopped, and ran her fingers down the smooth, damp trunk of a holly tree. "Last night he wore a tunic like the one Airt had. A tunic that must have been made for him by Coiteann, the mistress of the dye, who no doubt added something extra to those particular black dyes . . . something dark and binding and just persuasive enough to turn the head of a man already inclined to look in her direction."

The gentle voices again floated out of the night.

"Yet you were certain that the only one Donaill looked to was you."

"We are certain of this, too."

"Was the magic in this dye so strong it could compel him against his will?"

Rioghan shook her head. "I cannot believe it could be so strong," she said, "and yet the fact remains: he is with her." She tightened her fists again. "But how did she persuade him to accept such a gift from her at all? Why, if he had chosen me, would he allow her close enough to let her do such a thing to him?" She closed her eyes as pain threatened to overwhelm her again.

"We agree," said another voice, "that he did not lie to you."

"Coiteann's powers are not great enough to force his will."

"There must be something else—something more—that she has done."

"But what? Who would help her with such darkness, such power, such evil? No one that I know, not at Cahir Cullen and certainly not among you. I know she must despise me for helping Sabha get her justice—and for the things I said to her yesterday. But hatred alone will not give her the power of magic."

"Again, we agree," said a Sidhe voice.

"None of us would have helped with such a spell."

"Not even any of the men would do such a thing."

Gentle arms hugged her shoulders before vanishing back into the night. "Yet we believe hope remains for you and Donaill."

"Hope?" Rioghan found herself caught between laughing and weeping. "How could there be any hope for us, after what I have seen this day?"

The voices came rapidly now, floating all around her in the night.

"There is hope because Coiteann had not the power to do this alone."

"Donaill would never have chosen her of his own free will."

"She would have to have used the darkest of magics to trap him."

"Such a thing is difficult to do, and even more difficult to hide."

"There is more here than any of us know."

"Find out how this was really done."

"Find out the truth."

Rioghan closed her eyes. "The truth may be that I have not the power to turn his will, either . . . or the strength left to try, after the grief that he has caused me."

"Yet we see that your eyes are dry."

"If you do not weep for your lost love, it is because of your anger."

"Anger at a woman selfish enough to steal away the beloved of another."

"And at a man foolish enough to allow such a woman to get close to him."

"This anger will give you the strength to fight for him."

"Do you wish to fight?"

Instantly, she raised her chin. "I could not do otherwise," she admitted. "And, if I lose, at least I will be certain of where his affection truly lies . . . and I will know that I gave the best I had to give."

"Then come home now, where you can rest, and heal, and know that you are safe."

But she shook her head. In the distance, beyond the trees, she could just see the low orange glow of the torchlights from Cahir Cullen. "I cannot," Rioghan said. "Not yet. I have one more task to do this night, if I intend to fight for him—and I do intend to fight."

Chapter Nineteen

Darkness found Airt still outside, pacing around the inner wall of Cahir Cullen with his heavy cloak pulled up over his head, unable to make himself go back inside the house that he had so happily shared with Sabha and then abandoned for Coiteann.

Now he was alone.

He could only look at the tall, solid gates tightly closed against the long winter night, and wonder if he should simply walk out through them tomorrow when they opened at dawn . . . walk out and keep on walking until he dropped, until thirst or hunger claimed him or the wolves tracked him down.

He did not know what to do. So many lives affected, simply for a little time spent alone in the company of Coiteann!

His beloved Sábha had left him, going back to

her family at Dun Orga after her marriage had been destroyed. Coiteann had shown her true colors by stealing Donaill away from Rioghan, destroying their newly forming and very promising relationship. Donaill was poisoned with dark magic, just as he himself had been, and Rioghan had lost the man who loved her.

There seemed to be nothing left for him here . . . or anywhere.

He continued to walk, staying close beside the high, thick earthen wall that curved along the outer perimeter of the fortress, staying deep in its shadow—until he heard familiar voices.

Peering up, Airt realized that he was near the very back of the fortress, at the open space near the wall where the men often gathered to talk in the evenings. This night was no different, it seemed, for he heard Beolagh, Flann, Dowan, and Bercan talking in low voices.

Donaill, he noted, was not among them.

They fell silent as he approached. Beolagh grunted as he recognized the newcomer. "So, Airt, you have no one else for company this night?"

"I do not," Airt said quietly. "Everyone here knows it well. It seems that I am good for only one thing, and that is being the butt of every joke told at this fortress."

"Not every joke," said Beolagh. "There are a few at Donaill's expense, too."

"And not just a few," added Flann. "It's been extremely gratifying to watch the great and arrogant king's champion brought to heel by the best-known bush strumpet at Cahir Cullen."

"Perhaps she placed a spell of some kind on him," Airt ventured.

"A spell? That one? The dye woman? Ha! She has no such powers. She might be able to turn his head with some little charm, but that is all she could do. Donaill is there because he allows himself to be there."

"And now that he has turned his full attention to Coiteann," said Beolagh, "he has turned it away from Rioghan—and from Sion."

The men fell silent, but as Airt looked at each face he saw that all of them wore grim smiles and smug expressions. "From Sion?" he asked. "You are . . . you are planning to return there?"

"That we are," said Beolagh, looking hard at him. "Donaill is no longer the guardian of Sion nor the protector of the midwife. He is busy elsewhere. And we will do no harm to the Sidhe, not as long as they give us the gold they have no use for."

He took a step toward Airt, still fixing him with a glare. "Perhaps you would like to join us. You have lost much. A little gold might do something to rebuild your status, would it not? Perhaps even help you find another woman, now that you have lost two in two days."

Airt swallowed and looked away. "Would you allow me to go with you?"

Beolagh laughed. "That we would! You may not be much at keeping women about you, young Airt, but you are a good enough fighter to help keep the Sidhe at bay while we take their gold. And we know very well that the midwife would never come near *you*. She is a woman, after all, and we know how they run from you!"

All of them laughed uproariously, and Airt tried to smile. It was yet another joke at his expense, and he knew it was just the start of many more to come—unless he found a solution to his loss of face.

"I will go with you, if you'll have me," he said in a clear voice.

"Oh, we'll have you, all right," said Beolagh. "There's no one with better reason than you to gain some gold and raise your status."

"When?" whispered Airt.

Beolagh glanced up at the sky. "We'll need to do a bit of planning," he said, "but we don't want to wait too long. We cannot chance Coiteann changing her mind again and letting Donaill go, though I doubt she will now that she has the champion of the king. We'll go at the dark of the moon."

Airt nodded. That would be about ten nights from now. "The dark of the moon it is, then. I will be with you."

The house was as quiet as it had ever been. The low fire in the hearth did little to banish the cold and the dark, and Coiteann could almost see her breath in the cold air. But that did not matter. She was alone with Donaill inside his own house, and she would be here every night from now on because it would be her rightful place as his wife.

Excitement rose within her. Donaill, the king's champion, the carefree warrior who had recently begun an idle pursuit of a reclusive, manipulative little wretch named Rioghan, had forgotten all about that woman. Now he was bound to the powerful and enchanting Coiteann the way a mountain was bound to the earth.

She stood facing him beside the sleeping ledge, smiling up at him, wearing only a light linen gown even in the cold. The thin fabric draped nicely over her curves and hid little even in the dim light; but he seemed not to notice her at all. Her blond hair hung down long and loose, but when she threw back her head and allowed the gown to slip low over her shoulders he merely smiled at her and stood quietly, as though waiting for her to tell him what he should do next.

Coiteann sighed. "Would you like some hot wine? Maybe that would . . . relax you a bit."

"Of course," he said, still staring down at her. "Whatever you would like, I would like, too."

She smiled back. "Of course." She caught up one of the stitched fur covers from the sleeping ledge, threw it around her shoulders, and walked around to the other side of the hearth, where she crouched down to find the wineskin and a pair of wooden cups.

As she stood up with them, she was startled to see Donaill standing right over her. "Oh," she said, trying to smile at him. "I found the wine."

"You did." He stood still, watching her, waiting for her to do something else. When she went back to the sleeping ledge with the wine and the cups, he followed, then stood waiting once again.

He stood there the whole time and watched everything she did, never taking his eyes off her hands as she poured the blackberry wine into a small cauldron and set it on the glowing coals. In a short time the liquid was steaming and ready, and she poured a little into each of the wooden cups.

She handed him one, and he took it, but still did nothing but stare at her. "Drink," she said softly, and he obeyed. Coiteann downed her own wine in a single gulp.

She set down her cup, and he did the same, and at last she reached for him and took him into her embrace. He allowed her to hold him, but merely stood still with his arms at his sides. She got nothing in return from him but his beating heart and the steady rise and fall of his chest.

Coiteann stepped back and caught hold of his hands. "Come with me," she whispered, smiling up at his shadowed face. "Come with me, into the warm furs, where we can be together the way we were always meant to be together."

She pulled the fur cover from her shoulders and sat down on the edge of the wide ledge, sliding over toward the wall so that there was room enough for him to lie beside her. "Come here, Donaill," she said again, stroking the soft, thick furs covering the empty space beside her. "Come here."

Obedient as a child, Donaill sat down on the edge of the ledge, untied his heavy boots and pulled them off, and then stretched out flat on his back beside her. Quickly she covered them both with more furs and a couple of heavy woolen cloaks, and moved close to press the length of her cold body against his.

Now she had him where she could deal with him best. No one had more skill than Coiteann in the art of arousing a man. Now he would be unable to resist her, and she would make him her own. She would banish all thoughts of any other woman from his mind in such a way that he would think only of her, and desire only her, from this night forward.

But it soon became apparent that he was not responding to her at all. He lay back on the ledge and closed his eyes, and sighed as she pulled the warm furs over him, but her searching hands and caressing fingers had no effect on him at all . . . and after a time, she was forced to admit defeat and lie back on the cushions beside him.

It was only their first night together, she reminded herself. Some men were of little use to a woman once they'd had some wine and been taken to a warm bed. There was no changing the fact that he was entirely hers now and would always be hers. There would be time to make him love her later on—after they were married. Then their relationship would be consummated as it should.

And even if he never came to desire her, and merely stayed bound to her side the way he was now, she would still be his wife. She would still have all the status and property and prestige that went along with being the wife of the king's champion. She had still succeeded in taking him from

Rioghan . . . and there were always other lovers, if need be.

Beside her, there was only the sound of soft snoring.

The waning three-quarter moon was high in the sky when the door of Donaill's house swung silently open and a small figure in black crept inside.

The house was dark and cold and lonely, even though two figures lay close together in the furs on one of the sleeping ledges. Rioghan was very glad for the darkness so that she would not have to look on Donaill's face as he lay beside Coiteann.

There was no mistaking him, though. One glimpse of his shadowed profile was enough . . . as was the brief sight of Coiteann's long blond hair spread out over his chest.

For a moment the sickening anger came rushing back, but she fought it down. She had work to do, and it would require all of her concentration.

She moved to the ledge and sat down beside it in the straw. Donaill's hand lay along its edge, and she reached up and found his bare wrist.

His skin was warm in the cold of the house, as warm and welcome as fire's heat. Though she could feel the iron strength of his muscles even as he slept, the skin was smooth, and the fine hairs that covered it felt soft and alive beneath her touch. For a moment she forgot why she had come, and she closed her eyes and gently stroked the warm soft skin of his arm.

He caught his breath and began to stir. Instantly

Rioghan let go and bent her head low beneath the ledge. In a moment all was quiet again, and she reached up once more to touch his wrist.

This time she made herself concentrate on what she must do. With her free hand she reached beneath the neck of her black wool gown and took out the crystal of seeing, holding the crystal in one hand and Donaill's wrist with the other.

Tell me what happened to you, she thought. *Show me how this was done. . . . Show me. . . .*

The visions were dark and shadowed at first. He may well have been asleep, or even drugged, but if he was present his mind would have some recollection of what had taken place.

Show me . . .

She saw this house, Donaill's house, in darkness. Three men lay on the three sleeping ledges, each one dead asleep, and each with an empty cup dropped carelessly in the straw just below.

Coiteann walked through the house and closed the door and the windows tight, shutting out any trace of natural light. Only the faint glow of the coals in the hearth allowed her to see at all. From a small leather bag at her waist, she lifted out what looked like a heavy, dull, flat black lump of metal hanging from a thin iron chain.

It was the same amulet, the charm of binding, that Rioghan had made for her.

Below the ledge where Donaill lay, half asleep and half drugged into unconsciousness, his sword belt had fallen into the straw. Coiteann reached down to it, found the leather sheath that held his dagger, and pulled the weapon out.

She stood over him for a moment, speaking in a low voice. *Now you will become mine, and not hers. Never hers.* Then she moved toward him and crouched down beside the ledge, pulling his hand over the edge so that it hung out over the straw. With his own dagger she made a cut in the small finger of his hand and pressed it so that the drops of blood fell directly onto the amulet. Donaill flinched at the cut, but remained otherwise unmoving on the ledge.

Coiteann took the blood-coated amulet back to the hearth and placed it on the surrounding stone wall. Now, from a large leather sack in the straw, she lifted up an aged, fat, and nearly blind lapdog, too asthmatic to bark and too feeble to defend itself.

From the same sack she took a length of strong cord and looped it around the old dog's neck. Placing the animal's nose against the amulet, Coiteann tightened the cord and held it firmly.

In the span of a few moments, the helpless creature breathed its last terrified breath directly onto the charm of binding.

Coiteann placed the body of the dog back into the sack and then picked up a smaller leather bag. This one she emptied into a dark corner of the hearth, for these were cold ashes newly swept from Donaill's own hearth, a substance that had once been untouchable with bright heat but that was now cold and dead and dark—and entirely controllable. She rolled the amulet in these ashes and then held it up for one final look by the faint firelight.

The *luaidhe* stone had now been subjected to blood, and cruelty, and control, and would be an extremely dark and powerful charm of binding. Rioghan had placed only a gentle enchantment on it, one meant to be completed by a kiss between lovers, but after Coiteann's ritual it would carry an irresistible compulsion.

Coiteann took the charm to Donaill's side. Leaning over him, she slid her hand beneath his head and lifted him up just enough to get the amulet's chain around his neck. Then, with a great effort, she managed to raise up one of his shoulders and arrange the amulet so that it hung down his back instead of resting over his heart. The wearer would thus be pushed and compelled toward his enchantress, instead of lovingly and willingly drawn. It would bind him to the woman who had stopped at nothing to get him and would stop at nothing to keep him.

Rioghan dropped her crystal of seeing, letting it fall back against her breast. She let go of Donaill's arm and got to her feet, though her body shook and she feared her knees would give way. As quickly as she could she fled the cold, dark house, stumbling across the yard of Cahir Cullen with her dogs by her side, crying out to the watchman to open the gate and let her out, knowing she could never run far enough to escape the horror she had discovered.

Somehow Rioghan found her way home in the darkness, though anger and despair all but blinded her to the sight of the moonlit path. She was desperate to get home, but when she arrived at Sion she hurried past the opening of the cave and its welcoming warmth and light and ignored the dogs who tried to greet her. Instead she ran up the side of the mound until she stood in the ashes at the very top.

Alone save for Scath and Cogar, Rioghan threw back her head and sang out, a single rising note that floated out through the cold and misty forest. Though she knew that a few of the Sidhe always moved with her unseen in the forest whenever she left Sion, her wailing cry would bring them all immediately to her side.

It was not long before the gray figures began to appear at the rim of the mound, rising into sight as they climbed lightly up the side of the hill. Exhausted, Rioghan sat down on her black wool cloak and breathed deeply of the cold night air.

Gentle hands stroked her hair, her shoulders, her face.

"We are here with you."

"Take time and calm yourself before you try to speak."

"Look up at the beauty that surrounds you, and let it help to ease your heart."

Breathing slowly, deeply, Rioghan raised her head and looked out at the land around her. The endless pine trees reached up to meet the moon, their branches black in the deep night and glowing faintly in the mist and moonlight. It was peaceful and beautiful, as it always was . . . but now she knew that to the north, where the fortress of Cahir

Cullen lay within the holly grove, there was a darkness that even the brightest moon and most shining starlit sky could never banish.

At last she turned toward the waiting Sidhe. It was difficult to see them, for their faces were hidden by colorless cloaks pulled up high over their heads. They were all moonlit silhouettes against the starry night sky, occasionally bright with reflected starlight on their gold and bronze and polished jet brooches. Yet she knew they were there to listen to her, and comfort her, and give her what help they could.

"I have learned the truth," she began, "and it is dark and tortured and cruel. And I do not know how I can fight it without being just as ruthless and just as evil."

In silence, the Sidhe turned to glance at one another.

"Evil can never be used to fight evil."

"Both evil things would be destroyed, should that be tried."

"It is not your nature, nor is it ours, to use such methods, my lady."

"Then I will tell you what she has done," Rioghan whispered. As they gathered close, she told them all that she had learned of Coiteann's dark ritual and of the terrible binding curse she had placed on the amulet—and on Donaill.

"Only the deepest darkness could break such evil," Rioghan said again, and closed her eyes.

"Not the deepest darkness—but indeed the most

brilliant light," said one of the soft voices surrounding her.

"Each of those three curses can be fought."

"We will help you find a way."

Rioghan looked up at their shadowed forms. "How?" she whispered.

The Sidhe turned to each other for a time, murmuring softly and exchanging whispered words and gentle touches and even signals made with hands and fingers. Then they came back to Rioghan and surrounded her again, standing in a half circle before her with hands folded beneath their gray cloaks.

"The power of light—the greatest power anyone can wield—will be needed to break this curse."

"You must bring Donaill to the stone circle at sunrise on the winter solstice."

"That is the most powerful place."

"That is the most powerful time."

"The sun returns at the winter solstice, and its rays are the most magical at dawn on that day."

Rioghan shook her head. "He would never go with me to the stone circle. He might follow Coiteann, but she would never allow him to get near it."

"You must find a way."

"Or he must find a way."

"Somehow he must get to the circle at dawn on the solstice, or he will remain as he is now for the rest of his life."

Rioghan could only look at them. "*If* I could get him to the circle . . . what must I do then?"

"The blood that soaked the amulet, blood taken by force and without consent, can be washed away by tears."

"Tears of sorrow, wept for his loss by one who loves him."

"Your tears, Lady Rioghan, for you are the one whose love for him is true."

The Sidhe spoke to each other for a moment, and then turned to Rioghan again.

"The final breath of a captive creature, forced to die in pain and fear, permeates this amulet."

"The living breath of a free, wild thing will counteract it."

"Bring a wild creature willingly to your side as you stand within the stone circle, and allow its breath to touch the amulet."

Silence fell again. The only motion was the faint mist weaving among the trees down below. "And the final task?" Rioghan asked.

"The *luaidhe* stone was coated in ash, dead and dark and cold."

"It needs the warmth of a flame started from the rays of the winter solstice sun."

"A flame kindled with the crystal you wear over your heart, for a crystal is like a living piece of the earth. It has beauty, constancy, and longevity—just as a true love has."

Rioghan could only look at them as the trembling began again. "I know you are right," she said to them, "and yet I cannot think of how these things could possibly be done. For even if I could bring Donaill to the stone circle on the morning of the solstice, and lure a wild thing to my side, and kindle a sun-fire with my crystal . . ."

She shook her head. "I have no tears to give him. There is too much anger—at Coiteann for her cruelty and at Donaill for his carelessness. There is anger, and pain, and terrible loss . . . but there are no tears."

She could not use the Sidhe's advice.

Chapter Twenty

Ten nights went by, ten long, cold nights during which Rioghan could think of nothing else but Donaill—try as she might to push him from her mind. The Sidhe, kind as they were, had brought back the gold and bronze and crystal that they had hidden away from the invading men. It had once brightened the inside of her cave, and so they set it all out again in an effort to cheer her, but she could hardly bring herself to look at it. It only reminded her of how Donaill had come to Sion to help protect these same beautiful things, and now she despaired that he even remembered being here at all.

She felt torn in two, torn between wanting desperately to go to Cahir Cullen and do her best to persuade him to leave Coiteann of his own will . . . and fearing there was nothing she—or anyone—

could do to break such a spell. She could not use the Sidhe's method. Now that she knew what Coiteann had done, knew the darkness and cruelty that had gone into putting such a terrible curse on the amulet, she saw no way to overcome the curse without spells of far greater cruelty than even Coiteann had used.

And then she would think that perhaps Donaill deserved to stay where he was. He had allowed Coiteann close enough to him to drug him, curse him, and bind him to her forever. It had been his choice to spend time with her, even when he had just offered Rioghan a courtship and told her that he wanted only her.

Donaill had known very well what sort of woman Coiteann was. It would never have happened if he had simply stayed away from her. Perhaps it was better, Rioghan told herself, that she found out about him now . . . found that he was simply one of those men who would never give up the pleasure of other women's company, no matter how devoted he claimed to be to one.

Yet even as she told herself these things, she would remember, again and again, his smiling face and laughing eyes . . . his great broad shoulders and boundless strength as she sat behind him on his horse . . . his determination in driving men like Beolagh away from Sion and from the Sidhe, even though they were his own men. . . . And most of all, she recalled his gentleness, for all his great strength, when he had smiled at her and taken her hand and then bent down to kiss her.

Rioghan knew that she would never meet another man like Donaill.

The Sidhe told her that he still seemed to be himself when doing normal things among the other men: hunting, fishing, playing fidchell, or simply sitting outside and talking during the long, cold winter nights. But he looked at no woman but Coiteann, would speak only of Coiteann, insisted he would marry no woman but Coiteann.

His own people might be willing to leave him to his fate—but could Rioghan so coldly do the same?

At last it was the night of the dark of the moon. Rioghan stepped out of her cave, her heavy black cloak swinging about her feet. She looked up at the dark sky, shrouded in cloud, and wrestled with the thought that would not leave her mind. Despite what the Sidhe said, it seemed certain that only a power as dark at that used to curse the amulet could ever hope to break that same curse. But if she must do something so terrible to get Donaill away from another woman, was he really worth it?

Would anything be worth it? Rioghan had only to close her eyes to see his bright gaze and laughing face once again, and then would come the sickening vision of Donaill trapped at Coiteann's side, his eyes dull and patient and his face as serious as that of a scolded child.

She could not leave him this way. No matter what. The realization came to her that there was nothing she would not do to bring him back to the way he was, even if he was no longer hers. No one deserved to live the way Donaill was living now. Trapped. Controlled. Entranced.

Rioghan looked out into the darkness of the surrounding pine forest. If she was going to use the power of dark magic to save Donaill, the time to gather the things she needed was now, at the dark of the moon. In a moment she found herself walking through the forest, alone in the dark, damp woods save for Scath and Cogar . . . and, she knew, a few of the ever-present Sidhe.

She walked slowly, almost reluctantly, keeping her eyes fixed on the ground. She was barely able to see anything in the faint light of the few stars that managed to shine down through the broken clouds, and as she walked farther and farther from the clearing she began to doubt she would find what was required.

Then something caught her eye.

Beneath the brush, hidden at the roots of one of the largest pines, lay something small and broken and dull white in color. Rioghan bent down to look closely at it and found bones—bones from some small creature, most likely a hare, which should be left to return in their own time to the earth, but which she could put to other use. The proper ritual would extract the last of the essence that had once inhabited them, and might release enough power to turn the will of a man under the darkest of curses.

As she gathered the bones, her fingers found something else within them: the rusted, broken blade of an iron dagger. At the cold bite of the metal she instantly dropped it, knowing that this was the weapon used to kill the wild hare whose bones she now hoped to use. But in a moment she lifted it up again, slowly and carefully, for this too would be a powerful talisman if used in the proper spell.

Once the bones and the iron blade were safely gathered up and placed in a small leather bag, she began to dig in the bare earth where the bones and blade had rested. Directly below she found a stone not quite as large as her fist, buried so deep in the earth that it had never seen the light of day. This, too, she placed in her leather bag.

Last of all she cut a piece of deep root from the ancient pine. This root was intended to feed nourishment to the tree, and though the tree would not die it would suffer some harm when its root was torn away—especially when that beneficial root was used to nurture dark power instead of growth and life.

She stood up again, brushing the damp earth and pine needles from the front of her black gown, feeling the very heavy weight of the leather bag that held her collection of dark, hidden, holding, binding things. Did she dare to hope that she could use such things to overpower Coiteann's dreadful spell?

There was no answer for her now. Rioghan could only lift the heavy bag to her shoulder and turn back down the path that led to Sion—but just as she took the first step, Scath and Cogar shot past her in a mad race toward the clearing as if in answer to the frenzied barking that reached her through the pines.

The clouds closed in overhead, shutting out the

starlight. Rioghan had no choice but to find her way in near-total darkness, picking her way along the path and searching out the familiar tree, the fallen log, the crooked boulder that showed her she was getting closer, even as her heart pounded and she wanted nothing more than to bolt through the darkness and get back to Sion.

Finally she could see spots of light ahead through the trees, as the barking of the dogs grew louder and louder. At last Rioghan raced out of the forest into the glaring torchlight of the clearing—and stopped dead at what she saw.

Chapter Twenty-one

The dogs were indeed barking fiercely, and doing all they could to attack the intruders, but their raging was for nothing. Every one of the animals, including Cogar and Scath, thrashed and struggled within the entanglements of three heavy rope nets.

As before, Beolagh and his men had invaded the clearing, though this time they felt free to ride at their leisure or even walk on foot through the grass, since there were no warriors to defend Sion—and all of the dogs were now hopelessly trapped within heavy nets. And so, Rioghan saw with horror, were a few of the Sidhe.

The men of the Sidhe must have come running, as they always did, when the dogs sent up the alarm—but why would they have come out in the open to be get caught like animals in Beolagh's nets?

Then she saw why. Within the cave, glaring torchlight created harsh moving shadows. The black cowhide hangings were ripped down and thrown aside, and two men walked out of her home with their arms piled high with every last item of value that had lined the walls of the cave.

"Stop!" Rioghan shouted, but her voice was lost amid the noise of her barking, shrieking dogs. She hurried toward the cave, but another movement toward the road forced her once again to stop.

Two men on horseback drove a group of Sidhe ahead of them at swordpoint—and every one of the Sidhe, men and women both, carried a pile of beautiful gold and crystal objects, shining bright in the flaring light of the torches.

"Kieran! Luath!" Rioghan cried, and started to go to them—but then one of the riders drove his horse across her path and dragged the animal to a stop right in front of her.

"Do not, my lady," said the rider.

The voice was familiar. Looking up, blinking in the torchlight, Rioghan saw Airt looking down at her, holding his sword above her head.

"You?" she said, ignoring the upraised weapon. "You are a part of this?"

"Stay back," he told her, as his horse swung around. "Stay out of the way and you will not be harmed. You have my word."

"Your word! The same word you gave to Sabha? The same—"

"They only want the gold. Just stay back, and—"

"Better listen to him, midwife." Another horse slid to a halt beside her, and she saw Beolagh grinning down. His eyes shone with greed and triumph. "We'll have the gold, and the dogs and the Little People will not try to stop us—or they will regret it." He raised his iron sword and pointed it at her, and then jogged his horse over to the netted, struggling dogs and Sidhe. Holding his sword above them, he glared at Rioghan again.

"Will you stay back?" he shouted. "Or shall I silence them? It would be so easy. They are all trapped, and no threat to us any longer."

Airt turned his horse to face Beolagh. "Leave them. There's no need to do them any harm. We have the gold and that's what we came for."

Beolagh stared hard at the other man for a moment; then to Rioghan's great relief he lowered his sword and turned his horse away from the nets. He fixed his gaze on the growing pile of treasure, and he trotted past Rioghan, his eyes lighting up again as he looked at it. "You're right. Let's get our treasure home. Bercan! Flann! Get it all in the sacks, and then get the nets! Time to go!"

Airt wheeled his horse around, leaning down to grab two of the large cloth sacks clanking with heavy gold. As soon as Airt and three other men were loaded down, Beolagh and Dowan rode back to Rioghan.

"We're going to pull the nets off now," Beolagh

said. "If you value those creatures' lives, you'll call them off." He wheeled his horse around, and then he and Dowan leaned down from their horses, grabbed a corner of the net, and rode back with it so that it peeled off of the dogs and Sidhe. In a moment, the trapped and struggling creatures were free.

"*Madra! Madra!*" called Rioghan, and to her relief all of the animals immediately came to her. In a moment the other two nets were pulled off.

Victorious, all the men rode away, jogging down the road with their great load of gold and treasure and dragging their heavy nets behind them.

The dogs stayed close to Rioghan as the Sidhe got slowly to their feet. "Are you hurt? Did they wound you?" Rioghan cried, trying to look at each one in the darkness.

"I do not believe anyone is hurt," said Kieran, rubbing one arm, "but we should go and see to your home."

"They were all inside the cave," said another voice.

"We could not stop them," whispered a woman, and began to weep.

Rioghan took her by the arm. "Come with me, all of you. If no one is hurt, then I do not care what they might have done with mere objects. Objects are not everything. Even objects of ancient power."

Together the little group walked through the deep darkness, making their way through the roving, agitated dogs until they reached the mouth of the cave.

Lines of soft orange light glowed at the bottom

of her home's hearth. Kieran picked up one of the men's fallen, burned-out torches, and he touched it to the coals to light it. As he raised the small, flickering torch, they all stepped inside the cave . . . and Rioghan caught her breath.

A quick glance showed her that the shelves and niches and ledges of the cave walls had all been stripped bare. But the men had not stopped there. They had all but demolished the small interior of her home. They had started near the entrance, where her wooden chests of fabrics, gowns, and cloaks had been overturned. The clothing had been tossed onto the straw in their search for any gold that might be hidden within. The furs and cushions and heavy wools of the sleeping ledge had all been swept to the floor.

But the far end of the cave was the worst. Every bit of food had been thrown down and broken open—the clay jars of grain, the shelves of dried fruit, the small store of smoked meat. And all of her carefully gathered herbs and medicinal plants had been torn from their hangings on the walls and ceiling and ground into the dirt floor beneath the straw.

Clenching her fists, her breath coming hard, Rioghan looked at the bare walls of the place that had been her home. "It was not enough for them to take any shining, sparkling thing that gained their attention. They had to destroy all that was here in the bargain."

"We are so sorry, my lady."

"We will do what we can to put your home to rights."

"We wanted to stop them, but there were not enough of us."

Rioghan whirled to face them. "It was not your place to stop them!" she cried. "It was for Donaill to stop them! Or their own king! They are his own men, and Donaill made a promise to all of us here that he would not let them harass us again!"

"Yet he did not come," said a whispered voice in the shadows.

Rioghan nodded, looking into the distance, looking at nothing. "He did not," she answered, her voice soft. "He is with *her*. He allowed *her* to get too close to him, and now he is with her."

A group of Cahir Cullen's warriors sat outside together near the rear wall of the fortress, talking, laughing and drinking as they so often did in the evenings. On this windy, misty night, a small fire burned in the stone-lined pit and they all gathered close against the bone-chilling damp.

"I'm surprised to see you out here alone tonight, Beolagh," said Irial. "For each of the last four nights you've had a different woman in your house."

"Why, that's because none wished to return for a second course!" said Lorcan, and all of the other warriors laughed.

Beolagh scowled briefly, but then shrugged. "I do not see any of you with so many women you can barely keep track of them. And it seems to have escaped your notice that Dowan and Flann have suddenly become quite popular, too."

"So they have, now that you speak of it," agreed Lorcan. "But it seems that only the same few women are dividing their time among you all. Serving girls, young and foolish."

"Pity Coiteann is occupied, or you would be getting even less sleep." Irial laughed.

"Coiteann!" Donaill, who'd been sitting quietly by the fire, leaped to his feet. "Do not speak ill of the woman I will marry. She is everything to me. I will not have any of you mocking her here at this fireside!" He placed his hand on the hilt of his sword and glared at the gathering of men.

"Then I apologize to you," Irial said to his brother. "Though I admit I do not understand your choice, it is your choice to make, and none of us will interfere."

Beolagh smiled. "Some of us are quite happy with your choice, Donaill, for it allowed us to finally gain something that should have been ours all along."

Donaill merely stood quietly, but Lorcan raised his head, astonished. "Did you take it?"

"Take what?" Beolagh asked, fingering the frayed edge of his cloak.

"The gold. The Sidhe gold."

"We took nothing," Beolagh answered, grinning now. "They gave it to us!"

"Gave it to you?"

"They did! They were so impressed with the sight of us that no sooner did we ride up than they brought out their gold and bronze and crystal to us!"

"How many of the Sidhe were hurt?" asked Irial, his eyes narrowing.

"None of them. Not one! Nothing has changed for them except that their useless gold is gone from them, and given to someone who does indeed have a use for it!"

"So you do," Irial said, nodding slowly. "Buying the favors of foolish servant girls."

"It is ours to do with as we wish," Beolagh said in a growl. "No one has been harmed. Not the Sidhe, not the servant girls, and certainly not you."

"I thought my brother ordered you to leave the Sidhe and their gold alone, or else face a hearing by the king," said Lorcan.

Beolagh grinned, and glanced at Donaill. "Your brother no longer has any interest in the Sidhe, or in the midwife who lives among them. It is a man's privilege to change his mind, is it not? As I said, we did not harm them. We simply took what they had no need for."

Irial and Lorcan both turned to face their brother. "This is still true for you? The Sidhe no longer have your protection, even though Beolagh and his men have taken their gold?"

Donaill only shook his head slightly. "I have no thought to protect any but the king and the people of this fortress, especially Coiteann, to whom I am bound."

"Not even Rioghan, the healer of Sion?"

Donaill hesitated. "I have no thought for any woman but Coiteann."

His brothers looked doubtful, but could only

shake their heads. "The choice is yours," Lorcan said. "Coiteann does not hold you at swordpoint. You are a free man and can certainly choose the woman you want, no matter what others might think of it."

Donaill smiled faintly. "I thank you. And if all of you are agreeable"—he pulled his heavy red cloak closer around him against the cold, misting rain—"I will retire to my home. Coiteann will be there very soon."

Beolagh laughed. "Go, Donaill. There was a time when I would have envied you, but that was before the Sidhe so kindly gave us all their gold."

There was a silence, broken only by the dripping water from the trees beyond the wall and the snapping of the little smoky fire as the mist soaked into it. Donaill nodded to his brothers and turned to go, walking along the rear wall until he was out of sight of the men.

Somewhere in the back of his mind, it seemed he should be concerned about the Sidhe and their gold . . . but already the thoughts were fading. Far stronger was the image of Coiteann that was always with him, like a heavy weight against his back pushing him ever closer to her.

Suddenly he stopped. Someone was following him; he could feel it. They were following quietly, but making no effort to hide the sounds of their breathing—

He whirled around. And there behind him were two enormous dogs, two wolfhounds, one black with a gold collar and the other dark gray with a bronze collar.

They seemed familiar. They were not from Cahir Cullen, but he had seen them before. And then slowly, as though from very far away, the memory came back to him.

These two dogs were from Sion. They were two of the many that belonged to the midwife there. The healer. Rioghan, who always dressed in black. Or nearly always.

He began to recall that she was younger than he had thought, with fair, flushed skin and shining black hair and green eyes that sparkled even in the soft light of the hearthfire inside the cave where she lived.

The dogs came to him with lowered heads and wagging tails, standing close to him and pressing their noses into his hands. He stroked their great shaggy heads, his fingers running over their gold and bronze collars—and then he noticed something else around their necks.

Each of the animals had some kind of sphere hanging from a leather cord around its neck—a small golden ball, he saw, with a hole bored in each end. The surfaces were dotted with a fine pattern of tiny holes.

They were far too pretty and delicate to be used on the collars of dogs. Yet they were strangely heavy for all their delicacy, he thought as he lifted them up to look at them. And he knew for certain he had seen them before—seen them not on a pair of dogs, but on shining braids of smooth black hair.

Rioghan's hair. The same long black hair that was knotted through each one of the delicate spheres.

The dogs broke away from him and frisked for a few steps, as though inviting him to play . . . or to join them in the chase. And with the feel of the fine gold spheres still on his fingers and the picture of Rioghan's green eyes remaining in his mind, he followed the two great dogs across the dark and windy grounds . . . followed them toward the fortress gates.

Rioghan waited anxiously in the deep darkness of the holly grove, straining to see any sign of activity from the misty, smoke-shrouded fortress. The smoke from the torches and the mist in the air glowed with the light of the flames, leaving the place with a shining, unearthly look. But she was watching the gates most closely, hoping against hope that somehow they would open and she would see—

Donaill.

There he was, walking down the road in the direction of Sion, walking past her but not seeing her.

It seemed that the pair of golden spheres, the same ones she had worn in her hair for him on the night of the feast, had done their work. Yet she knew it had not been the spheres alone that had drawn him out. It had been the ritual she had performed over them, the darkest of any ritual that Rioghan had ever done.

For three days and three nights, the two delicate

golden spheres had been buried beneath the earthen floor of the cave that was her home . . . buried atop the bones of the frightened hare that had died only after long agony from the broken iron blade embedded within it.

On one side of the spheres she had placed the stone that had never seen the light of day, a stone that had existed always in darkness and been pulled from the earth at the dark of the moon. On the other side of them had rested the piece of root cut violently from the tree. Sprinkled over it all were a few drops of her own blood, drawn with the same broken blade that had so painfully taken the life of the hare.

She did not like having to use such methods. But it seemed she had been right to try them, for this alone had been able to get through to Donaill. Like a shadow she stepped from the forest and stood on the grassy area of land between the holly trees and the road.

"Donaill," she said softly, holding very still.

He stopped, looking in the direction of Scath and Cogar as they trotted over to meet her. For a long time he seemed to study her, as though he had seen her only once, long ago, and was trying to place her in his memory.

"Do you remember me?" she asked, taking a step toward him. "For I do remember you."

"Rioghan." He nodded slowly. "I know you. Beautiful, solitary lady . . . the midwife and healer who lives alone in the cave of Sion."

She smiled, and took another step. "Would you

like to see that cave again? Would you like to come with me to Sion, and stand once more atop the mound and see the beauty of the land beneath the mist and the night?"

He seemed to consider this for a time; then he began to smile. "I would like that," he said. "I would like to see Sion again."

"Then come with me now. We will walk down the road together," she said, reaching for his arm. "It is waiting for you; it is—"

"*Donaill!*"

The cry tore through the quiet night. Rioghan jumped and whirled around, even as Donaill slowly turned and the dogs set up a fierce barking just in front of him. "Donaill! Where are you going?"

Coiteann ran down the road just as the gate closed behind her. She was breathless and agitated—angry, though she tried not to show it. "Donaill, I was so worried about you! I searched everywhere for you! Why have you come out here?"

Rioghan's heart went cold as Donaill walked away from her, pulling his arm away from her hand as he moved. He walked straight to Coiteann, steadily and methodically, as if his feet knew what to do even if the rest of him did not.

"You must come home at once!" scolded Coiteann, taking tight hold of his arm. "It is late. It is dark. It is raining, and it is cold. And there are all sorts of creatures prowling about." She cast a murderous glare at Rioghan and her dogs, and then turned back to Donaill.

"Come home with me, my lord," she said

sweetly, stroking his arm as they walked. "Come to our home, where a good fire and hot wine await you, where we can hold each other close in the warm furs and—"

"Donaill."

It was only a single word, but it carried all of Rioghan's hopes . . . and as her heart threatened to race right out of her chest, he stopped, and then turned around.

Coiteann clung to him, trying to pull him back toward the fortress, but he ignored her and began walking toward Rioghan. The blond woman dragging at his arm might as well have been a fly trying to stop a magnificent bull.

"Come with me to Sion, and leave this evil that you have found," whispered Rioghan. "Come with me; come with me now—"

"Stop! Wait!" cried Coiteann, but Donaill kept walking steadily toward Rioghan.

Coiteann ran to him and slapped her hand down hard on his back, holding it there, pressing it hard against him. He stopped instantly, staring straight ahead.

Rioghan knew that the woman was pressing the cursed amulet hard into his back with all the strength and anger she possessed, forcing its dark power to envelop him even more strongly. "Now, Donaill," she said, through clenched teeth. "Now you will turn and go back with me."

Slowly—very slowly—he began to turn to go with her.

Quickly Rioghan reached down to the two dogs

at her side. She caught hold of the cords holding the golden hair ornaments, the ones that she had hoped Donaill would recognize, and pulled them over the dogs' heads. Both of the ornaments felt heavier than they should, weighed down as they were with the ritual of binding that she had performed on them.

Thinking fast, she pulled off her own black leather belt, slipped it through the loops of cord holding each golden sphere, and retied the belt. Then, before Coiteann could force him around, Rioghan ran to Donaill and threw her belt over his head so that the two golden spheres hung down over his heart.

Coiteann grabbed at the belt. She intended to pull it off, but Donaill extended his arm and swept her aside. He began to walk toward Rioghan, and she could see something like clarity, like recognition, beginning to return to his eyes.

So her use of the dark power was justified after all! The two gleaming spheres, these delicate ornaments that she had worn in her own hair, would never have had the power to overcome the *luaidhe* stone on their own. But with the touches of darkness, of heaviness, of binding, that she had placed upon them, Donaill had found the strength to turn away from Coiteann and walk toward Rioghan.

But the blond woman followed him, closing in behind him and reaching to the front of his belt. She drew his own jet-handled dagger from its sheath, and as she pulled it she allowed the sharp iron blade to gash his arm.

Donaill hardly seemed to notice the bite of the

dagger, but Rioghan flinched in horror at the sight of the dark, wet stain that suddenly shone on the blade. Coiteann held it up, glaring at Rioghan once again, and Rioghan saw her throw Donaill's red cloak aside. Then came the ripping of woolen fabric as the blade tore his tunic wide open and exposed the cursed *luaidhe* stone.

Rioghan did not have to see Coiteann's hands to know that she was coating the amulet with more of Donaill's own blood. She was adding the power of stolen blood, taken by violence and deception, to the amulet's own considerable strength. Coiteann pressed the amulet hard into his back with one hand and held the blade out with the other, pointing it directly at Rioghan. "Now we will go home," she said in a hiss, and turned Donaill away.

Standing in the road, watching them go, Rioghan tried desperately to think of one more thing she could do, one more effort she could make, to release Donaill from this terrible spell. There must be something. Something!

She clenched her fists in frustration. It would take power. Great power. Where could she hope to get power enough to—

Scath came to stand close by her side, and Cogar soon followed. They stood beside her in the dark and misty road, waiting patiently for her to choose which way she would go.

Power. There was no greater power than that of a loyal living creature that had devoted its life to her. There was no doubt that the power of its sacrificed life, running in a river of red over the cursed amulet, would let her break that spell once and for all.

Cold with shock, Rioghan turned away from the horror of such thoughts, turned and ran down the road toward the quiet and peace of Sion. "Scath! Cogar! Come with me! Come with me! Come . . ."

The two dogs ran with her, happy to be going home. After a moment she slowed and stopped, and they came to her, wagging their tails and licking her hands and greeting her as they always did. *Never could I do such a thing . . . never will any harm come to any of you. Never again will I walk the dark path. I am a keeper of the light, not a wielder of death and pain.*

She turned one last time toward Cahir Cullen. Donaill and Coiteann, her hand still pressed hard against his back, had nearly reached the open gate.

"Donaill!" Rioghan cried. "Donaill! You must come to the stone circle at dawn on the winter solstice! I can do no more for you unless you can find your way there! You must come at dawn on the winter solstice! I will be there waiting for you!"

The gate slammed shut behind them, echoing into the cold and misty night.

Chapter Twenty-two

Three more nights went by. Rioghan stayed close to her home, leaving only long enough to return the animal bones, the broken dagger, the stone, and the tree roots to their proper place beneath the unspoiled earth.

She could only do her best to make right what she had done, for it was well known that dark magic had a way of turning back on those who dared to use it. Any cruelty used in the pursuit of power would result in far greater cruelty being visited on the wielder.

Rioghan had not herself done harm to the little creature which had died here, but she had tried to use the essence of its cruel and painful death for her own ends. Now she returned the remains of the hare to the earth where it could rest peacefully and undisturbed, putting things to right as best she could and leaving all as it was meant to be.

At last she returned to Sion and tried to prepare for what was to come on the morning of the winter solstice, when she would have one last chance to free Donaill from Coiteann's curse . . . and she tried not to think of what she would do if the sun rose that morning and Donaill did not come.

As the night sky cleared to starry black, Rioghan walked in silence to the ring of nine standing stones. In her hands was a single white candle with a bright piece of holly at its base.

The soft light of the candle shone on her hooded face, but there was no one here to see it . . . no one but the Sidhe keeping watch from the forest, as they always did, and her dogs, lying quietly beyond the trees.

She reached the center of the circle and stood facing the north, toward Cahir Cullen, toward Donaill. She faced the north, raised her face to the stars, and began to sing.

It was a song with words so ancient that none knew who had created them, and it was in a language that no one in Eire spoke anymore. But Rioghan knew that the timeless words spoke of love and longing, and of desire that could never be denied. And so she sent her song to Donaill, and sent all of her love and longing for him with it.

By the time the song was done, the stars had turned only a little in the sky. The candle in her hands had burned perhaps a quarter of the way down. But when she looked out toward the deep pine forest, she realized that the Sidhe were parting their ranks and moving back from the hidden path.

The dogs rose up, lining the other side of the clearing and looking intently toward the path, but all of them remained silent. A few even wagged their tails.

There, walking from the path into the clearing of the stone circle, was Donaill.

He had done it. He had broken away from Coiteann and her curse. But . . .

The dogs lowered their heads. They began to growl and show their teeth. And then Coiteann came tearing out of the brush, a stitched cloak of furs hastily pinned around her against the cold, her long blond hair disheveled and wild from being snatched and pulled by the branches of the pines.

She was nearly too enraged to speak. Her face was pale with anger, her eyes narrowed with hate. "Donaill!" she cried. "Donaill, you will come home with me now! Come back now; come home where you belong!"

He paid her no attention at all. He walked slowly and steadily between two of the standing stones of the circle, gazing at the little candle Rioghan held, and as he came to stand in front of her he looked directly into her eyes.

"You have come home," Rioghan whispered. She started to lower the candle, but then drew back as Coiteann threw herself hard against Donaill's back. "Come back! Come back!" she cried, her tangled hair falling in her face as she shoved her hand hard against his shoulders, as if she wanted to drive the poisoned amulet right through him She struck him again and again. "Come back! Come back!"

Slowly Donaill turned to face her, catching her wrist with one hand and holding it immobile. Coiteann twisted and squirmed but was held fast in the iron grip.

With his free hand, Donaill reached up to his neck and found the rusted iron chain. With great effort, he lifted the heavy, evil thing up over his head and took it off; then he held it out toward Coiteann.

Her eyes widened as she saw the dark *luaidhe* stone hovering near her. "Get it away from me. Get it away!" she wailed, trying to turn away from it. "Get it away! Don't do this to me! Don't—"

But Donaill held her wrist so strongly that Rioghan feared it would snap. As she struggled, he dropped the chain with the cursed stone over Coiteann's head and around her neck.

Coiteann shrieked, tearing at the chain as if it burned, and then fell to the ground as Donaill released her. Lifting herself to her hands and knees, she tried to stand, but the stone seemed so heavy she could barely raise her head.

She got hold of the rusted iron chain, frantically digging her fingers under it, but was entirely unable to lift it. In a moment she collapsed to the damp and muddy grass.

Clawing at the chain and gasping for breath, Coiteann rolled onto her back, held down by the evil stone on her chest. Her hands fell open against the earth and she stared up at the black night sky, unable to do anything but open her mouth and struggle for air.

Just like the dog, Rioghan realized. Just like the poor, unfortunate dog that Coiteann had forced to breathe its last upon the stone. Now she was suffering in the same way, feeling the breath forced out of her body and living through the overwhelming terror that went with such a death.

Rioghan started to go to her, but Donaill held out his arm to block her way. He shook his head, and Rioghan stood beside him. She could only watch as Coiteann lay flat on the ground, making a terrible whistling sound as she fought to breathe and waited to die.

But she did not die. Before long, the whistling stopped. Rioghan saw that Coiteann still lived and could breathe normally now. But she still could not move, pinned to the ground by the weight of the *luaidhe* stone. By the wavering light of the candle Rioghan could see her already pale skin becoming whiter and whiter, until it looked as white as death.

With a chill Rioghan knew that Coiteann was paying nature's price for taking blood not her own. It was as if the amulet drew out the essence of her own blood and took it into itself, leaving her as pale and as weak as though her blood had actually been drained away.

The woman lay motionless, a white shadow on the dark earth. Rioghan took a step toward her, holding out the candle, and caught her breath as she saw the deathly white skin begin to take on a gray pallor.

The dull gray spread throughout Coiteann's skin, and even through her hair and fingernails, until she was no longer fair and blond but as rough and gray as ash—the burned-out ash from Donaill's hearth, which she had stolen and then used to coat the cursed stone.

Rioghan's candle flickered and went out.

Donaill lowered his arm. Rioghan set down the candle and then went over to crouch down beside Coiteann.

She was alive, and would remain so, but the soft light of the stars showed Rioghan the dull, sickening gray pallor that had invaded Coiteann's skin and hair. And it was not just the color. Coiteann looked old and worn far beyond her years.

Rioghan looked down at her. "The cruelty you have done is now evident in your face, and your skin, and your eyes, and your hair, for all the world to see. It will remain with you for the rest of your days, the natural result of the darkness you tried to wield.

"You saw no wrong in what you did. You wished to have a man, and none would begrudge you that; most women long for a man to be their mate and companion. But you chose the cruelest of ways to get one. You tried to steal him from a woman who already loved him . . . first a man from Sabha, and then one from me.

"Now the hurt and suffering you have caused your sisters will be a mark on you that will never be erased. You will serve as a warning to all those who think there is no harm in stealing a little of a man's attention, when he is already loved by and bonded to another."

Rioghan reached out for the cold, rusted iron chain around Coiteann's neck, raised the woman's head a little from the ground, and lifted the heavy chain and stone away from her. Coiteann groaned, and stirred a little, and slowly sat up.

"Get up, Coiteann," Rioghan said, stepping back from her. "Get up and make your way back to Cahir Cullen. No doubt they will let you stay and continue to work among the servants . . . but no man there, or anywhere, will ever look at you again."

Without a word, without a look, Coiteann got to her feet, pulled her fur cloak close around her rough and ashen skin, and walked with her head down and her dull hair hanging until she disappeared into the forest. In a moment she was gone.

Rioghan closed her eyes and breathed a great sigh of relief. It was over. The curse had been broken. Now Donaill would be free to stay with her, only with her, to look into her eyes and see no one else, be forced to think of no one else.

She turned to him and looked up into his eyes, and then tried to take him into her arms . . . but he stood immobile, as unresponsive as a stone anchored to the earth. As her arms fell away from his sides Rioghan knew that Coiteann's curse still lay heavy on Donaill.

With the last of his will, Donaill slowly turned so that his back was toward her, and then stood unmoving and unseeing once more. Quickly Rioghan threw aside his heavy red cloak to look at him—and her mouth dropped open in horror.

Even in the faint predawn light she could see the dark and hideous black stain on his skin between his shoulder blades, left there by the deeply cursed and monstrously heavy *luaidhe* stone. So long as that stain was still there, the power of the curse would still control Donaill . . . and as Rioghan ran her fingers over his skin, careful to avoid the ugly mark, it seemed to her that the stain reached far down through his skin and flesh and seeped all the way to the bone.

How could she hope to fight such evil? She rested her forehead against his shoulder, reaching up to hold tight to his arm with her hand. And then, almost imperceptibly, he flexed the muscles of his arm, as if trying to reach for her but being held fast against doing so.

Rioghan straightened, still holding his arm. He had done his part by getting here to the circle, but he could do no more on his own. She would have to finish it for him, if there was to be any help for Donaill at all.

Chapter Twenty-three

Rioghan stepped away from Donaill. She tried to think of what must be done next, of what she would have to do to lift such a deep and terrible curse from one she loved . . . but found that all she could do was struggle to control her own rising emotions.

A small motion at the edge of the clearing made her look up. The gray-cloaked Sidhe were moving out of the forest to stand just outside the ring of stones, each one holding a stick of pine. Their words came back to her now:

. . . tears of sorrow, wept for his loss by one who loves him.

. . . bring a wild creature willingly to your side as you stand within the stone circle, and allow its breath to touch the amulet.

. . . a flame kindled with the crystal you wear

over your heart, for a crystal is like a living piece of the earth. It has beauty, constancy, and longevity—just as a true love has.

She would have to try to use the ritual of the Sidhe after all. It was her last hope, and it would take all of her strength and all of her skill . . . as well as all of her love.

Rioghan tried to gaze at the *luaidhe* stone, which still hung heavy from the iron chain in her hand, but found that it was difficult to see. Her vision was becoming blurred and hazy . . . and then the stone seemed to darken and glisten as her tears fell upon it, tears shed at last for a man she loved with all her heart but who might now be forever beyond her reach.

Tears of sorrow, wept for his loss by one who loves him.

Composing herself, folding her hands together with the chain of the *luaidhe* stone wrapped around the left one, Rioghan moved to stand in the very center of the stone circle. Donaill remained a few steps away.

Crouching down, she held out her right hand. "*Madra,*" Rioghan said softly. "*Madra.*"

Several of the dogs padded softly out of the dark forest to stand close beside her, wagging their tails and greeting her but otherwise making no sound. With her hand on the gray shoulders of Scath, Rioghan lifted her head and began, once more, to sing.

But this time there were no words. She sang a pure, clear, primal note, one from deep in her throat, and soon she was joined by her loyal dogs who also raised their heads to the sky and sang the same deep, calling, primal song.

After a short time the dogs fell silent. Rioghan did the same. And all of them kept very still as a new visitor appeared at the edge of the clearing.

Slowly, quietly, the wild wolf made its way into the circle to see these strangers who had called it. It greeted the friendly dogs, who were both curious and accepting of their wild cousin. Then, head low, it walked over to the one whose call had been the most insistent.

Rioghan held very still as the wild creature approached. Gently she held out the chain with the *luaidhe* stone. The wolf turned toward it, breathing in the cold scent of the heavy stone, its own damp breath covering it in warmth and wildness and with life that could be controlled by no one.

With a quick glance at Rioghan, the wolf turned and trotted back into the forests, vanishing almost before the dogs knew it was gone.

Bring a wild creature willingly to your side as you stand within the stone circle, and allow its breath to touch the amulet.

The sky in the east began to lighten. The Sidhe moved closer to the stones of the circle. In just a few moments, the winter solstice sun would rise.

Rioghan sent the dogs back into the forest. They obeyed in silence. She took Donaill by one arm and slowly turned him so that he stood at the very center of the circle and faced the east.

Rioghan, too, turned to face the east, and then

knelt down on the cold ground. She began to rake her fingers through the grass and soon had a little stack of dry grasses and pine needles and sticks . . . and from the white candle she had set down on the earth, she took the piece of holly at its base. It was the same piece of holly that Donaill had given her at the feast, and she laid it down atop the pile of kindling.

Last of all, she took the crystal of seeing out from beneath her black gown and held it out before her just as the Winter Solstice sun shot the first gleam of light above the horizon.

Blinking against its light, Rioghan held out the crystal and focused the brilliant beam directly onto the piece of holly. In the space of just a few heartbeats the wood and leaves began to show a thin curl of smoke. Then a tiny red glow appeared . . . and then the smallest hint of a bright yellow flame.

Rioghan sat back. The little stack of tinder she had gathered flared up into light, especially the piece of holly, which always burned with the hottest, brightest, fiercest yellow light.

Quickly she held out the iron chain and let the heavy amulet hang directly within the bright flame. The fire hissed and flared and spat as soon as the dark thing touched it, instantly leaping up as if in anger to attack the cursed stone.

A kind of vile steam began to curl up from the amulet, writhing up into the air in dirty gray-black tendrils. Then, suddenly, the chain on the stone broke and the cursed *luaidhe* stone fell straight into the fire. Rioghan dropped the chain in after it and quickly sat back, shielding her face as the blaze flared up bright as the sun and the filthy smoke from the stone and the chain exploded up into the air.

A flame kindled with the crystal you wear over your heart, for a crystal is like a living piece of the earth. It has beauty, constancy, and longevity—just as a true love has.

After a time, the smoke faded to something like normal, and the fire eased until it burned as pleasantly as any hearthlight. Rioghan watched as the last of the iron chain and cursed stone were consumed by her magical fire—and then she felt a touch at her shoulder.

Rioghan rose to her feet, turning swiftly to see Donaill standing before her and just beginning to smile down at her. As she stood in front of him she looked searchingly into his eyes, and to her joy saw warmth and recognition there. With the pale winter sun shining straight into his face, he drew her into his arms. "Rioghan," he said. "Rioghan."

She could say nothing, but simply held him as closely and as tightly as she could, pressing the side of her face hard against his broad chest and listening to the steady, strong, natural beat of his heart.

Quickly she broke away and ducked behind him. She caught hold of his arm and turned him so that now he faced the west, and then threw his heavy red cloak up over his shoulder so that the rays of the new sun shone directly onto the bare skin of his back.

As she watched, the last of the awful black stain

faded away, and his skin was once again clean and perfect.

Together they turned to face the east, letting the pale rays of the winter solstice sun wash over them. The Sidhe stepped forward to stand just inside the stone circle. They, too, faced the east, and began to sing an ancient song of welcome for the newly returning sun, taking turns touching their pine sticks to the fire Rioghan had kindled and raising their torches to the dawn.

As the soft voices surrounded them, Donaill turned to Rioghan and pulled her close to him, wrapping his heavy red cloak over her and gently stroking her long black hair. "It is over, dear Rioghan," he murmured. "And I have come home, thanks to you."

"It was not I alone," Rioghan answered, the side of her face close against his broad chest. "You found the strength within you to come to this place at the right time. I could have done nothing for you if you had not had the will to be here."

"Nothing could stop me from being where you are. Not the lure of brightest treasure, not the cruelty of darkest magic. From this day I wish only to be where you are, and I can only hope that you might wish to be where I am."

"I *do* wish it," Rioghan whispered.

"Then . . ." He stepped back so he could see her, and raised her face so that he could look into her eyes. "Lady Rioghan," he said, as the rising sun grew ever brighter, "will you do me the honor of being my wife, my only wife, my only love, for all the rest of your days?"

She looked up at him, into his shining blue eyes. She wanted to say, *I will! Oh, I will!* but found that the words were not quite there.

He saw the hesitation in her face. "You still fear betrayal," Donaill said quietly.

She looked away, and nodded slowly. "I do. And yet . . ." Rioghan looked into his eyes once again. "No man could have broken a spell such as that one without the truest desire to do so. I believe you will and truly mean what you promise. And I can think of nothing more important in any marriage."

"Well, I can say, dear Rioghan, that if ever there was a lady whose actions matched her words, it was you. And I can also say that I have learned a thing: no other woman should be allowed close to me, no matter how innocent her purpose may seem, for that is your place and yours alone."

He smiled, and then bent down to give her the softest of kisses. "None can ever say with certainty that they will never betray another—but I believe with all my heart that if ever a man and woman could remain true to each other, you and I could remain so, Lady Rioghan of Sion."

She smiled back at him, still looking straight into his eyes, and then nodded her head. "I will marry you, Lord Donaill of Cahir Cullen. Oh, I will."

Together they embraced in the cool light of the winter solstice sun, as the chants of the Sidhe rose up all around them and the fire burned down until nothing was left but cool white ash, shining in the winter sun.

That evening beneath the blue-black sky, Rioghan and Donaill climbed up the mound of Sion. They found the Sidhe already gathered at the top, standing beside the stack of cut logs and deadwood that now covered the bare ashen spot at the center. Five of the Sidhe stood to one side, and each one held a blazing torch.

The five approached them, and Rioghan greeted them with tears in her eyes, suddenly feeling as though she might never see them again. Donaill turned to her and reached for her hand, and then he spoke to all the gathered Sidhe.

"This is the last night your lady will spend at Sion. At dawn tomorrow she will go with me to Cahir Cullen, there to become my cherished wife."

The Sidhe all turned to each other upon hearing this, murmuring softly among themselves. "Yet you have this promise from both of us," Rioghan said. "Sion remains yours, as it has always been; but Donaill and I together will serve you as its protectors and guardians and help you in any way we can. Indeed, if this place is safe for you now, it is because Donaill has seen to it that Men will not return. Sion is once again a haven and a home and a place of power for the Sidhe, as it was intended to be.

"You know that I have always served you, and this place, in whatever ways I could. And you have seen, of late, that Donaill too has done as he promised me, and more than once driven off those who would steal from Sion and do it harm.

"Both of us will see that Sion, and her people, are protected from any who might do such harm ever again. I, Rioghan, swear this to you now, by the sacred light of the winter solstice flame."

"And I, Donaill, swear this to you also, by the sacred light of the winter solstice flame."

The Sidhe lowered their torches and began to speak.

"We thank you for all you have done for us, Lady Rioghan."

"And we thank you as well, Lord Donaill."

"You will both be greatly missed here at Sion."

Donaill tried to smile, but could only shake his head. "I wish I could have prevented the theft and destruction that happened here. I was not . . . I could not—"

"Do not trouble yourself, Donaill."

"Sion needs no gold to be of value to us."

Rioghan took Donaill's hand and smiled up at him. "It is time."

The five Sidhe stepped back and bowed to Rioghan and Donaill. Then, carrying their torches, they moved to surround the stack of wood. The crowd fell silent as they began to speak.

"This is the night that follows the winter solstice."

"From this time on, the nights grow shorter."

"From this time on, the light of the sun returns to us."

"We light this fire that all may mark this night."

"We light this fire with the flames of the sun itself."

The five Sidhe stepped forward and extended their torches until the flames touched the stack of wood. In a few moments the fire crept through the wood, spreading and growing and taking hold in larger and larger spots, until at last the flames leaped up to the dark sky and the entire stack was engulfed in bright yellow fire.

All of the Sidhe stepped back from the great mountain of flame, making a circle around the edges of the hilltop and sending their own chants up to the sky along with the roaring and the crackling of the fire. Two of those who had lit the bonfire walked to Rioghan and Donaill and handed each of them a burning torch.

"Take this, the light of the sun and of Sion, and keep it with you always."

"We will see that it burns forever in the hearth of Sion, and we will be the keepers of the light."

"We will care for this place, now and always, and welcome you here whenever you return."

Rioghan embraced them both, and then together she and Donaill started on the path down the side of the mound. The sounds of the fire and the chant floated after them.

The cave of Sion sat dark and quiet. Only the faintest glow remained deep in the bottom of the stone-lined hearth. She and Donaill placed their torches down in the hearth, where the pine sticks could burn through and provide comforting heat and light on this long winter night. It was as if a little of the returning sun had been brought inside their very home.

Rioghan walked through the place where she had lived alone for so long, still saddened by the sight of its bare stripped walls. Yet in the places where all the beautiful gold and bronze and crystal had once rested, Rioghan found small stone lamps and white beeswax candles, new and clean and ready for lighting.

Very soon all of the candles were lit and casting their soft and wavering light throughout the cave and over the fur-covered sleeping ledge. The pine torches in the hearth snapped and burned pleasantly. Rioghan stood beside the ledge and turned to Donaill, waiting for him there in the shimmering light.

He came to her, took her face in both his hands, and leaned down to kiss her gently. Rioghan reached up to him, taking him in her arms and losing herself in the feel of his broad back and strong arms and soft, gentle mouth.

Yet his kisses did not remain soft for long. They became more insistent with each passing moment, even as Rioghan felt the rising passion within herself strengthening to meet his own. It seemed that as he grew stronger, she grew more yielding, ever softer and more pliant, raising her face to his until her head fell and her long black hair covered his hands. She leaned back against his strong embrace so that her entire body was open to his, and pressed up warm and soft against the iron hardness of his chest and hips and thighs.

It seemed that the light of the candles faded away. There was only cool darkness and rapid breath, and strength she had never before imagined holding her upright on swaying legs. Strong fingers pulled the golden brooch from her cloak and let the black wool fall heavily to the rushes on the floor of the cave. Next her leather belt was loosened and pulled away, and then her boots untied and slipped off.

With sudden gentleness and care, the half-rings holding her black wool gown and linen undergown were eased away, and the gowns allowed to fall down off her shoulders and slide down to the floor on top of the cloak.

Quickly, for the midwinter air was cold, those same strong arms lifted her up through the dim light as though she had no weight at all, placed her on the softness of the cushions covering the sleeping ledge, and covered her with thick furs.

A small sound in the rushes told her that Donaill had unpinned his heavy red cloak and let it drop. Without needing to see him, she knew that he was taking off his belt and boots and breeches and tunics. Then his tall heavy body was beside her on the furs, close and hot, and as hard and strong as the very stone of the cave itself.

Yet despite all his strength, despite his urgency and rapid breath, he was gentleness itself as he raised himself over her. "Rioghan," he whispered, a dark shadow in the soft light of the candles. "Beautiful dark-haired lady, Rioghan who is to be my wife . . . let me show you the love I have for you, and will always have, now and always; let me show you how we can truly become as one and never be separated again."

In answer she reached up and slid her arms up over his back, stroking the smooth, hot skin of his shoulders and pulling him close, so close, yet still not close enough. She was beginning to feel the insistent hunger of her own body, which told her he could never be close enough.

Just as she was the one growing more eager, more anxious, more insistent, Donaill eased back from her slightly, and she could feel him smiling down at her in the darkness. Slowly, slowly, he lowered his head until his lips hovered just above hers, until she arched her back to reach for them, until she was the one who pressed her mouth to his and returned his long and loving kiss.

Even as he kissed her, Donaill began to caress the bare skin of her body, tracing over every rise and curve and every tender place, moving so gently, so carefully, so deliberately, that even through her own haze of heat and emotions and desire Rioghan knew he did not forget that never had she been touched in such a way by any man.

At last Rioghan felt as open and yielding as the soft earth when it is warmed by the summer sun; and when she could wait no longer, she pulled Donaill to her, so that his comforting weight pressed down upon her, over her and around her and finally deep within her, and Rioghan knew, as she held him close and wrapped her arms and legs around him, that she would never feel incomplete again.

Chapter Twenty-four

The following morning, a gray mist lay still and silent on the grounds outside Sion. It seemed to invade even the cave itself, hanging on the damp ground and clinging to the bare walls. "It is so sad to see it this way," Rioghan said, as she stood near the entrance and looked back inside her home. "So empty, so alone."

Donaill smiled at her as he buckled on his sword belt. "It will not be this way for long," he said, walking toward her. "By tonight, some of the Sidhe will be living here as you did. This fire will never go out." He nodded at the hearth, where neatly banked coals glowed beneath their covering of ash.

"I know that. They will care for it well. Yet . . . the walls—I wish . . ." She fell silent, and smiled up at him. "Let us go home."

He stood before her, sliding his hand beneath the long dark hair behind her neck and gently kissing her forehead. "I am so sorry, dear Rioghan, that all of the beautiful things that should be here have been lost. I promise you—I will not rest until I find this treasure and return it to its rightful place. The fault was entirely mine."

"Oh, Donaill, it was not. They would have succeeded one way or another. They were determined to take the beautiful ancient things of the Sidhe for their own selfish reasons, the way a child might take another's plaything—never realizing the value of what they have stolen."

"Yet I should have done whatever was needed to prevent such a loss. Most of all I should never have let myself be tricked and enslaved by one not fit to clean the mud from my boots."

His face grew dark at the memory of it, and Rioghan reached up to touch his cheek. "Do not think of it again," she said. "It is over now . . . and you and I know that it will not ever happen again." She smiled. "The Sidhe are the masters of creating beauty where there is none. And we will help them, you and I."

She took her hand away and started to walk from the cave. "Please, Donaill. Take me home."

He smiled back at her, and nodded. Together they walked across the misty clearing with Scath and Cogar alongside, and started on the road toward Cahir Cullen—toward home.

* * *

Three days later, two riders left the fortress in the early morning light and walked their horses—one black, one gray—along the road toward Sion. With them was a shaggy pack pony carrying as many large woven sacks as could be tied to its saddle. Two huge dogs trotted alongside the horses and roved in and out of the forest's edge. The gray and black dogs were easily seen against the grass and the holly and the pine trees, for on this particular morning all was lined with pure white frost.

"Rioghan, I fear there will be no food, no wine, no linen, and no woolen cloth left at Cahir Cullen," Donaill said with a laugh, as his black stallion snorted and broke into a high, prancing trot in the cold morning air. "You have brought it all for the Sidhe!"

"Oh, there is still a little left," said Rioghan, smiling up at him from the back of her small gray mare. She wore the same clothes she had worn on the night of the feast—the gray linen gown with the green woolen dress over it, a belt of gold links, and the mantle of silver-gray and deep green with just a few lines of bright red. "And I will be glad to prepare all the bread that I can bake and all the meat that I can dry, and weave all the cloth I can weave, if it will help the Sidhe and reassure them that they will always have our protection."

Donaill smiled sympathetically, and eased Cath back to a walk so that the pack pony could keep up. "I know you have always felt close to them. They are your family, in many ways."

"They are. But there is another reason. They were

the ones who helped me to break the curse that rested on you. Without their help you might have been lost to me forever, no matter how much love I had for you."

Donaill could only gaze at her, and try to coax the slow pack pony on a little faster.

The rest of the journey was a peaceful one. The horses walked calmly along the good road, and gradually the mist began to burn away as the brightening sun broke through the cover of cloud.

Though it had been only three days, Rioghan's heart leaped as she once again approached Sion. She loved her new life with Donaill, her husband, and their fine house at Cahir Cullen; but this would remain a special place for her, she knew, for all the rest of her days.

There seemed to be a special brightness, a certain gleaming light, coming from the clearing in front of the cave . . . but she supposed it was just her eagerness to see her old home again, and a reflection of the love she would always have for it.

Then they rode into the clearing. Donaill and Rioghan stopped their horses and stood very still.

The clearing did indeed shimmer with light, for on every frost-lined branch of pine hung beautiful things of gold and bronze, copper and crystal, moving gently and flashing bright in the early-morning sunshine. There were plates and discs large and small, cups and armbands and torques and rings, and figures of all sorts of animals, turning in the slight wind almost as if they were alive.

The horses snorted a bit and shied away when

asked to move forward, for dapples of light danced across the frosty grass, and the very trees glittered in their eyes. "How is this possible?" Rioghan said under her breath, glancing quickly from branch to sparkling branch. "All of their treasure has returned . . . and like this!"

"Let's find out," Donaill said, and persuaded Cath to step into the clearing. The pack pony and Rioghan's gray mare followed him closely.

As the horses walked toward the entrance to the cave, three of the Sidhe came out past the cowhide hangings. All, it seemed, of the others appeared at the edge of the forest. And the happy gray and black dogs came bounding up to greet their former mistress and romp with Scath and Cogar.

Rioghan slid down from her mare and gave the reins up to Donaill. She walked toward the cave, toward Luath, and could not help but smile. "So beautiful!" she said, almost laughing. "I am so happy that it has been returned to you! How has this happened?"

Luath walked forward and took both of her hands. "A man has brought it back to us."

"A man? How could this be?"

Luath nodded toward the forest's edge. "This man."

Rioghan and Donaill turned—and there, just within the cover of the trees, was a man standing beside a horse. When he saw that they were staring at him, he led the animal forward and came out into the open light of the clearing.

"Airt," Rioghan said softly.

He walked toward them, stopping only a short distance away. "I had hoped you would be here on this day," he said. "I knew you would return soon, and I hoped to see you again before I left."

"You have done this?" Rioghan asked, glancing around at the bright, shimmering clearing.

He smiled. "I have. I knew where Beolagh hid it, and it was little trouble to bring it back to its rightful owners. It was the least I could do to try to make things right again."

Rioghan nodded, watching his face. He was somber, but there was a peaceful feeling about him as well, as though he had come to a decision and was determined to carry it through. "You said you are leaving?"

"I am. I am on my way to Dun Orga, there to win back Sabha no matter what it takes."

Now it was Rioghan's turn to smile. "That will be a difficult task," she said. "But it is a worthy goal."

He nodded, his face serious and still. "I understand that now. I was a fool to try to collect women the way some men try to collect pieces of gold. I should have considered myself lucky to have one woman who truly loved me, instead of taking pleasure in having two forced to live in jealousy and tension and pain while they competed for my attentions. That is the dark side of love. I would much rather have the light once again."

She reached out and gave him a gentle embrace. "Go with the light, then, Airt," she said. "And tell

Sabha for me that she might do well to consider you once again."

"I thank you, Lady Rioghan. I hope that Sabha and I will see you again one day."

She stepped back, and in the gleaming silence of the clearing Airt mounted his horse and rode away into the forest.

There was a soft footstep behind her. Rioghan turned to see Luath standing there, looking all around him at the shining, glittering trees. "Do you approve of this ritual, Lady Rioghan?"

"Ritual, Luath? Tell me about it. I have not seen such a thing before—but neither have I seen anything so beautiful, so magical."

The Sidhe started to walk slowly across the clearing, and Rioghan walked with him. "When this man, Airt, returned our treasures to us, we found they had all been badly used. These beautiful things had been stolen, hidden, and used in trade to get that which should be freely given. And so we have hung them outside, in the pure light of the newly returning sun, to celebrate both its return and the return of our treasure . . . and to allow the gold and bronze and copper and crystal to regain their purity once more, to become as they were when the Ancient Ones made them so very long ago."

"It is wonderful, Luath. A marvel. Perhaps this ritual should be done each year, both to celebrate the return of the sun and to simply enjoy such beauty."

Luath smiled down at her. "We will consider it, Lady Rioghan."

She glanced back at Donaill, and her eyes widened. "Oh! I nearly forgot why we came! Luath, please gather your people around—we have brought things for them all."

The Sidhe all glanced at one another, but then came to stand near the pack pony. Donaill slid down from Cath and began unpacking the big cloth sacks, and in a moment both he and Rioghan were handing out skins of good blackberry wine, bags of dried wheat, thick folds of bright woolen cloth, and lighter stacks of the finest linen weave.

"We cannot thank you enough, Lady Rioghan and Lord Donaill," said Luath. "These midwinter gifts will help us get through the remainder of the darkest, coldest season. You have been most generous to us all."

"Far less than you have done for me, all these years," Rioghan answered. "Yet I hope that I might ask a favor of you now."

"Of course, lady."

"Ask whatever you wish."

"There is nothing we would not do for you."

Rioghan folded her hands and looked around at the many faces gazing back at her from the bright clearing. "Sion has been my home, and that of my family, for more years than I know. Now I have gone to live with my beloved husband at Cahir Cullen, there to make a new life with him and, I hope, to serve the people there as I have always served you.

"But you must know that we will never forget you, never abandon you. We have brought you these gifts this day to show you that this is true, and we shall continue to do so on this day for every year that is to come. That is how important to us you are.

"In return, we hope that you will continue to live here at Sion, for it is safe for you now, remaining the guardians of this place and of the stone circle—and call upon us whenever you might have need of us. Would this also be your wish?"

The Sidhe all turned to each other, and then turned back to Rioghan and Donaill.

"This is our home, and yours, now and always."

"We will forever be the guardians here."

"Both of you, too, may call upon us, if ever you have need of us."

Rioghan smiled at them, and stood close to Donaill, taking his arm. "Then I will go in peace to my new home, knowing that my husband and I will always have one here."

He bent to kiss her as the Sidhe looked on, and when Rioghan opened her eyes she heard the lively sound of a harp and a drum and saw laughing, dancing Sidhe whirling and leaping all through the sparkling clearing.

"Lady Rioghan! Lord Donaill!" they cried. "May this day be a merry one for you both, now and always!"

"And for you as well." Rioghan laughed, and reached up to kiss Donaill once again in the bright, dancing light of the winter morning.